V.I.P Plus One
Samantha Jon

Contents

Dedicated to Jimmy Fallon.

I will never forgive you

PROLOGUE

IF I WERE WRITING this scene in a script, my marriage wouldn't be ending in the cramped conference room of his real estate office. With the damp smell of the low ply, faded blue carpet barely covered by the reek of bleach, leaving behind the scent of a red flag. Nor the worn leather executive chairs which are squashed around a chipped oval table and a too large TV, alluding that they're not the only outdated things in here. I wouldn't be here on a beautiful Saturday afternoon, the kind where the golden rays catch every speckle of dust that dances its way onto the floor, stuck waiting for an explanation, half expecting the camera crews to jump out at any moment and yell *gotcha*.

If I were writing this scene in a script, Trent wouldn't be wearing a pair of ass-less chaps that cup too tightly to his crotch, making me want to itch and tug at my own leggings, while he scrubs at his face trying to find the words to tell me what the hell is going on. The images of Rebecka, our newest intern, playfully tying him up with rope, her bedazzled boy briefs sparkling *rodeo* across her butt when she moves, wouldn't be on repeat on my mind. This moment wouldn't be ticking by like a broken record I'll be left to clean up in therapy sessions for years to come.

If I were writing this script, it would be classier.

It would be emotional.

Heartbreaking even.

It would be everything it isn't. And it certainly wouldn't be happening to us.

The tail end of whatever Trent is saying pulls me from my thoughts.

"Do you even care, Vicky? You just found out I'm cheating for fuck's sake and you're staring off into nothing."

He shakes his head, grabbing at the back of his neck in frustration as he paces.

"Don't you want to know how long? Or if it's serious? Anything at all?"

I stay silent, wondering if he remembers that the curly cues from his backside are on full display. He goes on with no encouragement, content to fill in the empty space of me just fine.

"We both know we've been over for a long time. You put us on autopilot, and you never took back control. I thought... Well, I'd *hoped* I could snap you out of it. I've loved you the best way I could for almost my entire adult life, and I've tried..." He twists his hands before biting out, "I've fucking tried everything. Even this, as callous as it is, was my attempt to make you *feel* something. To come back to me, even if you were angry. I did this for *us*. Tell me you feel *something*."

There's an ache in his words, fighting to be heard. I want to be indignant at that ache. To scream, or to cry. To call him a fucking liar, that he did this for himself. Every Carrie Underwood song comes to mind, finally making sense and the desire to crank them up loud and do damage sends shivers down my spine in want. I'm angry at the audacity, at the injustice. But it isn't enough because he's also a little bit right. I've known something was off for months... years even, but I've willfully ignored it—the fear of losing the life I built more palatable than just losing my husband. He shakes his head again, taking my hands softly.

"I know you're oblivious sometimes, but could you at least recognize what you're doing to me? What you've done to *us*."

My heart squeezes in embarrassment. He pokes at the places that are bruised. The memories that are gaslit and fuzzy, the ones that should make me want to curl up around them to staunch the pain. I don't. He doesn't wait for a response, instead releasing my hands so he can walk to the door and back. Honestly, I can't imagine what he expects. I hardly want to recall this moment later and see myself broken by a man who doesn't even have the decency to cover his balls that are slapping at his thighs as he paces.

So, instead of arguing or acquiescing, I continue to sit silently, barely glancing at the man I swore to spend my life with. The man I've relied on to make everything easy and safe. To uncomplicate things. The guy who's blown my carefully laid plans to smithereens with every body part on display and cowboy boots that squeak a bit when he walks. When I finally get to his eyes, they scream in pain, and even though I think I might hate him, I can't force myself to hurt him further by pretending any longer.

Trent finally goes still, waiting for me to say anything. Normally, I would. Or I might. But my non-response speaks louder than I ever could. He's stopped his pacing and, as if he's had enough of the silence and the stares, his hands slam down onto the table. Its old linoleum squeals at the force, pulling my attention from all the other distractions.

"Dammit, Victoria!" His sigh runs down to my bones. "We're over. You've made sure of that. I'll be sending you the divorce papers first thing Monday." He runs his hands down the front of his chaps, realization at what he's still wearing dawning on him. He hangs his head in defeat. "In the meantime, I'll be staying at Rebecka's if you need anything."

Good ol' Trent, a shoulder to cry on 'til the end. A real nice guys finish last situation. I refrain from rolling my eyes. How would he break if I told him the truth? What if he heard, for once, that I was tired of only writing love stories and that, if I couldn't live them, I at least wanted to sell them to give others a chance who could. That maybe I would've been content with him if the rest of my life hadn't lacked such color. That somewhere along the line, I had lost myself. Would it magically heal our marriage? Would it spark a fire that burned out long ago?

No. Not now, after Rodeo Gate. I don't think it ever would have.

The words fall mute in my throat. Trent would never understand. *Who would give up perfect for messy*, he'd say.

His hesitation to leave is just enough to try, but I let it pass. His boots scuff across the carpet, then the door breathes closed. I wait for my heart to shatter like all the movies, the songs, the books... but it doesn't. Instead, a million possibilities flutter through my mind. One hundred new choices to create a life I dreamed, with romance and writing and excitement. With desperate need and sticky want. Messy in all the perfect places.

Instead of chasing the freedom that sits at my fingertips, my mind betrays me and clings to the loss, leaving me with only one thought; *how the fuck am I supposed to start over now?*

ONE

THE WORLD MAY AS *well be ending*, I think as I stare into my thumb at the last chip of *blushing babe* nail polish that's still holding on. I'm not normally so dramatic outside of my scripts, but it's the only way to accurately describe to my heart what's happening. Sure, thirty is supposedly the new twenty (cue infomercial voice) and *there's a whole big world out there* (end cut), but that doesn't mean losing everything I've struggled to hold together for the last decade of my life doesn't hurt like a bitch.

We'd been building his business together since we were twenty-five, our relationship for longer, and it is all falling apart. *Fallen apart.* I've lost my husband, my job, and my house all in the last few weeks—there isn't much further to go. It's like I've hit every *fuck my life* rung on the way down, too. At 22, Trent had given me the first place I'd belonged since my parents had died, my first glimpse of a family of my own again. Even if a small voice inside of me thinks it ending might be what I need, I still miss the stability of my old life's fears. The devil you know and all that.

I scratch desperately at the last vestige of that life, trying to keep my mind off my impending flight and the prospects of what Monica has promised me in return for boarding it, is. I go back to flipping between taking notes for a script I've been working on in my phone and reading a book I've been desperate for since it came out, unable to concentrate on either. A baby screams directly into my ear while sitting in her wild-eyed father's lap. Every wail seems to say *you shouldn't be here*. A disgusting veil of wet coats his cheeks, a tiny droplet splashing on my skin as I grind my teeth against my urge to join in the tantrum.

Hell has got to be a vacation spot compared to this terminal.

I stand up, pulling along my rolling luggage. It's *clack, clack, clack* echoes behind me, as I pace back and forth in the tight space. I desperately want coffee, black and bitter, to bring some solitude into my nerves. My anxiety at missing my plane and spending money I do not have demands I stay. The fear of flying and the ringing in my ears tells me to go. My worry is at war with my want. But the need to move and the call of caffeine wins out.

Coffee at this point is worth every penny in my bank account.

My eyes are puffy, and a headache isn't far behind, forming a companionship with the other bleary-eyed travelers that nod at me as I pass, a silent agreement not to judge our disheveled states a given. We're all just trying to make it somewhere. Even with being faceblind, unable to remember their faces or recognize them again, there's a kinship with this odd assortment of strangers. It sits like swallowed gum, my body unable to process it entirely. *Maybe in seven years?* Or maybe it's just the 2-week-old, frozen burrito that Cheri wasn't sure I should eat before we left, that I'm feeling.

Katie and Cherie dropped me off a little over an hour ago, but with a hundred miles between me and my divorce papers, it could be a lifetime. I've written a dozen bad poems, named a castoff-dipshit-side character that I instantly killed off after my ex, and said goodbye to every brick, restaurant, and favorite picnic spots I had. Even with movie therapy (which entailed a full 48-hour loop of *You've Got Mail*) this chapter has officially ended, and it painfully pulls at the roots I've grown, making time take on an indefinite quality. All the years are slipping through my fingers with nothing for me to hold on to.

The line to the coffee shop comes into view and I hesitate, clasping at my phone as nerves rattle in my chest. I need a pep talk before I decide to hell with this whole idea and leave this airport, and this dream, behind. I pull up my favorites and hit dial. The phone barely rings before a stubborn voice I know as well as my own picks up.

"Victoria Irene Pencheske, do not tell me you have cold feet already," Cherie says, exasperated.

My full name rolls off her tongue before I can process it is even fully mine, and I cannot help but flinch. I imagine she's stretching with an exaggerated yawn that screams she's tired of my shit. She rarely, if ever, calls me anything other than Vip, and it breaks my heart hearing her frustration. I roll my eyes to cover the pain, knowing it is her intent. There's the thick sound of a slap on skin before Katie's motherly voice interrupts.

"Cherie! Don't be a cow! This is a pretty big freakin' deal. Let the woman breathe," she says. "You doing okay, hon?"

Her voice is full of concern that beads across my skin, looking for a break in my armor. She's always doing that. Ruining an otherwise safely shallow moment with feelings and emotion, asking me to be vulnerable in ways I'm not sure I'll ever be ready to be. Seeping in my waters of regret and worry, like a tea bag who hopes to make things better with a handful of flowery herbs. But she doesn't fool me, it's still dirty leaf water. And I'd rather not get sticks stuck in my teeth when I'm thirsty, thank you very much.

I can't articulate to *myself* how I feel, let alone someone else, so I seal my lips, unwilling to sink her in guilt, too. Thankfully, Cherie, obnoxious as ever, answers for me.

"Of course she isn't. That's why she's heading to the big show and why we booted her ass out to go. Vip, you cannot come home. So, suck it up and put those big girl panties on! You've got places to be and people to meet," Cherie sings.

Tears well up in my eyes. It's not that it's a bad idea to leave. There will be writing opportunities in California that I cannot find in Winlock, or Seattle for that matter. Not to mention no one will know who I am. I can be anyone I want which holds its own type of romance. I lost myself for so long in other people's expectations that going out on my own feels big and limitless. The question is, would I be able to find myself again? It's all a risk with no guarantees.

Still, my friends don't think living should-I-get-coffee-or-food broke or this-anxiety-might-actually-kill-me feelings are valid enough reasons to stay. Ever since Monica called to tell me she got me a job *and* the possibility of a meeting with a studio; the only choice was to go. And now, I have run out of time. I had to be there today, or else Monica was coming to get me.

"How do you even know I'm questioning staying?" I ask, innocently enough.

Katie heaves in a sigh, because we all know I'm not that dumb and neither are they. There's only one reason I'd call this close to boarding. For all I knew, they installed a tracker in my bag and thought I was leaving.

"Vip, you have to go. You have been bothering us since junior high about testing your writing chops in Hollywood. You've wanted to create for as long as we've known you. Then Trent came into the picture and you just," she sighs again, "never got around to it. But you still write stacks of romance scripts on that stupid little phone app. And receipt paper. *And* in all those spiral notebooks I somehow ended up with in my already stuffed office. I bet there's even more you haven't told us about. Some part of you must still want your dream. And this newest one is your best yet. It only takes you giving it a chance to sell, I'm sure of it."

The nickname soothes my soul, but before my heart can love her too much, Katie rips the band aid off.

"Well, ma'am, Trent is g-o-n-e. It is your time to shine. You're getting on that plane and that's final."

Her voice is firm, leaving no room for argument. And once Katie puts her foot down, she means it in a scary consequences type way.

I lower my voice, giving words to the fears that have been hounding me all morning.

"You both realize I'm not really a *writer*, writer. Those scripts are just for fun. And yes, when I was younger, I had big dreams, but until the divorce is final and I sell the house, I'm broke. Like, mid-freshmen year college level broke. I need a real job with a real paycheck. I'm thirty and have nothing to show for it. Can you imagine how embarrassing this is for me?"

I breathe back the tears that threaten to overwhelm my words. Unwilling to be anymore truthful, I reign myself back in.

"Yes, Trent had a lot to do with not leaving Washington after college, but we all know I will never make it in LA. There are too many people. Too few patterns I can remember. I cannot even recognize my own family when they're not where I'm expecting. How am I supposed to network at parties with strangers? With different people every night... I will make a fool out of myself before I even have a chance. Asshole or not, Trent was right. The entertainment industry is too messy for me. Why should I press my, clearly thinning, luck?"

My breath holds, stomach sinking at the thought that they may actually agree with me.

"PLEASE. You are not using the faceblind excuse again, are you?" Cherie huffs out. "Girl. We've *talked* about this. Your inability to recognize people isn't the problem. Your fear of getting your butt off the proverbial couch and putting yourself out there is!"

Cherie is on fire, each 'r' dropping and rolling out more and more with the New England accent of her parents.

"You've got it handled. And as far as the ticket goes, we bought it. Your accommodations? Are free. And your sad excuse of having no job, which might I add is a bold-faced lie. Monica has one waiting for you—and is just another reason you have to go. This town is worn out for you. Bigger things lie ahead. We believe in you—and now? It's time to throw baby in the deep end."

The soft whisper of Katie saying, *swim, swim, swim, little fish,* floats in the background.

"You guys are real sticklers for my safety," I groan. "What if the plane crashes? You know I hate flying. What if something *else* happens? How do I tell people about... this?" I slowly gesture from head to toe, encompassing all that I am, even if they can't see me. "What do I do if I fail?" I whisper.

"Easy. You don't," Katie says. "I mean, eventually you'll have to explain, but you tell them the truth and move on. Just like you've done here, with all of us. Besides, Monica will be there. You aren't going alone. She has the best of intentions, and when push comes to shove, she's got your back. And we'll always be here, whether you live in Washington or California. But you'll never succeed if you don't at least try, Vip."

Cherie snorts. "Yeah, and we'll never hear the end of it. Besides, if you get murdered, it's not like knowing who did it will change anything and being broke gives people less incentive to target you. The plane is not going to crash. That's statistically improbable. So, stop being such a baby."

I grab at my forehead, staving off the headache of both their wisdom and their sarcasm.

"You're both horrible and I'm writing you out of my memoir," I say, deadpan. Still, they're right and we all know it. "Alright guys. There's a line forming and I'm not about to continue this day without some coffee. Call of the SWAT, I'm getting on the plane. Love you both."

I hang up the phone to the shouts of their 'I love yous' and slide into line, my sneakers squeaking across the polished floor. I try to refocus my worries on the soft pinkish hues of a California sunset. Of how I can wake up with a coffee and a pen and relinquish the quiet, with no other plans than the ones I make. I think of the parties and people; of the choice of shadows to hide and lights to shine in.

I can be anything or everything I've ever wanted. I can find the girl who loved to crank up Bonnie Tyler music videos and force her friends to recreate them. Who didn't have to only jot half sentences of scraps of purse paper in the grocery store line but would drop everything for an hour because an idea wouldn't leave her alone. The one who took every opportunity to experience a moment that could blossom into a whole new story. A girl I locked away when my marriage became everything I was.

My breathing shakes in anticipation, a genuine excitement taking hold.

That is until I lock eyes with the woman in front of me. She keeps looking back, irritation marring her mouth, a frown pulling down at the corners. Every time her hair floats off her neck when she turns, I smell roses, and déjà vu hits. I'm beginning to wonder if there's something I've done wrong, if I've said something I thought I was only thinking about, or if I'm in the wrong line. If

I might know her. Her eyes dart around, like a rabbit caught too far from her den. I try to break the tension that's slowly seeping into my resolve.

"Is this the line for the caffeine IV?" I ask her, going for the safety of being casually funny.

Her nose scrunches up, lips still turned comically down. I cannot help but picture the green fuzz of the Grinch doing the same, making it impossible to hold in my smirk.

"Funny. You are *so* funny," she sighs out, looking around and back at me.

She says it in a way that tells me she clearly does *not* find me funny. So, I do what any thirty-something adult woman would do.

I sigh deeply back and say, "I am, aren't I?"

She rolls her eyes and turns her back to me. I'm not sure what I've done to elicit such open dislike, but there are bigger things for me to worry about than some ashy-blond bob sashaying in front of me. As soon as I have a mind to pretend she has never existed, a man steps up behind her, effectively cutting the line. Now, I'm usually one to live and let live, but I cannot stand a line cutter and today is not the day that I am capable of staying silent.

"Excuse me, but the line starts back there," I say as venom seeps from my voice.

Never get between an anxiety attack and her coffee. I'm positive it is how all murders start. An unknowing, obtuse husband too early in the morning. A shit boyfriend who pushes it just *that much* too far after a long night. And this asshole who thinks all 5 foot 4 inches of me won't shove my suitcase handle so far up his ass, he'll have to go through baggage claim.

At least five other people have piled in behind me. Seeing their gratefulness for someone speaking up for the complete lack of manners bolsters my chest and strengthens my spine. The guy, now in front of me, hunches his shoulders clean up to his ears. I smile ruthlessly in anticipation of where I now can throw all these jittery feelings deservedly.

"Victoria?" His voice is incredulous, saying my name before he turns around.

My heart picks up its pace as fear sticks to my throat. I'm unsure how I know the two in front of me, now realizing he's holding hands with the bob, but it's obvious I do. My back, once standing so tall, curls in. The whirring of my brain tries to focus as he faces me, flipping through the mental Rolodex of everyone I have encountered, the unique attributes of their person filtering in every available thought and trying to match any of those details I can to the man in front of me. *Balding. Dull eyes. Brows that need to be badly trimmed. Hair along his first knuckles.* I pull on a stoic face, hiding the panic.

"Yes?" I say a touch friendlier than I had been, too worried about burning bridges. "Forgive my manners, but I've had a very early morning and no coffee yet. My brain is just mush."

My lips pout and I tip my chin pointedly at the coffee bar in front of me. The best-case scenario is this is someone who knows I can't recognize them, and we can laugh about this as I firmly reiterate that they still should not be cutting. This *is* a coffee line in Seattle, of all places. Worst case, they take my excuse as a joke without being offended and apologize as they move to the back of the line. Either way, how bad could it be?

As if the world is just dying to prove me wrong, the guy rolls his eyes like he's a thirteen-year-old girl who I just told Dad must supervise her at the mall.

"Seriously?" He shakes his head. "You give a third of your life to a woman and she still doesn't have the decency to remember who you are." His unmanicured brow bends in frustration as he reaches for the woman beside him. The words sound like a joke, but the simmering rage with which he delivers clears up any confusion. "It's your ex-husband, Vicky. Does that ring any bells?"

My cheeks flush, heat rising to the point of becoming an inferno. I'm mortified and furious. The surrounding people no doubt hearing Trent's seemingly justifiable irritation and judging me like I'm a contestant on *America's Got Talent*. If only being a cold-hearted-bitch could get you as many standing ovations as it does side-eye. My ears burn a little more. It's not like I want to forget his face (though I do); I can't help it! He knows that how much time I spend with him doesn't matter. I have no control over when I recognize someone and when I don't. My brain is like a fucking roulette wheel, with black or red being my memory. And I hate that I give a shit about any of their opinions, but I do.

"Yes, Trent. As a matter of fact, it does." Before I can think better of my temper I spit out, "you're the no-good, cheating with your employee, assless chap wearing dick head that left me. How could I forget?"

I tap my finger to my chin. If he wants me to play the bitch, I'll play.

"Oh, yeah—because I just so happened to erase your memory well enough to not even recognize your hipster slouch, or that left corner bald spot you try to cover. You're not fooling anyone, *bro*. Who knew my faceblindness would be so handy?"

Rebecka is already pulling at Trent's arm, vacating her spot in line, while the people around us turn towards my raised voice. The heat in my face intensifies with embarrassment knowing that I'm causing a scene, and I almost regret it.

Trent fidgets as if he has more to say, steam practically billowing from his ears and circling said bald spot, so I simply glance over his shoulder. He deserves what I've said, but I can't start this adventure off this way with another fight with Trent.

"Just... go away," I practically beg.

We've done enough damage to both our days, and I just hope he'll understand that without it needing to be said. I am worn by his presence and I'm over his backhanded words. One day, maybe, we can be in the same room, at the same airport, together, but that day is not today. I see Trent's boots plant on the scraped tile floor before Rebecka whines, tugging his hand and begging him to move. I've never been so relieved to hear her high-pitched squeal before.

"C'mon, Trent. We can get coffee on the flight. Don't let her spoil our vacation. This was just for us, remember?"

I hate the way her voice wraps around the word *our*. Not long ago I was the other half of "our" and "us". I was someone that was part of something more, who could be called and counted on, to help make decisions or memories. I used to be wanted, too.

She can have him, I think, instead of wallowing.

I watch as Trent's shoes shuffle out of my vision and count to ten before lifting my head back up. A few pairs of eyes shift away in guilt. I no longer have someone's shadow to live in, and I'll be damned if I mourn that part of what

I'm leaving behind, so I tip my chin up higher insisting I'll meet any stare and mold myself into the line, careful to keep my eagerness to get away from these people and their pity hidden. I never wanted to be a spectacle, but now that I am, I won't let them win by shaming me back to a corner.

Readying my sweaty, slick plastic card to pay, I order the bitter fluid that will keep me sane. The dollars and cents register in my mental checkbook, and I can't help but wonder, *what the fuck am I doing?* I could have avoided this whole thing if I just tuned out and realized I really didn't have the money for this.

"Don't worry. This one's on me."

The barista smiles as if we share a secret. Though I'm angry at her for seeing my embarrassment, for shrinking who I am into this tiny moment, I still smile and nod back. *Baby steps, Vip.* I gingerly take the hot cappuccino from her hands, the rough cardboard of the cozy bringing me back to myself and out of this disaster. My feet can't carry me away fast enough from these people, back into my little corner of the airport where I can await my true escape in peace. This is probably the most eager I've ever been to get on a plane in all my life. And that's saying something, being that I am deathly afraid of flying.

If ever there was a villain origin story for me, this had to be it.

\#

You'd think this early in the morning there would be another empty seat in the terminal but the only ones that are open surround where I originally started, stuffed between frazzled travelers, that I'm not even sure I could squeeze my butt into the seat. I sigh, opting instead to push my bag up against the farthest wall and slide down beside it.

My eyes close as I try to stop anticipating the minutes before I need to board. A quiet throat clearing jerks my eyes open, only to catch a blue-eyed attendant crouching down in front of me, her blinding teeth and minty breath infusing my space.

"It seems like you've had a long day, and it's only 7 am. I... well, I saw what happened at the cafe line. And guys like that, they really yank my chain, ya know? How about I get you an upgrade?"

She smiles, her words throwing my already volatile mood off. I pretend to glance back and forth before coming back to the attendant in front of me.

"Who me? I've already forgotten anything that may, or may not, have happened before this moment," I say, desperate to not start my trip with witnesses, to be known as *that* girl.

The attendant's smile just widens as she nods her head in knowing affirmation. Part of me wants to say no, to hide from the embarrassment that I can't stop exuding to the world that I need help and ignore her understanding eyes. I want to start this do-over without taking the easy way. The handouts. The things that got me into this situation in the first place.

"C'mon. I've got the best seat around with your name on it," she pressures.

My internal battle dilutes. I can't take back what's happened or ignore the boost that I so clearly need. I might as well take advantage of whatever perks come from that ridiculous ordeal. Besides, I bet they have better barf bags in first-class, anyway. I heave myself off the sticky airport floor, dusty fluff balls sticking to my hands that I quickly wipe down the sides of my favorite joggers, praying it doesn't show.

"Thank you," I whisper, allowing her to guide me away from this morning and all the people in it.

I leave my irritation and pain at the threshold of the plane, only taking my imagination, my fear of flying, and my new first-class ticket. Destiny is showing good fortune and never one to question karma, or a free ride, I scan in and walk the boarding hall right into a death tube of luxury.

Then the panic attack begins.

TWO

Victoria / Roman

Maybe this is exactly what I deserve.

Another friendly attendant greets me at the entrance to the plane as I try to force my breathing from marathon level pants to something resembling normal, which is a Herculean task. She escorts me to my seat—a window seat, second row—which, to my amazement, is empty. I breathe a fraction easier, knowing no one else is here to witness my meltdown. I must be doing a good enough job of hiding it since the attendant doesn't even seem to notice that I'm swallowing down air like it is an Olympic sport. Either that or they see this often enough, it's no longer a spectacle to behold.

I look between the large, cushioned seats until my eyes snag on the open oval window and I cannot hide the nerves that take over at the thought of seeing the clouds beside me. The attendant snags up my small roll-on into the overhead compartment, fluid in her movements, clearly trying to speed this along. She's oblivious to my gaping mouth and shuffling hands as I try to work up the courage to ask if I can switch. I don't want to make a gracious gesture a headache for her, but I also worry I may lose my breakfast, or consciousness, if I don't. Unfortunately, she decides for us both as she vanishes before I can make a sound.

I snap my teeth together and breathe deep, reciting the technique my therapist taught me the last time I had a trip to take. *In, one, two, three four; out, four, three, two, one.* It doesn't do much more than make me self-conscious that I'm standing in first class, counting to myself and people are staring. I choose to chance another passenger's anger and plunk myself down in the aisle seat, tossing my bag into my assigned seat instead. *If anyone comes, I'll move. All I need to do is make it through take-off, turbulence, and touchdown. Easy. No big deal.*

My heartbeats tick down a notch at the plan. Anxiety and excitement still pool in my belly, but it's manageable. I sport the first genuine smile of the morning as I sort through the literature in front of me to locate the barf bag. Just in case my luck doesn't last.

The vibrations of Trent's scowl filter through me, as I cannot help but wonder what he might be thinking with his mocking laugh and consolidation that my dreams were too much, but that I fit just right into the life we had. Comfort swells at the belonging those words gave me, even as bright quirks and eager parts of me were being killed.

My marriage wasn't violent. It wasn't loveless or abusive or scattered. It just wasn't enough. For either of us. That's the most painful part of it all; that I had something many could be content with, that many wish to have, and yet, I couldn't make it work. I couldn't be alive and fulfilled and still be overlooked. I wasn't sure how to split the difference between everything I once thought I could have and what I'd settled for. And Trent couldn't be faithful to someone whose attention had slipped.

As hard as it was to lose someone who knew me, it was freeing to slip into the hope that now I could change. I could finally do something different with my life. Something that resembled the stories that I spun, that I clung to when I was shoved back into who I was when I stepped ever so slowly toward something new. I could become anyone in a city layered with possibilities.

People pass, filling the seats beyond first class. The throng of boarding slows, and a shiver of anticipation runs through me. I watch the entrance for the equally beautiful and terrible moment when they seal us all in. I have to believe the flying gods must be on my side this morning.

To distract myself, I sort through my bag for my eReader, a grateful exhale at the prospect of being alone for the entire flight leaving my chest. I settle in for a perfect three-hour read, when I watch from the top of my lashes a three-piece suit's long strides eating up the aisle. My gut sinks, not sure how, but knowing he's headed straight to me. Unsurprisingly, he comes to a halt at the edge of where I'm sitting, not even a little out of breath, eyes narrowed.

"I believe you're in my seat," he says as he eyes my tucked in legs, glowering deeper at every inch he takes in.

His voice is honey drenched in spice, thick and syrupy and irritated, as if his words don't want to leave his body. I don't blame them. If he wasn't addressing me, wanting the seat I'd already claimed, I wouldn't want to leave his lips either. But he *is* talking to me. My own irritation pricks underneath my skin, cheeks flushing in both frustration at having a seat mate and the embarrassment at my assumption that I would be alone in first-class.

Slowly, I remove my bag from the window seat, standing so I can slide into it and stash it between my legs. I'm careful to take up minimal space as he folds his enormous form into the space. Fighting the urge to beg him to switch, I count my breaths, fear spiking as I glance at the tarmac. I remind myself that I only have this first-class seat because of a favor, and it could easily be taken away if I misbehave. Hating to fly is always better in the plane's front than in the back. At least unless we crash, then it obviously doesn't matter. But agitating my panic attack now to a full-on fit will only cause me pain for the next few hours. I swallow the butterflies and work to be normal, trying instead for polite conversation.

"Sorry about that. I thought the seat would be empty. A girl can dream, right?" I ask.

He ignores me as he works his phone out of his pocket. For the sake of keeping the peace, I try again.

"I'm Victoria."

My hand reaches out to him. He stares at it pointedly until I relent, slowly bringing it back to my lap.

"Charmed," he mumbles, before going back to his phone.

I stare, agape, and can't help but size this guy up. I notice a small expensive leather messenger bag tucked at his feet that oozes wealth from its seams. The shoes that surround it are polished with matching black socks that barely peek up the sides. His suit is black, darker than any black I've ever owned, not a crease to be found and freakishly clean. In fact, that was the best way to describe him.

Clean. Cut. Cruel.

His entire demeanor screams money. From the perfectly trimmed hair to the manicured nails. Even the way his jaw is set feels expensive.

I fidget, pulling my eyes away, seeing my three-year-old joggers, slightly fraying at the edges, with their matching soft knit hoodie. I've loved this outfit since Katie pulled it off the discount rack and shoved it into my arms, insisting I had to have it. Although I wouldn't wear it to a party, it makes my skin pop with its dark blue cotton and has that perfect worn in comfort that is more than suitable for a quick plane ride in coach.

Except, today, I'm not in coach. And now, I look more like I might rob first class than buy a ticket for it.

The glory of the extra leg room dims to a light sunbeam, and I immediately shrug away the cloud. This man knows nothing about me. I could be wealthy and confident, my outfit a big middle finger to the classism of the world. I mean, I come from the capital of grunge wearing millionaires. And if I *was* said sassy money bags, I wouldn't let this man, someone who obviously doesn't appreciate the luxuries he treats so flippantly, make me enjoy them any less. It's only a few hours, but I can think of no better time to try on a new persona instead of bending over backwards to please this asshole.

My body immediately spreads to take up more room in defiance and I check the man in my peripheral still fussing over his phone. His dark stylishly unkempt hair falls across his forehead, eyebrows scrunched, trying to keep the strands from reaching his eyes. He glances over, catching the corner of my gaze and I jolt away, focusing my attention instead on the attendant currently closing the airlock, afraid he can see right through me. I remove my elbow from the armrest. Maybe I'm not as ready to be someone else as I thought.

Everyone buckles themselves in around me and I quickly do the same, ready to be anywhere but here. My shaking fingers catch on the buckle, my stomach dropping out. My new seat mate sighs at my clumsiness, and the tingling across my chest turns into an inferno in my cheeks. I watch as he shoves headphones into his ears before going back to whatever he's been doing on his phone. I'm not sure if I'm more annoyed, terrified, or embarrassed, but I wish I didn't have an audience for it.

Sure, he was hot, but he wasn't *Henry Cavill hot*... at least, I didn't think so. After the run in with Trent, I hesitate to make any final assumptions, unsure of my instincts to recognize anything. Another peek has me checking for the classic Henry smile or jawline as I try to imagine them, then decide to play it safe. I secretly search out Henry's picture on my phone and compare, relieved when I don't find the blue eyes or chin dimple. I smile dumbly to myself. Of course, he wouldn't be on a public flight. Or so completely rude. Or sitting next to you, *ever*.

I shake my head to get the daydreams out. If I am ever going to make it in entertainment, I need to get my imagination under control (ironic; I know). It is bad enough I can't recognize anyone. It will be worse if I am constantly second guessing myself. I cannot use an Internet search every single time I share space with someone.

Treat everyone as if they're someone.

It's a mantra I've been using all my life, a reminder that I do not have the luxury of picking my mood or my personality based on my surroundings. I need to be consistent and confident in my actions. Playing a character, while fun, is not realistic. At least, not outside my scripts or my head. It only took me less than five minutes of trying to realize that.

So, instead of pushing into the facade of belonging here, I make a vow to ignore my seat mate for the rest of the flight. I pull up my eReader and dive right in, desperate to distract myself from the window and the ungodly rattle the plane is making through takeoff. I avoid his ire for approximately ten pages into my book, right after the seatbelt sign dings off and the worst of takeoff is over.

The romance book glowing up at me has my skin tingling from anticipation. I both love and hate the sex scenes that are equally taboo and consuming all at once. The love interest, Antonio, has professed his love for his college roommate's girlfriend and there's nothing holding their passion back any longer. Antonio is the guy who would take you to your favorite movie in the park without forgetting the popcorn and makes you measure every real-life man against. He's been the one from the start and Jo, the roommate's girlfriend, is finally accepting the passion between them.

Jo is about to scream his name as Antonio continues to do unspeakable (but very readable) things to her while she wriggles in vain, when a choked sound interrupts me. My side-eye game is strong as I try to ignore it, pretending instead it's part of Antonio's moans, but he persists to the point of recognition.

I sigh out, "*What?*"

His shock and embarrassment hit with the force of a hot oven wind.

"Do you think that's appropriate for... for *public* consumption?" he asks, shock dripping from his tongue.

Had we just been reading smut... together?

My cheeks flare to life of their own volition at his audacity. He had to have been reading for a while too, because the truly racy parts don't happen until over halfway down the page. A small cartwheel whips through my gut before my irritation consumes it.

"Yes. As a matter of fact, I think *what* I'm reading isn't the problem here. You want to know what I think the problem is?" I sneer back, irked by his judgements.

I've dealt with guys like this. *Trent* could be a guy like this, and I was done being shamed for liking or wanting anything. I tip my head as if I'm about to tell him a secret. Spit already wetting my lips as his shoulders slouch toward me, a moth drawn in by the flame.

"The problem is the sleazy prude in first class sitting next to me reading *my personal property!*" I yell the last part, heads spinning in our direction from the aisle next to us.

The sleazy prude in question, with a voice I'd like to hear read this instead of condoning it, eyes widen and mouth slacks open. I'm not sure what he was expecting, but it certainly wasn't that. His surprise turns to anger, slowly creeping over his body. Reddened cheeks tint through the olive tone of his skin, stretching his coloring past a point of no return and his chest might grow another million feet from the breath he's holding, hands circling a crushing grip on the arms of his seat. His chin is still leaned towards me, angling him enough to invade my space. I marvel at how similar bursting with passion and exploding with anger actually looks like and imagine if his cheeks tint the same color when he holds in his laughs. Or his moans.

He opens his mouth to say something I'm sure is nasty but before he can, a flight attendant sashays up to our row, polite and the picture of perfection. He closes his mouth but doesn't immediately turn to greet her. His eyes promise retribution. My eyebrow pops up in challenge before I quickly tear my gaze away from his and let the biggest bullshit smile I've ever had, grace my face. The young, polished woman stands next to him, and I am grateful both for the interruption of this conversation and my own thoughts.

\#

"Hello, Mr. Wh—"

No. No way is this, this *mess* of a girl next to me is learning my name. As soon as she hears *Mr. Wheatley,* she'll gush, her eyes widening from narrow slits as she assumes all the ways I could help her make it once we reach California. *Roman? Roman Wheatley? The director?* she'll say. Then the praise will come, hoping to gain favor, whether or not she likes my movies. Or worse, she'll sneer down her nose and think that she's better than me after reading who knows what gossip rag, despite my expensive clothes, first-class ticket, and the dozen awards I've been nominated for.

Why didn't I buy both seats on this godforsaken plane again? In fact, why did I even get on it?

I catch her from my peripheral and her smile could rival the sun. And just as my dislike for the desert, it grinds against my eyes like sand to my skin. I should have run the moment I saw her sitting in my place, her tattered bag taking up the window seat with *Victoria* scrawled across a dirty travel tag. If she doesn't realize who I am already, she will if I let this conversation continue, and all my successes and all my failures will be laid out with a single name.

I won't stand for it.

I turn my head from the irritating woman and my eyes clash into the tight bunned blond standing next to me. Her crystal blue eyes and classic looks, no doubt seeing the juxtaposition of my seatmate and me. I cut the questions off before they can begin, quick to interrupt this catastrophe as she flinches back a step from my gaze.

"It's fine. I'm fine." My words are clipped, the old money arrogance I've perfected, crisping every word. "Except, I would love something sharp to drink, if you could. Whatever you have that will numb the next few hours of this flight."

My smile is tight and grows even more strained as the wreck beside me pipes in, "make that two."

The poor blond mirrors my smile now, all hope of civility gone.

"No problem, sir. I will be right back with that."

She scurries away without acknowledging my seat mate. Victoria has ensured only one of two things will happen now for the rest of the flight; either the attendant will be slow to fill every order placed from this point on or she'll rush to fill us with liquor, hoping to calm the obvious tension we're seeping into the cabin. Either could be a disaster. I am so glad this flight is a short one.

The ghost of Victoria's gaze rests on the nape of my neck. I hesitate to turn back. She's beautiful in all the ways a girl like her can be—careless, because no one is watching. At the very least, no one is *documenting*. Her lips and cheeks are full and flushed, a rosy hue making her hazel eyes glow. It irritates me all the more. Pushes my anger past a tolerable level under my skin. I've been on this tipping point since my rat of an agent called demanding I be on this flight, and Victoria just happens to be the one extra grain to tip the scale.

"So. Are you just going to pretend I don't exist now?" she quips.

I lose the battle of looking away and find Victoria inspecting her fingertips.

"Because I tried that, and it was you who couldn't mind your own business for long. I was perfectly content reading my, rather pleasant, book."

Her voice is firm. Rooted in what she's saying, humor creeping in at the edge of her tone. I don't intimidate her enough to quiet the need to defend herself. It makes me want to laugh. A cruel laugh my father taught me. One that only comes when someone is so clearly outmatched and pathetic that it warrants no other response. I shove that down deep into my throat. I would rather choke on it.

Just because I need his praise does not mean I want his likeness. His nose and eyes are enough for me, thank you. Despite all the churlishness this woman exudes, I'm man enough to realize she doesn't deserve my anger, even if I can't exactly stop it from seeping out. It wasn't the book, really, that made me lash out. I had seen, heard, and read more filth than I needed to. But seeing the flush rise from her chest to her cheeks, combined with the rejection of my apology from Lauren and this stupid fucking trip, had me on edge.

My head drops into my outstretched palm, elbow resting on the aisle side, still turned away. I scrub at my face and brows, the grit of my facial hair sanding my fingers, knowing I'm being too sensitive. I try to stretch out the crease and tension that has taken up permanent residence in my forehead, neck, and jaw. Control is what I need. To provide, at the very least, in difference. We have hours left to go seated next to each other, after all.

"Perfect."

Her lips pop out the word before I can pull myself together and face her to start over. Everything tenses back up as I hear the dramatic effect of rustling, turning to see buds being angrily stuffed into her ears. She's twisting herself up, leg popped up inside of her seat, facing the window, her back to me. She forcefully slams the window screen shut, as if just realizing it's there, her hands noticeably shaking.

Fuck. Is she scared of heights? She could have simply asked me to switch seats with her if that was the case and I would have happily done it. Well, maybe not *happily*, but I would have switched. That's all that matters.

I try to let it go, even as a shred of guilt tugs at pieces of my heart I didn't realize were still around. I pull back up my phone, determined to make it through this flight with no further incidences. An email from the studio has come through reminding us of their plus one service again, which I quickly delete. The last thing I need is Victoria reading that over my shoulder and hearing her snickers. Instead, I reopen my downloads and begin reading the numerous scripts sent to me. Or failing to read. I can hardly get through the titles before my attention shifts back to Victoria.

I'm working up the nerve to ask her if she wants to switch seats when the attendant finally makes her way to us with our drinks. She's taking her time, no doubt working to staunch the flow of alcohol to us. Option one it is. Her instincts must be good, realizing it would be like adding gasoline to an already raging fire. I would applaud her if I was a stranger looking in. But I'm not, so my scowl only grows. She has two plastic tumblers on her cart, golden liquid peering out. They're only half of the way full, but it'll have to do.

I tap Victoria on the shoulder to get her attention, my fingers barely brushing against her sweater, not wanting to make her any more uncomfortable than she clearly already is.

"WHAT?" she yells, her headphones at a volume unbecoming of a closed in tin.

Narrowed eyes barely reach over her shoulder to me before she realizes the attendant standing at my side, cup in hand.

"Oh! I'm sorry," she yells.

My flinch must tip her off as she quickly removes the buds, mumbling *sorry, sorry,* as she readjusts in her seat and reaches for the drink.

Time ticks into slow motion, Victoria bending into my space. Her arm almost touches my chest, and the heat from her skin burns through my thin dress shirt, as she leans further out to the attendant. The warm smell of spiced vanilla reaches me all at once, skating across my skin in a swell, my eyes focusing in, and I'm engulfed in her. Her smile is like a visceral thing as she mouths *thank you,* her delicate fingers trying to wrap around the plastic.

Only they don't. She tries to pull too quickly, or the attendant tries to give too fast. Something in the span of a moment goes horribly wrong. The liquid falls directly in front of me, its golden waves splashing every side before tumbling upside down, landing firmly in my lap. It seeps through my suit onto my inner thighs. Wet, sticky fabric clings to my crotch, outlining areas I would rather keep private. I jump at the sensation, effectively slapping my chest against Victoria's arm and my head against the attendant's.

"FUCK!" I yell.

Both women scoot back from me in horror. Victoria, lips moving like a fish out of water, lunges for the napkins currently in the hands of the attendant and starts dabbing at my crotch as soon as she gets them.

"Oh, my god. I am so, *so* sorry. I didn't mean... I cannot believe... I am such a klutz."

She's rambling and if she rubs any harder, there's going to be an even bigger embarrassment that arises. I fling my hands out, pushing them both away.

"Stop. Just stop already!"

I'm flustered, and a bit turned on. Embarrassment tumbles around in my stomach and I decide my best course of action is to leave this space before we both get convicted of a felony. My reputation cannot afford it.

I move like lightning is at my heels for the bathroom. Both Victoria and the attendant are calling to me, apologies and what sounds like giggles, which I ignore. People are staring and one person already has their phone out. Another attendant is quick to stop it, knowing the frailness of his first-class passenger's privacy. Appreciation for the attempt at discretion has me nodding.

The bathroom clicks, and I can finally breathe behind its locked door. I look in the tiny plane mirror and recognize my furious face well. It's the face I've worn often throughout my entire life, the pinched dark brows, and wild pupils. My eyes have always been ensconced in black, but lately, the stress has somehow made them darker. I hardly remember what color lies beneath. At least they're one thing I got from my mother. The sharp lines and dark hair are all Wheatley blood. I run the sad excuse for a faucet and throw a small paper towel under it.

Black has always been my friend, but right now, not even it can save me. You can hardly see the liquid outline that could easily be mistaken for me pissing myself, but as soon as I run the towel on the fabric, it pills leaving behind a visible trace all the way from my thighs to my hip. Flashbacks of private school come rushing back of the obnoxious pranks pulled on unsuspecting students. Hand in water while sleeping was always a favorite, followed by pictures posted by dorm mates throughout the halls. I sigh. My whole life is a series of spaces ruled by humiliation in some form or another. Perfect lives have nothing better to do for entertainment, apparently.

My trousers are already drying but far from the spill not being noticeable, and I've done the best I can do with myself. I'm not ready to leave this room. I don't want to go back to my seat, or more specifically my seat mate. Still, what other choice do I have? We're on a plane where there is literally nowhere else to go. The longer I mope in here, the worse it'll be. I steel myself for explanations and apologies, fully calm when I open the door. Out in the hallway is the blond attendant, my messenger bag strapped over her shoulder as she protects it tightly. My face puckers in question.

"Mr. Wheatly, your seat is... no longer a viable option, given the...dampness. We would like to exchange seats for you for the rest of the flight with our sincerest apologies. We will also provide you with a credit to the airline's VIP bar upon landing for all of your troubles."

Her cheeks are pink, obviously embarrassed she even needs to have this conversation. The smile that blisters my face and my ego, however, clears up her concern.

"That sounds wonderful. Thank you," I say.

I am so relieved that I won't have to face Victoria again that I cannot hold my stoic appearance any longer. It's not that I wish her any ill will, I just don't want her bad luck rubbing off on me anymore than it already has. Both literally and figuratively. My smile slips as I realize I am being escorted back to the same row I had occupied previously, sans the woman seated next to me.

"Here you are, sir. You have the entire row now and can sit in the window seat, which is free from any liquid. Again, our apologies on this mishap."

She gestures for me to sit, so I do. Then she hands me a full drink, ensuring my hand has fully grasped it before letting go.

Before she can leave, I cannot help but ask, "What happened to her?"

"Oh. We've moved her back to coach." She wrings her hands as if she is personally responsible for the mix up before continuing. "She was upgraded this morning. We are truly sorry. Please let me know if you need anything else."

Thank you is all I say before waving her away.

I sip at my drink, an ugly inkiness gnawing at me. I shake it away. *Good riddance.* Maybe I'll be able to make this flight in one piece now.

Besides, I protest to myself, *it's less than an hour now. She'll be fine in coach for an hour.*

I pull back up my phone and continue reading script titles. If I don't choose one soon, the studio will pick for me. I can't have that. Thoughts of Victoria are shoved into nothing more than a memory as I become consumed with trying to figure out how in the hell I'm going to get through this next movie.

THREE

Roman

THE VIP BAR NESTLED into the private alcove of the airport puts me at ease. I have been dreading the photographers that troll the Los Angeles airport all day and am more than happy to put off crossing their paths anytime soon. To hell with Davis. If he wants to have a meeting with me, he'll have to do it here. At least until the credit the airline has given me runs out. My cell phone vibrates on the bar, the glow bringing it to my attention. *Agent Asshole* blinks up at me. I hit silence again.

I'm right here, buddy. Come and get me.

At ten in the morning, the bar is understandably empty, for which I'm grateful. The bartender slides by and I order breakfast along with an exceptionally large, and rather fruity, mimosa. The over garnished orange and red drink arrives, sugar practically dripping from its rim, just as a familiar laugh ricochets from behind me. My tense shoulders finally relax, and a small smile lifts my lips.

"You know you didn't have to come all the way to California to get a fuck ton of sugar this early in the morning, right? You could have just, I don't know, gone to 7-Eleven and ordered a Slurpee."

Thoren's hand grips at my shoulder and his laugh fills the space. My younger brother's smile comes fully into view as I swivel toward him. His dark eyes crinkle, leaving his cheekbones high and prominent on his face. He's shortened the sides of his hair, keeping the top long, and even gained a little muscle since the last time I've seen him.

"Where's the fun in that?" I clamp back at his own shoulder before sighing. "Besides, you know as well as I that Wheatley's don't drink from such clownish cups. Our sugar must come from the finest sources and most expensive dealers," I drop my theatrically pompous speech, "it's good to see you, T."

He rolls his eyes and slaps his forehead before replying, "right. After being away from the estate for so long, I must have forgotten that." His smile widens. "I've missed you too, Roman. It's been, what? Eight months? That's too long."

He's right, of course. Eight months for the Wheatley brothers to spend apart is unheard of. We've always found ways for all four of us to drop our lives, if just for a few days, and fly to each other to catch up. Even the heat of my exile from my father's good graces didn't stop that. But the last eight months have been different. I've been different. Losing everything will do that to a man.

"I know." My smile slips as I hold his eyes. "I'm sorry, Thoren. For all of it."

I couldn't mean anything more deeply if I tried. I was sorry for needing to follow my dream of being a director. I was sorry for climbing to the height of fame and then destroying that dream with my failure. I was sorry for losing the woman who was all our friend and should have been my wife. Not to mention the fucking yacht. But most of all, I was sorry I let him down. That I had drug him to California only to leave him here while I hid away to tend to my pride in private. He didn't deserve my abandonment, but I'd done it all the same.

He shrugs off my apology, like he always does. "I know, Roman."

He adamantly stares into my gaze a second longer to show me he's heard me before moving on. His eyes dip down to take me in before his laugh comes on full force again.

"Damn! What the hell happened to you on that flight? Did you join the mile high club and get your pants stuck in the toilet during the deed?"

Looking down, I notice the faint water outline in my crotch is showing, along with the small fuzz balls left behind by my attempt to clean it up in the bathroom. I swivel back to my seat, effectively hiding my lower front in the bar. I scrub at my face with both hands before taking a large gulp of my drink.

"It's a long, irritating story that is in no way as fulfilling as the account you just gave, I promise you," I reply. "Sit down. Order breakfast and *maybe* I'll tell you about it. But only if you tell me what's been going on with you."

"Deal!" He says with gusto.

As my brother regales me with his hilarious LA exploits over the last several months, I shoot a quick text to Davis, *bring pants from my luggage when you come actual pants not sweats don't be incompetent and late.* I should probably be nicer to someone I am expecting to do something for me, but since it's his job and we're currently having a difference of opinion, I leave the message as is and hit send.

There's no doubt he'll be here with the pants I've requested. The studio has made it clear; make Roman happy. It is bad enough that I've disappeared from the spotlight after I crashed and burned across every major tabloid known to man, but they still cannot afford to lose me when the public is currently so invested in what I might do next. It is all over the internet and gossip sites. Conspiracy theories, fan sites, petitions to bring me back. Everyone loves drama that isn't theirs. They need me.

That's why, after eight months of trying to coerce me back, they've brought out the big guns. If I didn't direct my next film in the next four months, they were going to sue me. For everything. I could never work again, my non-compete activated to its full capacity until either my debts were repaid, or my movie made. They could come after assets I've already spent. They could come after my inheritance to pay it back. If I even still had one. My father would disown me. I would be stripped of the Wheatley name for good.

I had every high-priced lawyer I could find pouring over the contracts before I got on this flight. The best of the best. They are ironclad. It didn't escape my notice that those same lawyers had been the ones to help me draft and revise them in the first place. I had been so worried that my first big break might be taken from me; I had wanted to make it impossible to lose it. Wanting out in less than three years had never crossed my mind. I was a fool.

My thoughts drift through the whole turn of events again—Davis calling me with the threat, the ticket to California already sitting in my inbox. The yelling with the lawyers, my oldest brother trying to calm me as he explained there's nothing to be done. Getting on the plane from Connecticut to Washington, directly disobeying the flight path, hoping that I could show up and Lauren would let me in to apologize. I at least owed her that if I was going to come back here. To no one's surprise, she did not. Then, getting on the plane, headed here to California. The land of imbeciles. Angry and reminded of why I left in the first place.

Victoria floats into my mind, her name on the cusp of being forgotten. I'm a fool *and* an asshole. Now, with liquid gold filling my veins and not just my pants, I can see I took my frustration out on her. I could have been nicer. Switched her seats and avoided the whole mess. I could have told the attendant to bring her back, that there were no hard feelings, and we could be more than tolerable for the rest of the trip. I could have done more. It appears I'm more like my father than I want to be.

Lauren's deep brown eyes take over Victoria's hazel ones. Even if I'm glad we're not married, I didn't want it to end like that. The guilt creeps in and I quickly stuff them both into the back of my mind. If I think about my ex-fiancé now, or even a new girl I've wronged, I might just do something incredibly stupid. I've had enough of that for one day. Not even an hour into being here and I'm already buzzed and loathing.

I hate California.

I tune back into Thoren's wild tale about his latest online date, a young woman who was...

"Wait." I hold out my hand to him on the bar. "You're saying she was a... circus performer? Like... a clown?"

My brother's eyes dance mischievously as he giggles at my interest.

"No, Roman. Like an acrobat."

His eyebrows wiggle, and I can't help but laugh with him.

"Alright, alright. I see why you stayed. But did you have to tell our poor, innocent mother that you've been looking for a wife then?"

My eyes pin him to the seat, a little ribbing necessary. He sobers up, straightening in his seat.

"Hey! I *am* looking for a wife. This girl was just in town for a few days—she travels a lot—and wanted to have some fun. But I promise, most of them are *not* this type of fun. Scout's honor." He holds up two fingers as a pledge that he's doing right by our family.

"Good. I'm glad to hear it. Both that you're being honest and that you're having a bit of consensual fun." I smile at him. "It really is good to see you so happy."

My tone tightens, and he reaches for my shoulder again, giving me a tiny shake as he does.

"You know, Roman, I wish..."

Before he can finish his wishes for me, ones that I'm sure come with advice I've already heard and actions that are, for now, impossible, we're interrupted. A short, trim older gentleman hustle up to us, snagging the other seat beside me. Davis. There's a dribble of sweat that mars his perfect tan, slicking his thinning black hair into even thinner pieces. His crooked nose sticks out like a hitchhiker's thumb in the wind. He's trying not to pant as he hands me a thin, reusable black bag.

"Mr. Wheatley! Good to see you here in beautiful California finally! Did you enjoy your vacation?" Davis asks.

He's the guy who could step right into dog shit and tell you it was time for a new pair of shoes anyway, as he continued whistling down the street. His positivity doesn't tire easily. He has that used car salesman, last man standing on the lot, attitude and I absolutely despise him. I stare at him as he waits for a response Hell's going to freeze over before he gets.

"Okay! Well, here's the pants you requested. Nice black slacks. Figured it'd go with the wardrobe if I know our boy, and don't we know our boy there, Thoren? Huh?"

He smiles across at my brother, who only reaches up and pats my cheek in condescension.

"That we do Davis! That we do," Thoren responds.

I want to punch them both. Instead, I stand, excusing myself to change. As I do, Davis notices the issue with my current pants, his eyebrows raising in interest. He knows better than to say anything by the promise of murder that is surely written across my face, telling him he shouldn't have noticed in the first place.

By the time I come back in my fresh slacks, I find Davis and Thoren huddled next to each other, eating my food. They've practically demolished half my plate, a piece of bacon still greasing my brother's fingers. My patience threatens to come unglued, but I'm ready to be out of this airport and into a bed. A public fight will only delay the inevitable and create a front-page story I am trying to avoid. I've been up too long to deal with any more shit.

"Let's go," I announce to them both.

They startle, the bacon falling from Thoren before he scoops it back up, quickly shoving it into his fat mouth.

"Sorry, bro. We were just sampling the menu a bit," he says around the food.

Davis is quick to jump in. "No sir. Thoren was sampling. I ordered my own."

I sighed, shrugging up my shoulders.

"Fine, but I am ready to leave. If you're ordered to babysit me, let's go. Otherwise, enjoy your meal, by all means."

My tone harbors no love, and I can see the longing Davis has at wanting to wait for his meal.

"It's okay Davy-Dave. I got this. I can get my brother safely to our condo and keep the pap at bay. You can just drop his bags off on your way out. I promise he won't be a flight-risk." He thinks for a minute, hand caressing his jaw. "At least, not for tonight."

His shoulders shrug in good humor, and Davis laughing right on cue. My brother loves nothing more than a willing audience and Davis is always looking for a show. Two peas in a moron pod, they are.

"Sounds good enough. A Wheatley promise is as good as gold, I hear," Davis jokes.

He smiles big at Thoren and me before sitting back down to wait, the bartender refilling his glass.

"But not as good as our contracts apparently," I dig.

Davis loses his smile. I turn and walk away, Thoren close at my heels.

FOUR

COACH. I CANNOT BELIEVE they moved me back to coach. Over a stupid, *accidentally*, spilled drink. Sure, I couldn't help the laugh that shook me to my bones as the heathen walked away. I was nervous, and it was *funny*. No one would have been able to resist it. No one, except the lovely woman who had upgraded me in the first place, apparently. She let me know how big a mistake she had made as she escorted me to my seat, right next to the screaming baby.

The luggage carousel finally produces my bag, and I push forward to snag it before I have to wait for another rotation. *Love of My Life* by the one and only Jennifer Lopez blares from my pocket, the vibration pulling at my already sagging joggers. I readjust my carry on over my shoulder and scoot off to the side with my bags before both pulling up my pants and my phone out. Monica's name flashes across my screen along with a flawless selfie she no doubt took and saved in my contacts.

"Kind of busy, Mon, trying not to get trampled by baggage claim." I curse as one of my tiny suitcase wheels collides with my toe.

"Well bitch, I'm here!"

Her voice is cheery, with only the slightest undertone of importance. With Monica it is never *what* she says, it's about how. Learning nuance is a require-ment for being her friend.

"What's the code this time?" She asks casually.

I plant my feet, steadying myself for the embarrassment.

"You know what the code is. I'm sure the three of you monsters have been waiting patiently for this since the moment I stepped into the airport. Maybe sooner."

Her laugh is like velvet, my opposite in every way. Where mine is vibrant and loud, stubborn as an uncut diamond, Monica's is the engagement ring. Perfect, understated, glamorous. The one everyone wants to have in their possession. I sigh dramatically before hanging up the phone without another word and begin my trek to the pickup line outside.

The line of cars is steady, ranging from standard mini vans and cabs to limos and town cars. There's plenty of bustle, but not enough to miss the sign being held up by the platinum blond standing next to her pristine white Lexus convertible. Her sky-high stilettos give her just enough height over her already tall figure to be seen from the automatic door currently whining at me to move. Her smile is wide and blinding. Every cord of muscle in my body threatens to rip it right off her face.

"NOBODY PUTS BABY IN THE CORNER" glares from the poster board in bright pink marker. I see others taking in the sign as well. Some chuckle under their breath, or to their loved ones. Others scoff, looking around confused to see who could possibly answer to this salutation. I take a deep breath in, let it out, and then make my way to Monica.

"You know, I haven't needed this since we were in high school? And you make a terrible Swayze!" I yell across the last few people between us.

"There's my Frances!"

She walks to meet me, the sign finally falling to the wayside, as she pulls me in for a side hug and kisses my cheek. The scent of rosewater with a hint of clove hits my nose, threatening a sneeze.

"I know you don't, but someone has got to keep our superstar humble. And Swayze could *never*."

We break apart as she flashes me her heels along with a coy smile. I take my luggage to the trunk with an eye roll before piling into her car. The leather burns under my butt before the car starts and the AC blasts icy wind into my face.

"How was your flight?" she asks.

"Well," I begin, unsure how much I should tell. "I got upgraded!"

My smile is trying to be sincere, but falls short. The shrug of my shoulders giving me away entirely. Monica stares daggers at me.

"Spill, Vip. Now." Her all-business tone has come out to play and arguing now would be futile.

"I *did* get upgraded... that is until I got downgraded again, mid-flight."

She turns her face fully to me.

"WATCH THE ROAD MONICA!" I yell.

She obliges and then laughs at full volume.

"You... you, what?!"

I can barely understand her through the gasps.

"It wasn't my fault! I was minding my own business, just reading my book like a delightful guest of first-class. Then Mr. Hottie-Underpants-In-A-Twist decides to be cranky. We both order drinks, which seemed appropriate at the time."

I'm rushing through my story, not wanting to dive too deep into embarrassment, knowing I'll never hear the end of it. The heat still burns on my skin and an odd mix of righteousness and guilt turns in my gut. How did this day get so screwed up this early on?

"Oh no. Tell me you didn't. Tell me your clumsiness did not make an appearance," she whispers in horror.

"Mon! It was an accident! I didn't mean to drop the cup in his lap. I would never intentionally soak what looked like a very expensive suit. Even if he might have deserved it. He talked shit about the book I was reading. Despite that, I tried to... help clean it up." My hands wave as I defend myself. "I should get a medal or an award or something for my kindness!"

Her laugh has died down, not even a single crease in her makeup to be found. She lets out a few more snickers as her head shakes in disbelief. Monica has seen firsthand the extent of my ability to make a situation awkward without even trying. My body somehow senses I need things to go right and will immediately do the opposite. Throughout school, people cruelly called me Bubble Girl, implying I needed to be contained in a bubble or wrapped in bubble wrap. Some even thought it should be both.

"So, you..."

Monica makes a rubbing gesture around her crotch. I close my eyes, lips folding in, as I admit my mistake,

"Oh. My. God... You're right, that is *some* kindness Vip!" She laughs, then refocuses, "OK, OK. but... he was hot?"

She smirks, navigating her car dangerously onto the highway. Monica has always been the one to ask the important questions.

"So not the point. I could have been arrested for molestation or something," I groan.

My face is in my hands as I try to cool down my flaring cheeks.

"Please. If you were getting charged, they would have apprehended you on the flight." She rolls her eyes and continues, "Was he... you know, at least worth getting booted for?"

She sizes me up in her side eye, before gesturing with her hands over her steering wheel what I can only imagine is an acceptable length she's trying to convey.

"Oh. My. MONICA! I'm not doing this with you. You are driving! I can't talk dicks when my life is in your hands!"

Her laugh echoes in my eardrums as I crank up the music to end our conversation.

"I'll take that as a yes!" she yells over the sound anyway, before a song she loves comes on.

She turns it up to an almost unbearable level and focuses instead on what I can only assume is her music video audition tape. My head bops to the deep bass pumping through the car, letting it pull me away. I think about the man I spent my morning next to and how I wish I could remember more. His features have already faded in my memory, his name never provided. Still, I don't think I'll be forgetting the feeling he gave me anytime soon. Like a character in one of my scripts, he comes back to me.

It was like being on a roller coaster. Watching him walk toward me in a crisp, tailored suit; the tick-tick-ticking of the car going up through the tracks slogging its way to the top, my anxiety building with every tick. The argument we had briefly; anticipation of sitting on top of the world, readying yourself to dive headfirst with both excitement and terror. The final conversation: my glass falling from my hand and into his lap, *fuck* ringing from his lips like the breath from my lungs as I'm plunged into the blur of sky meeting ground. Then being kicked back to coach; getting off the ride unsure of what the hell just happened and realizing I'm discombobulated, detached from my life before the fall.

He is a reminder of all I've missed. Sure, I could do without arrogance and judgements. The fury at his entitlement was still pinging through the edges of my anxiety from the flight. But even if he *was* an asshole, the experience made me more alive than I've been in years. And the pages I had scribbled in coach, of what should have happened with a meet-cute like ours if we wouldn't have been *us*, were good.

I could change them to take place on a ship instead of a plane and it would fit right into my current *Cruising for Love* script I planned to pitch first. Or they could be the start of something completely new. I haven't decided yet. But they were there, on paper, ready to be molded. I couldn't stay mad at that. Besides, I would never see him again. There was no lasting harm done, meaning I could let it go. Chalk it up to another memory. Another scene in my story.

By the time we make it to Monica's apartment in Studio City, Katie has called three times, the car radio swallowing any chance I had of answering. Monica grabs my carry-on as I lug my larger-than-life suitcase inside. Monica's apartment is livelier than I expected, bright orange hues greeting us from carefully picked walls. She notices my looks of disbelief and shrugs her delicate shoulders.

"It's the art district," she says as if there's nothing to be done with it. "I'd rather be able to afford a full-service building here than a dump next to the studio. Besides, it gives me a reason to use the Lexus."

Her smile is devilish, and I can't help but laugh.

"I cannot believe you kept it in the first place! You have no shame."

An old nudge, one that she appreciates because it's true. It's one of her most admirable qualities. Something I wish I had more of.

"Well, if Charles didn't want me to keep it, he should have never put it in my name and then slept with my roommate." Her shoulders shrug again. "I like to think I taught him an invaluable life lesson."

Our laughter follows us into the building, the concierge's head popping up in distaste as we make our way to the elevator. My chucks tap to the beat of the voiceless pop song softly playing from the speakers as we go up, up, up. The lulls of conversation with Monica have never been comfortable, not like they are with Katie and Cherie. She weeds out my weaknesses, finding places to pick at until she gets to whatever it is she's looking for. They're filled with a need for acceptance, a want for her to consider me her equal but having nothing of importance to say.

The elevator does not come fast enough as I shoot out before the doors even fully open. I will need to get used to it being just us, without the filler our friends normally provide. They've always been the buffer to our delicate balance. A way we can easily swing from uncomfortable to relaxed again. But my mood is slightly better when I notice the discomfort on Monica's face too.

"This way," she calls as she strides past me in the hall.

The apartment is chic, tidy and very Monica. It's a one bedroom that looks out over the district and catches the sun as it rises. There's a beautiful bar with a marble top and three barstools tucked tightly beneath it. The couch is a black and buttery sectional that takes up most of her living room space with blankets and pillows folded and tucked nicely on its end, facing a large flat screen. The coffee table is neatly ordered with a few design books, crystal coasters, and the remote control. A small desk is tucked into the corner next to the TV, sorely sticking out of place both in its newness and style.

"I know you haven't been to the new apartment, but this one is only a one bedroom, so you'll be crashing on the couch," Monica tells me. "All I ask is that you fold up your blankets and store your clothes in the dresser in the hall coat closet."

She folds herself onto the couch, heels easily slipping off as if she's done this a million times.

"I, ah, I also got you that desk to use for your writing. I know it's not much and you can always use the common space in the lobby, but I figured you might like a space to work up here too."

Tears prick my eyes. "It's perfect. Thank you."

Walking over to her, I bend down to give her a small squeeze before joining her on the couch folding my toes into its cushions.

"I really appreciate all you've done and for letting me crash with you while I'm figuring this all out. I know it's not easy to have someone invading your space."

She waves away my concern like it doesn't bother her a bit, even though it does.

"It's fine. That's what friends do, I'm told." A small smile threatens before being squashed down by another thought taking over her features. "Speaking of, I need to tell you about the job I have for you. Well, more like a proposition. A *mutually beneficial* proposition."

My guard immediately shoots up as her negotiating voice comes into play. *This cannot be good.* My stomach tightens, making breathing difficult. I knew that the job couldn't be that easy, being that I didn't even apply and Monica was being very hush-hush about the details. It would be just like her to have holes in my proverbial lifeboat. My brow raises and I motion for her to go on.

"You know I am an executive assistant for Timothy Oliver and Daniel Beckson at Dreamaway Studios, yes?"

She's stalling, so I roll my eyes and shake my head.

"Just get on with it, Monica. Obviously, something has happened with the job."

She sighs. "No. The job is still there, just as I promised. I'm glad you think so little of me," she sneers before continuing, "We had a bit of an issue come up the other day with some of our actors. Apparently, they are dateless for this season's parties and quite fussy about the usual selections—one of them had an incident with a plus one trying to upstage him, and he's been blabbering about it to anyone who will listen. It has them all spooked."

I don't like where this is going. My skin beads in anticipation.

"What on earth does this have to do with me?"

Her eyes narrow in, finally ready to land the arrow in my heart.

"I mentioned you staying with me to my bosses and your *unique* ability to forget people. He suggested you could be our plus one for the season." The objection is hot on my lips as Monica holds up a finger telling me to shh. "Now, before you lose your temper, we're willing to pay you, very well I might add, *and* I'll be able to take your script directly to acquisitions. They are currently in a rush to fill a director's opening for production and yours would float to the top of the pile."

The heat is rising into my cheeks, rage coiling into my joints, tendons, and bones. A sweet, slimy sickness has taken residence in my stomach squeezing organs I need to breathe. I knew Monica was selfish. From the moment she spent all her money buying erasers at the book fair only to sell them to all her friends at a premium, I knew. And I knew that being here would have strings. I was prepared for chores and parties. I was prepared to be her champion and wing-woman. I am not, however, prepared for this. This is lower than I thought she would go. Words have escaped me, but Monica has more.

"Before you make any final decision in that stubborn brain of yours, you need to know that I already told them you would."

I'm going to strangle her. Right here, right now. The reenactment for true crime TV flashes before me, the horrors of this moment living in infamy. My stand-in, grabbing Monica's stand-in by the shoulders, clawing into her bob before they pan the camera to my stand-in holding the bloody vase above her. It wouldn't be glamorous, but it would be accurate.

She continues, "Honestly, Vip. This is too good of an opportunity. You told me you were broke. You told me you needed to sell your script. You said you had to start living an actual life and stop running scared. This gives you all of that." She ticks the points off on each finger, "Money. Opportunity. Adventure. Something you can shove in that asshole ex's face. It is everything you came to

California to find, and I couldn't let it slip away from you. Not when it was handed to us on a silver plate *and* came with accolades for me. It is the perfect solution. You see that, right?"

"Monica... What the fuck?" I seethe, unable to say anything else as my mind lets her reasons sink in.

It wasn't perfect. Not in the fucking slightest. Going out with a C-level, grade-A douche bag was not my idea of putting myself out there. My last bad first date was in college. Did I really want my next one to be a paying opportunity? I cover my face in my hands, needing to break eye contact with Monica before I rip her face off in passionate rage. She didn't even *consider* how I might feel about her making this decision for me!

I breathe deep, trying to push down the fear of people knowing I won't recognize them, the fear that I will forever be marked as the girl who did that thing once, and try to think through her offer. I am a big enough person to admit to myself; it does provide *some* benefit. Not enough for me not to hold this against Monica for the rest of her fucking life, but maybe enough for me to agree. This once. Maybe.

A tiny butterfly flaps its way through the sickness as I think about my script being considered by the top studio, Dreamaway. My characters *finally* coming to life on-screen. If that happens, I might be able to forgive Monica sometime this century. Maybe. I inhale a deep breath before lifting my head and catch the legitimate worry etched all over her face. I hope she's realizing just how far over the line she's stepped this time. I wait a few more beats, watching her face fall even more into panic, before putting her out of her misery.

"Fine," I grunt. "But fuck Monica, you've stepped way over the line this time. I am not forgiving you. And I'm not doing anything else for you—no other strings while I'm living here, do you hear me? This is your onetime free pass. For anything else, you go directly to jail. You do not pass go and you do not collect $200. Understand?"

My voice is solid, deadly in its seriousness. I cannot risk her trying a stunt like this again.

She nods rapidly. "Yes. Of course. I've overstepped and I'm sorry. I really have the best of intentions with this. But I promise, never again."

She crosses her heart over her chest, and I have no other choice but to let it go. I've agreed, she's agreed, and I need to accept where that's landed me. For everyone's sake.

I've just sunk my body into the resignation of my fate when her voice chimes in, "One more thing. The date? It's for tonight."

She's fucking dead.

Monica is more athletic than I remember. She outruns me around her apartment for a good ten minutes as I scream obscenities until finally, I lose my breath. I settle for chucking a pillow at her ass, accidentally breaking a cheap white IKEA vase in the process before I calm down enough to have some semblance of normalcy. Then I call and tattle on her.

"She did what?" Cherie screams into the phone, "I'm going to kill her!"

I can't help the chuckle that escapes me. Monica sweeps up ceramic while mumbling incoherently to herself across the room from me.

"That's what I said. I broke her vase, but we are not remotely even."

Katie is stunned silent, but Cherie laughs in glee.

"Good. You get your revenge, girl," she says to me before yelling to what I can only assume is Monica, "I HOPE IT WAS AN EXPENSIVE ONE. You hear me, Mon. EX. PEN. SIVE."

The patience Monica has been holding over this argument's cliff thins before snapping her into free fall.

"THAT'S IT!" she squeals. "If you have something to say to me, Cherie, get your ass down here. I *apologized*. I admitted I was wrong. But it HAPPENED. Can we move on already? Even as messed up as you think this is, I am doing more for Vip's future than either of you. I don't see you guys opening career doors for her. But I am. SO, WHAT if it's going to a couple parties with successful guys? SO, WHAT if it helps me too? That doesn't negate what it's going to do for her!"

Her neck is turning purple from the strain of having to defend herself.

Katie cuts in, quick to disrupt whatever tirade Cherie had in mind.

"We get it, Monica. I see why you didn't grasp the full consequence of doing this to Vip, but I'm hoping now you do."

She's silent for just a beat and as if she can sense Monica's head shaking in affirmation on the other end of the line, she continues, "Look, ladies, what's done *is* done. Vip has agreed and I'm positive there are plenty of precautions being taken for her safety."

"Of course there is," Monica scoffs. "I'm not an idiot. They are vetted dates. Vip has her own car service and driver to ensure she gets there and back safely. We also have security at these parties and have briefed them on the situation. She couldn't be any safer."

"Security?" Cherie pops in. "So, these are like, BIG deal parties then?"

Monica rolls her eyes. "These are awards parties, industry parties, *insider networking* parties. We weren't sending her to a random club or dinner and drinks with a sleaze ball. Who do you think I am, Cherie?"

"A selfish social climb… Ouch! What the hell Katie!" Cherie cries.

"We love both of you very much," Katie coos into the phone. "Vip, call us and let us know all the dirty details."

The line clicks before I even have a chance to say goodbye. I sigh and turn my head to Monica, who's washing her hands in the kitchen behind me.

"See? I told you it wasn't that bad. They didn't even freak out much," she says.

"That is so not the point."

I shake my head, but I'm done arguing. Insecurity swells inside me, fear of who I'll meet and what they'll think and thoughts like, *I can't believe I'm actually doing this.* I don't want to dwell on them, so I hurry to move on.

"I'm glad to hear all the steps you're taking to keep me safe. What else was set up?"

Her smile returns and she glides to the couch to sit beside me.

"We get to go shopping. Completely paid for. You'll need a few outfits, so you don't stick out like a country bumpkin. And as a onetime apology from me, you'll be getting your hair and makeup done, too." At that, she grabs my hand and squeezes. "I would never put you in any danger, Vip. I love you the best way I know how."

Her eyes are wide as saucers, and she holds contact until it's painful to continue.

"I know, Mon. I do," I say, then pull her to me. "For better or worse, we're in this together. I just hope, if this is a horror film, you're the one who gets killed off first."

FIVE

Victoria / Roman

I RUN MY FINGERS over the chain of my wristlet, the weight of my phone forcing indentations into the pads. Shopping was a montage. Seeing Monica in her natural habitat, ordering people to their respective jobs and picking out several pieces that flattered me with barely a second glance, was astounding. It did its job of keeping my mind off the failure my life had become. Laughing with her reminded me of all the reasons we'd been friends for so long. Reasons that don't seem to hold up in the silence of the town car currently zipping down the interstate.

My driver's name is Stanley, who I've lovingly been referring to as 'Stan the Man'. He doesn't seem to mind one bit if the toothy grin he keeps giving me is any indication. A thick gold hoop earring in one of his ears makes me think of that movie the internet claims never happened. His neon purple shirt is visible beneath his split, tailored black suit. All of it clashes horribly with his red mustache and freckled bald head, making it, if nothing else, hysterical. But Monica was right when she told me it would be impossible for me to mistake him. In this getup, he is truly one of a kind.

The smoggy sky of LA is just starting to get inky. I'm on my way to meet my date at the venue—a hole in the wall club that's been rented out for this event. I'm told it's a perfect spot for Dreamaway's guests to go unnoticed. A small kick off to the season's other parties—and an evaluation of my worth since tonight is my trial run as being a plus one for the studio. If I do well enough, I'll go to the bigger parties a couple of nights a week for the next few weeks.

Monica promised it would be nothing too extensive or time-consuming. I'm required to attend from arrival until midnight at the earliest, and for every date I complete, five hundred dollars will be deposited into my account. It's practically magic. Although I'm uncomfortable being paid to hang out and look interested, who am I to argue? Until my house sells, or I sell a script, it's either this or paging through job boards. And this at least has an *in*.

I try to let go of the sinking feeling in my gut I get every time I think of all the faces I won't know. Or the scowling voice of Trent incensed I would throw it all away for *this*. I won't even try to imagine what my parents might say if they were here, even if I'd like to think they'd be proud of my reasoning.

We pull up to a curb and come to a stop. Stan the Man turns back to me, his grin shining over the seat.

"Now, you be careful in there. Should be a lot of fun, the bosses don't expect any trouble, but if you find you need saving, I'll be right here waiting."

He gives me a friendly wink, and I smile at him, a small *thanks,* slipping out of my mouth before he slides out of the car.

The alley we stop in is dark, buildings blotting out the streetlights. It looks like it should be boarded up except for the lone security guard standing in front of the fire exit. The street is stained and dirty, no bricks of gold laid here. Stan opens the car door for me and waits as I straighten myself into something presentable. The black mini clings to my thighs, among other parts, as I stride toward the back entrance of the club. An LBD would lend me the ability to blend in, but the bareness of my legs is an overlooked vulnerability. Thank God, at least, I went with a long sleeve.

Dreams have died up and down this walkway. I find them in the traces of gum that stick to my heels. I cannot even begin to imagine what my poor red bottoms must be going through without a knot forming in the pit of my stomach. They will probably be my first, my last, my only, and I wish my first night out in them wasn't wasted on this common, dingy club. Then again, I wouldn't even have them without this. The irony is not lost on me.

Stan nods to the security guard in a way familiar bros do before opening the door up, letting me inside. The narrow hall is lined with doors, only one of which is open. I duck in, as instructed by Stan. Inside there are two men sitting on a velvet settee and a young woman teetering precariously on sky high heels. Her head is leaning over her phone as she texts at a speed that makes my head spin. I knock softly on the open door, drawing their attention.

The woman's neck snaps up while the men's conversation abruptly halts, and their eyes catch mine. No one moves, the air in the room holding like a boat before the wave. Then all at once both men stand and the woman steps forward toward me, phone still perfectly poised in front of her.

"You must be Victoria," she says, no question in her voice. She looks at me up and down before turning to the couch. "This is your date, and for the sake of this evening, he's asked that you just call him Logan."

The man she's gesturing to clocks in just below my eye level in these heels. He's stocky, a clear complex to make up for his insecurity about his height and the rounded, rosy cheeks he's rocking. The royal blue suit he's wearing tailored so that every bulge can be seen from every angle. I'm uncomfortable with the tightness of his clothes and mentally take bets on how long I think the threads will hold.

One hour. Max.

"And this is your handler for the evening, Mr. Beckson. He will run any interference necessary for you both."

Or because of you. The unspoken warning rings clear and I nod in confirmation that her message is received. Mr. Beckson reaches out his hand in offer of mine, his nails trimmed into perfection, holding a single gold coin pinky ring that obnoxiously sits on his hairless finger. I take them, careful not to rip the mammoth off his hand in my eagerness to release it.

"Nice to meet you both," I say in my best Susie homemaker voice.

I want them to like me. If I'm going to do this, the last thing I need is bad press with the people who will be considering my manuscript and Monica's boss. Logan's eyes narrow before he turns to Mr. Beckson, ignoring me entirely.

"She's too tall. I've told you I cannot have a... a *nobody* towering over me in heels. I'm a goddamn movie star, Beckson."

His voice is whiny and high-pitched at the end, making it nearly impossible not to respond. A snarky comment is on the tip of my tongue as Mr. Beckson's arm wraps around Logan's back, escorting him through the door in quiet whispers. The woman is subtly waved over, following them out. Before I can even finish the deep breath I'm taking, she's back and digging through a ratty, black duffle bag that's hung over her arm. A pair of scuffed silver packable flats falls to the floor in front of me.

"You'll need to change. I'll have those," her finger points between my beautiful red bottoms, "returned to your car." Her arms cross in impatience.

"Seriously?" I ask as my feet slide out of my shoes. Of course, she's serious, but I'm livid with how this night has started. I roll my eyes as I hand over my shoes, grateful Beckson isn't in the room to note my childish behavior, and slip into the flats. "They're too big," I say.

Her shoulders shrug, a flair of sympathy crossing her face.

"You'll have to make do. This way."

I follow her out of the room and watch as she hands my shoes to security, who takes them and immediately walks out the back door. I mourn that I may never see them again. She leads me down the rest of the hallway; the flats fighting to slip right off my feet with every rat trap step. We end up in a large, lofted seating area that overlooks a dance floor and bar. Seated on a couch to my right is Logan, his royal blue shrink wrap standing out through the dimness, a drink already in hand. He has the smug look of entitlement in his smile as he gestures wildly to the men surrounding him.

The woman I'm following tilts her head towards him.

"I'm sure you'll be posted at that table most of the night. If you need anything, let the bartender or server know. They'll find Mr. Beckson for you."

She wanders back down the hallway, her nose already back in her phone. I stand frozen, my fists tightening at my sides. *Think about the money.* That doesn't help. *Think about Monica.* That certainly doesn't help, my anger only rising. *Think about the script, Vip. That beautiful, romantic, once-in-a-life-time script. Think about seeing the credits and your name under writer.*

The dream furls in my stomach and spreads like fire into my limbs. Everything I've ever wanted sits on the edge of a knife and tonight could be my chance to tip the scales in my favor. All I need to do is stay calm. Be kind. And deal with a pretentious ass for a few hours. I've done that for the last ten years. A single night was *nothing,* especially when so much counted on it.

My nerves calm down enough to paste a smile on and put one foot in front of the other towards Logan.

The club echoes. There's a deep thump of base that vibrates the floor every time the slippery heel of my flat touches it. The lights are all dimmed except in the dance area below, where streams of colored beams flash around in anticipation. Clusters of people spot the room, a light trickle filtering in from the doorways. I imagine it's still early for a party and the crowds will grow as time moves into the dusky haze of early morning and bad decisions.

Logan's eyes catch mine as I move closer, his gaze immediately traveling down to my feet before a giant smile lights his face.

"Here she is!" He bellows, reaching his arm to wrap around my waist and bring me down onto the couch beside him. Before instinct pushes me away from him, he releases me and turns back to his table. "Guys, this is Victoria. I am letting her follow me around for a few days for an article she's writing. Please be nice to her. I would hate your unruly behavior to color how she sees me."

The surrounding smiles are polite and curious. They assume something more is happening between us, or perhaps that Logan is making the whole thing up, but no one dares to call him on it outright. He may not be the biggest name in film, but he is here, and Monica was clear with me that these types of parties weren't for just anyone. I let the irritation slip from my face at being taken off guard and smile brightly.

"Nice to meet everyone. Please, just pretend I'm not here. I want to witness Logan in his natural habitat."

One man sitting next to Logan smothers his mouth with his hand, trying to hide the laugh. Logan glares daggers at the subtle jab but quickly moves on. He begins animatedly talking about his next role and the press tour they're spending a fortune for him to take.

"My biggest fans are in the Southern Americas after all," he drones on, sounding very much like the condescending idiot he is.

I decide to tune him out and focus my attention on everyone around me. The club is… normal. I'm not sure what I was expecting, but there isn't anything that directly shouts *celebrities* here. Sure, if you stare closely enough, you'll find designer clothes worth more than the median income in most states and snippets of conversations about promotional swag or Instagram followers, but you'd have to look for those things and when you were looking, you'd see pores, and wrinkles, and flaws. You'd see normal. Stunning sometimes too, but no more so than the 20-something barista on the corner of Hollywood boulevard trying to get in the door here someday. Being faceblind takes away the shine of reputation and lays people bare to be the base of who they truly are. It's the purest form of first impressions and it can be both calming and a little disappointing.

Before long, the drink I ordered is empty and dangling needlessly from my fingertips. Logan is still droning on, trying to impress his peers. I've managed to almost tune him out completely. The party is finally in full swing, crowds filling the dance floor. I itch to tug out my phone to check the time, only to remember it sits back with Stan to prevent me from using it and making a poor impression. A space at the bar has opened, and it calls to my empty glass like a Roomba to its charger. The man across from me must notice the desperate need for escape and the sadist drowns me with attention.

"So, you are writing a piece about our boy here," the bottom of his whiskey tilts toward Logan, "have you learned anything worthy enough to impress your readers?"

If my superpower was to shoot fire from my eyes, this dude would be ash. Why haven't I been thinking up responses to this stupid cover Logan has given me? My jaw clenches like a nutcracker at Christmas, frustrated with myself for getting too comfortable being ignored. I know nothing about Logan, and it's obvious these men do. I don't even know what movies he's been in or if Logan is even his real name or if it's a stage name...I know nothing. My eyes slide to him for help as a smile lifts the sadist's mouth below his glass.

Logan's eyes widen when he realizes I haven't been listening to a word he's said.

"Did you all hear about my tour? Yes? Well, did I tell you there will be a *one bed* situation with Carina? No? Listen to this..." He traps the rest of the guys into his story, an obvious lie if the gesticulation of his hands is any indication. I take the opportunity to slip out of the group and make my way to the bar, sneering at the sadist as I do.

As I move toward the open bar, a man slides in in front of me. He's wearing a finely made suit, expensively tailored to every curve of his backside. Perfectly combed blond hair waves down to his shoulders, easily pushed back from his face, the color graying at the temples. Age has graced him, but in a distinguished way that screams he's been well taken care of for an exceptionally long time. His eyes crinkle in a smile as I glide to sit beside him, his drink already ordered and waiting.

"What are you having? You look like you need a refill."

I've set my empty glass on the bar top but am no longer eager to fill it. Since this is a Dreamaway party, it is likely this gentleman knows who and where Mr. Beckson is and the sooner I can talk to him, the sooner I can leave.

"I'm okay, actually. I'm just here to ask the bartender for Mr. Beckson. You haven't happened to have seen him wandering around?" I ask.

His smile widens, something I've said obviously funny. He relaxes his elbows onto the counter, leaning back, his hips kicking out in the process. He does a magic trick of making himself look both as comfortable as if he were home, and as out of place as a commoner like me. The bartender sets down a drink at his back, a single glance thrown my way, before making his rounds to the other end, and I've missed my chance to snag him.

"Sometimes, at these parties, I feel like I don't know who anyone is. It's all just kind of a blur." He sticks his hand out to me. "Name's Brad, by the way."

I put my hand into his, a familiar warmth spreading. A contagious smile takes over my face. His charisma is catching, and I want nothing more than to relax next to him. I wish, not for the first time, that I could place him. He's giving off an old Hollywood vibe, and I'd love to know who he really is. I mentally note his energy, of the way his body rests into the bar and the confidence only someone who never accepts no has. He will make an astounding main character for a script someday.

"Victoria. It's nice to meet you." I let his hand go and rest my back on the counter too. "If it makes you feel any better, I actually don't know anyone here, so."

My shoulders shrug up as if it doesn't matter.

We've found a friend now, and that's enough. This must be what it's like to be star struck. I am consumed by his presence, even if I only know him as Brad. I've felt this way with only a few, and just like the others, I lock the feeling away, only to be shared in my stories. The first time I felt it at an eighth-grade field trip we took with two neighboring schools to a play in Seattle, I had made the mistake of trying to explain it to Cherie. She was so confused and concerned about my mental state that I dropped it and never tried again. Only in my scripts was I validated.

"So, it's the blind leading the blind," Brad lets out a whispery laugh. I want to join in the joke even if I don't get it since the only "blind" one here is me. "You be safe tonight, Victoria. I'm sure the bartender would be more than happy to help you find Beckson. And when you do, please let him know I said hello."

His hand rests on my shoulder in a friendly way as he picks up his drink, motions for the bartender, then saunters into the dancing crowd, taking his perfect backside with him.

His face I will forget, but those slacks... never.

The bartender interrupts my perusing.

"Can I help you with something, miss?"

He's indistinct, my eyes forgetting him the second they leave his face. I glance around as if I'm looking for someone.

"Actually, yes. I was told to come here and ask for Mr. Beckson when I needed him. It's Victoria Pencheske," I add as if it's an afterthought.

His head nods as he moves from the counter to the bottle behind him, unearthing a phone from its shielded place.

"No problem, Miss Pencheske. I will ask him to meet you here right now."

He fiddles more with his phone before walking off to take the orders of a rather obnoxious group that has just approached, clearly already drunk.

My fingers dance on the bar top in anticipation. My feet are slick with sweat inside of the disgusting patent flats. I'm positive I'm going to leave with, at the very minimum, a nasty case of athlete's foot tonight. I'm ready to shower, scrub and rub tea tree oil all over my body, then crawl into the couch for the night. I'm going to be using Monica's expensive stuff, too. All of it if I can.

Two men, amid conversation, walk toward me from the side of the bar. One nods his head in my direction, and I look down and catch a golden glimpse of a too large pinky ring. Beckson. I smile and nod back.

"Ah, Victoria! There you are. How are you doing so far this evening?"

His tone is bright, as if a few drinks have been thoroughly appreciated in our absence from one another. His mouth is soft even as the man next to him stares, brows furrowing in concentration. As if he's just realized a mistake, he throws his hand up onto his forehead.

"Sorry, sorry! It's Mr. Beckson. I was told to introduce myself to you *each time* we meet so you aren't thrown off," he looks to his companion, "she's some sort of blind... what is it called again? Propo... pragma..." He looks to me to fill in the gaps.

"The scientific term is prosopagnosia. But I'd rather just make it simple. I'm faceblind. Basically, I have trouble recognizing people." I smile encouragingly, careful not to roll my eyes at his condescending tone. Beckson is thin-ice-nice. His cheery facade can break at any moment, and I don't want to push my luck.

After all, he holds my script in the palms of his hands. One wrong word and it could all be over before it even starts.

"Right, right. Simple. I like simple."

He smiles, then looks to the other man still looking at me and back again, as if I have ruined his night. With all the unfortunate run-ins I've had lately, my hackles rise. He's giving off an energy of familiarity, as if he already knows exactly who I am. I obviously don't recognize him, but I want to steel myself in case he's not a friend.

"Oh, Victoria. This is one of our most honored guests! You're going to love being introduced. It's not every day someone like you meets a page six regular!"

He leans a little closer to me, excited that he has the ear of someone so elite to introduce. I breathe a little easier too, knowing there's no way I know this man and his bad attitude is just a mark of his personality.

"This is…"

#

What are the odds that I would run into the mess of a woman? The uneasiness in my gut at being recognized unfurls, as I listened to Beckson explain her unique set of circumstances. At least I don't have to live through the humiliation of our first introduction twice. My muscles relax and I take the opportunity to check her out.

I must admit, Victoria looks good. Her legs are on full display, the stretch in her dress being put to the test across her thighs. Her mouth pouts out, even as bare as it is, allowing her cheeks to round out the friendliness of her features. That is until we lock our gazes.

The irritation in her hazel eyes only solidifies the smoked look of her makeup, allowing her to hide her emotions in plain sight. She looks haughty and ready for a fight. If it weren't for the god-awful footwear stunting her, she might pass for any of the many eager entertainers and artists here. Before Beckson can embarrass me by name dropping, as he often likes to do, we're interrupted by none other than Logan Jones.

He's far drunker than he should be this early in the night. It's not even midnight, and he smells like the entire building might explode if a cigarette is lit within 30 feet of him. His face is red and splotchy, the carefully applied makeup unable to keep pace with him. There's a reason I never worked with him on my movies, and I have a feeling I'm about to be reminded of that now.

"'Cuse me Beck. Can I cut in?" A hiccup overtakes him as he slides his arm around Victoria's waist. Figures she would be here with him. "My date and I haven't had the chance to dance yet."

Victoria is visibly uncomfortable when I glance at her. The crease in her brow is practically a canyon, her frown so sharp it slices across her entire face. But within a blink, the look is gone. She carefully untwines his arm from her waist.

"Oh, Logan. I'm not a great..." she protests, but doesn't get to finish. Logan grabs her hand lightning fast, pulling her out onto the dance floor with unbelievable speed, given the amount of drunk he currently is.

"It's OK sweetheart, I'm a rockstar at dancing. I'll make us both look good." He's shouting to her over the music as they slip away to the outskirts of the dance floor closest to us. Instinct has me stepping forward to help Victoria before Beckson's hand shoots out to stop me.

"That's our newest plus one. My assistant came to me with the idea. Perfect, isn't it, Roman? A date who can't bother anyone because she can't recognize the greatness all around her."

"And you paired her with Logan? If he can't get a date without being recognized, that should be the final red flag. I don't know why you don't drop him already, Becks."

He sighs, knowing we've had this conversation before. "You know I can't talk about it. Everyone knows how Logan can be. Never one to give up any of the spotlight and thank goodness, this option came along. But they'll be fine. We've warned him—best behavior. I've got security watching. And it's just a dance," he explains.

Even though I know, *just a dance,* is a terrible excuse, there's not much I can do. So, I nod, but I watch, too. I can try to piece together the girl from the plane with the one on Logan's arm and it's a mystery. I never imagined Victoria to be the new plus one. The studio had passed along a few emails, offering me this same date for future parties while I'm here. I had declined without consideration, even though it intrigued me.

Who would I be if I could start completely fresh?

It wasn't a thought I put much time into. After all, it was impossible. At least, I had thought it was. Now I knew there was a chance. What if I could meet someone who didn't know about my family or my money? Who didn't know I was a successful director who then failed so badly I spiraled into a breakdown? Someone who didn't wonder about the girl before who broke off our engagement, or the public fighting and the paparazzo, or that stupid fucking yacht. Who would I be if I didn't have so much... shame and responsibility?

Watching Victoria being tossed about by a drunken Logan, I found myself wanting to know more about her, and her to know more about me than the terrible impression I made on the flight.

The DJ changes the song to an upbeat dance hit that leaves Logan howling in excitement. Victoria's eyes light in panic from here as his dancing only gets more chaotic. He's twirling her. Throwing her in and out of arm's reach, kicking his legs out in a jive and obviously stepping on her toes. Those horrible thin flats are not built to sustain Logan's heavy stomps, and I'm moving toward them before Beckson can stop me.

People around them are already giving a wide berth, many whisper-shouting to their companions, laughing at the embarrassing display. Logan either doesn't see or doesn't care about the scene he's causing and instead leans into all the attention with more exaggerated displays of his dancing. He's smiling madly, and the moment sharpens as everything falls apart.

Logan's foot comes down just as Victoria tries to take a step back, probably hoping to avoid losing a toe, but instead of the entire shoe moving, just her foot does. He traps the top portion of the clearly too-big shoe under his as he shoves Victoria out into an overly aggressive twirl. She has no choice but to go, her foot flying out of her shoe, shooting her across the dance floor. Before Logan realizes that he's put too much force into his swing, Victoria's hand leaves his, sending her ass straight to meet the hard, probably alcohol soaked, floor.

Before I can think about it, I dive for her, putting myself between her and the hardwood, scooping up under her arms. Her back pushes into me and I take several steps, losing a few breaths in the process. She's sticky with sweat and my arm's grip onto hers with both the force of the fall and my determination to hold on.

She's momentarily stunned, her body staying at a forty-five-degree angle in my arms. Everyone around us is in shocked silence, the only noise the pounding of the music from the speakers. Logan goes through a kaleidoscope of emotions: first disbelief, then anger and he finally lets his happy drunken self take over.

"WOOOO! The captain saves the day!" He yells to the crowd. "Who's next?"

The song changes to an upbeat, but slower, pop song. It breaks the crowd up, leaving Logan to sweep up a skinny brunette and disappear further onto the dance floor.

The guy is a fucking idiot.

"Are you okay?" I ask Victoria. She's still laid stunned in my arms, her back breathing into me. My voice seems to knock her out of it.

"That guy is a fucking asshole," she says, straightening herself up and glaring in his general direction. I can't help the laugh that overtakes me.

"That he is." I look down at her now barefoot, the toes already looking swollen. She's a mess, but no one deserves the aftermath of a drunken Logan Jones dance. "Do you need help to your car?"

She follows my gaze to her feet before her eyes close, head shaking. She looks back, hoping to retrieve the missing flat, but it's nowhere to be seen in the crowd. "Thank you, but no. It'll be fine. It can't get much worse, right?"

She starts to walk away toward the back exit, a very noticeable hobble where there was none before. My eyes roll to the heavens. I should mind my own business, but I can't stop helping even when people tell me they don't need it. Striding over to her easily, I pull her up into a fireman's carry, craning my neck to look her in the eyes as I do. Her hands grip into my shoulders, but she doesn't fight it. I take that as a sign to continue.

"I know you said you don't need help but, you're *hobbling*, Victoria. And you only have one shoe. There is glass and who knows what else on this floor. I can't in good conscious let you walk out of here." I sigh and look away. "If you really have an objection to me helping, I can grab security or see if there's a wheelchair or something to help you."

She stiffens in my arms before firmly shaking her head, shaking the lone flat from her foot so it flops helplessly to the floor.

"No. Please, no. I'm already embarrassed enough. I don't need any more people involved." She looks exhausted and her body deflates, letting me know I've won.

"Fine. Carry me out. And thank you," she adds, begrudgingly. A small smirk plays on my lips.

"You're very welcome."

Before I can say any more, I'm encased with light slaps on my arms and whoops of *way to go Captain*. The satisfaction I had just a moment ago is sliced away and my irritation returns. I hate this fucking city.

We make it out the back door and I nod to the security guard, a silent ask to have our cars called. He calls on his comm and I look for a safe place to set Victoria down. A black town car already sits at the curb, a skinny red-headed man hopping out of the driver's seat in a disturbingly bright shirt. Victoria laughs as she catches sight of him.

"That would be my driver," she says to me before calling out, "hey Stan the man! I needed rescuing tonight after all."

She's fully relaxed across my back at this point and smiling. I tell myself it's seeing the car and her driver and being able to end this night. Secretly, I want it to be me she's getting comfortable with.

What is wrong with me? Lauren has left me more of a mess than I realized.

Stan opens the backseat, and I deposit Victoria into it, tucking her damaged feet in securely before shutting the door. She quickly rolls down the window.

"Hey, thanks again for the rescue. I *do* appreciate it. Tonight was... well, let's just say I am glad it's over," she says.

"No problem at all. I couldn't in good conscious let Logan Jones continue to demolish you on that dance floor." I cringe in thought at the sight of her poor toes being stomped on.

"Oh, my, God. *That* was Logan Jones? Action movie sidekick, Logan Jones?" Her voice is in complete disbelief. "Doesn't he play like a 17-year-old in all his movies?"

I cough out a laugh, unable to hold it in at the horror on her face.

"Don't worry, he's actually closer to 30 than 17. You can see why he's a bit of an ass."

She's laughing with me and shaking her head. "Oh definitely. Poor guy. Always the Robin, never the Bruce. Those tights and man panties must have crawled WAY up there tonight."

I wish Logan was out here now to hear this. She's funny. Crass, but funny, and I find myself less appalled by our encounters than I did earlier this evening. She's still a mess, but at least she's an entertaining one.

"I would recommend you go straight home and soak those feet. It looked like he was practicing his river dancing all over them tonight." I tap the top of the town car. "Get home safely, Victoria."

Her hand lifts, and she does a tiny salute.

"Aye, aye, Captain," she says as she pulls away from the curb.

I look after her until the pocket of my slacks vibrates, a picture of Thoren flashing on the screen.

"Yeah?" I answer.

"You done with that shitshow yet? I'm heading to the hall in ten. You in?" he asks.

"I'll be there."

I hang up and slip the phone back into my pocket. A few games of pool would do me good, help me shake out the image of Victoria in that dress, the soft skin of her bare thighs in my hands, and focus on getting out of this place. Plus, knowing Thoren, if I try to just slip home, he'll only bring the party to me and I'm not in the mood for guests.

Victoria's smile dances into my mind, wondering if I should try to see her again. I dash the possibility from my thoughts. One day of Victoria will have to be enough. I've got bigger problems to solve. My town car pulling up doesn't come soon enough. I have meetings in the morning with a handful of writers which should have me heading for the condo, but right now whiskey is the only thing that will keep me from hopping a plane back east. It doesn't matter; they all know the gossip, anyway.

They'll get me how they get me.

SIX

Victoria

BREATHE IN, ONE-TWO-THREE, AND out, one-two-three. Now reach to your highest peak yet. The tv pulls me out of sleep, a soft gong disorienting me. The crust of my mascara tugs as I open my eyes to a full ass of sweaty pink yoga pants. Monica is giving her best impression of a tree, and I can't help but throw out my arm to knock her off balance.

"Hey!" she warns.

"Sorry, it's reflex. When I wake up to physical exertion of any kind, I get violent." I shrug and roll over, throwing myself into the cushions.

"You should probably get up any way seeing your meeting with the studio is in an hour and a half." Her voice is muffled and when I turn back around, she's back in her yoga form.

"I'm sorry—I haven't really woken up yet, and I thought you just said that I have a meeting in an hour and a half, which is *impossible* since I don't remember scheduling one," I say sitting upright. Monica sighs deeply, giving a good *namaste* before turning to me.

"You heard correctly. You didn't schedule one, I did for you, remember? It's the whole reason we fought, and why you went to an exclusive party last night? I promised I would get you a meeting, and I did. It's at noon and it's ten thirty now. So... hour and a half."

She rolls her eyes, and I swear to all that is sacred in this world that I will rip them from her head if her eyelids flutter like that even one more time.

"MONICA!" I scream. "Why didn't you tell me? Or wake me up sooner? Or do anything to remotely resemble a friend?"

"*Excuse me?*" she gasps. "I *got* you the meeting, you ungrateful baby. And I let you sleep in as long as you could so that you weren't extra cranky, which apparently did not work! How was I supposed to know you slept in your makeup? You know that ruins your skin!"

I'm scrambling up and hustling to the bathroom, letting out a moan as soon as my poor battered feet hit the floor. But I'm too tired and panicked to be lectured, especially when she's fucking right, so I push through the pain, cursing Monica and Logan and this whole city the entire way. I never considered my 'big adventure' to LA to include scoldings and physical ailments, especially so early in my time here, but that's what you get when you leave yourself to Monica's whims!

As I rub the makeup remover violently into my face, I mumble, "I wouldn't be sleeping in my makeup if I didn't come home battered and exhausted from a terrible night, you egotistical maniac."

By the time I've cleaned and prepped myself to the best of my ability and am padded out in Monica's robe, she's done with her yoga and is perusing a hanging rack of clothes. I have always envied her closet ever since we were teens. Monica always had the best selection and fashion sense out of any of us. Thankfully, it was one of the few things she didn't mind sharing. Any chance she got to make us her dress up dolls, she took. I was always a willing participant. Even now, as angry as I am, I know I'll give in. She selects an outfit, drapes it on the couch, and pats the ottoman.

"C'mon Vip, we don't have all day."

I fling myself down grumpily. She picks up a small first aid kit, and I feel tricked. She bends down and grabs my foot before I can stop her, fussing over the bruises before bandaging them up.

"You'll have to wear flats. I've got a perfect pair for this outfit in my closet you can borrow. No one will be the wiser."

She's completely focused on her task, and I relent, seeing the furrow in her pristine brows. I want to be the selfish one and whine, but seeing the reigning queen of that position with my foot in her hands, I stop myself. I put my hand on her shoulder to stop her, forcing her to look at me.

"Thank you, Mon. You can be a real asshole, but no one else would dress my toe wounds." She rolls her eyes, but this time I don't want to kill her so much.

In Monica fashion, she shrugs off the moment.

"That should do as long as you don't dance with anymore men with two left feet."

She stands, hurrying off to her room to grab the flats. I look at the outfit she's picked out, a thick black pencil skirt with a beautiful deep purple silk top with gold threading. It's another thing she's letting me borrow, the closest to an apology I'll ever have, but I accept it fully all the same. Monica lets beautiful things speak for her. It's her love language and I can appreciate the gesture for what it is.

I change into the outfit. Monica is quick to bring in the black and gold matching flats and a sheer black pair of tights to polish it off. Hardly a single bandage can be seen. I look at myself in the mirror and grin at the accomplishment I've become in only forty-five minutes. Thank God for excellent products and clothes.

"Ready?" she asks me.

I nod my head, move my purse items into my laptop bag, noticing the freshly printed and bound copy of my script already inside, and we are out the door.

The drive to the studio isn't far, but it is long. Traffic here is a mess and riding with Monica makes me so motion sick, it's like we're lost at sea. We arrive at the studio with just enough time for me to get my bearings before needing to march inside and sell myself unlike I ever have before. This is the part I dread most about being a writer and wonder, not for the first time, why the hell I don't hire someone else to do this part for me.

I'm broke, that's why.

I promise Monica that I'll text her when I'm done, agreeing to meet at the coffee shop in the lot. All at once, she's zipped off and I'm alone outside

Dreamaway Studios. I pull out the freshly printed script, hand running over the plastic cover page. I open it up, stick my face into it and inhale the fresh ink, then march into what could be *my* movie's studio.

The inside of Dreamaway is as glamorous as its movies. The lobby is clean and open; all steel and dark woods balanced against soft grays and crisp whites. Huge, picturesque windows let in the California sun, throwing off the glamourous vibe this city is known for. My heart floats in elation through my chest as I walk to reception.

"Hi! My name is Victoria Pencheske, I have a meeting at noon about adapting a script?" I say to the miniature version of Monica.

I am kicking myself for not asking who I was scheduled to take a meeting with before getting here. The concierge flips her long, finely straightened hair over her shoulder, continuing to type away, before looking up at me.

"If you would like to take a seat, I'll let them know you're here," she says, her eyes immediately floating back to her screen, annoyed that I bothered to interrupt.

"Can I ask one more thing?" I ask, the words popping out before I can rein them in. She cuts me a glare, the plastic in her chair crackling softly as she fidgets.

"Yes?" she says through clenched teeth, tensing her jaw into a severe line. I chicken out, knowing this woman will immediately rat me out if I ask.

"Where are your bathrooms?" My cheeks tint pink. She blinks once before pointing down an open hallway.

"Down there, to your left." She turns back to her computer and I'm frozen. "Anything else?"

"No, no, that's all."

I scurry away from her, avoiding the hall and instead opting for a seat next to the window. I move between watching the people come in and the people already mingling inside.

Finally, the guy having an animated conversation on the second-floor beelines to me. He's wearing a tailored gray suit—basic attire for many of what I can only assume are agents that work here wear. He's trailed by a shorter man wearing almost the exact replica of suit if only the suit had been purchased secondhand.

I search the guys for any hints that we've met and catch a ghoulish pinky ring on the one in the expensive suit. Mr. Beckson.

Although I'd bet the rest of my bank account on it being him, I can't come out and say so, but I still find comfort in knowing. Just another lovely requirement of having a condition no one understands. If you fall outside of what they think they know, you're cured! I roll my eyes internally at the stupidity of the whole thing.

"Miss Pencheske! It's Mr. Beckson. It's lovely to see you again so soon. I was at the club with you last night," he says as he holds out his hand, talking down to me both figuratively and literally.

"Hello, Mr. Beckson! Yes, I remember. Good to see you too."

I push down the irritation and smile, shaking his hand in mine politely.

He gestures toward the stairs as he says, "this way! Sorry to keep you waiting. Davis and I were discussing your pitch and got caught up without realizing you were sitting right here. I'm sure you know how that goes... Oh! Have I introduced Davis?" He points back to the cheap grey suit following us, "that's Davis. He's what I like to call a 'boots on the ground' agent. The guy who gets things done. Isn't that right, Davis?"

I look back toward Davis, a small nod and smile that he returns.

"That's right, Beckson! Boots on the ground indeed."

Mr. Beckson jumps right in, "but he won't be joining you today. As a matter of fact, neither of us will. It looks like we've double booked, so it'll be just you and Mr. Wheatley, the director. Which shouldn't be a problem for a hotshot like you! You had us all enamored last night. Just do the same thing and you'll be fine."

My breath hitches. I wasn't intending to meet with a director today. This was supposed to be a sales pitch. To an agent, or a buyer, or a studio exec. *Not* a director. I can't help the panic that lances through me. I want to say something, *anything,* to get a better understanding of what is going on, but we're already right outside an intimidating conference room, Mr. Beckson gesturing for me to go inside.

"Right in here, Victoria. Roman should be here shortly," and with that he leaves, the last word barely making its way in the door before he's back in hushed conversation with Davis out of sight.

What the fuck is going on? I try to smooth my skirt and hair down. My hands shake with each stroke. *Roman Wheatley had not been given my script.* The man was a legend in making blockbusters. He had put out several of the top ten grossing films of all time. Even if he was disgraced, it's unheard of to be in a room with him as a first-time writer. My body curls in as if to agree that my confidence is getting smaller and smaller as each thought rolls in.

I move my attention to the conference room before I have a complete meltdown. It looks like a grown, updated version of the one I left my husband in weeks ago, and my heart skips a beat. The sheer embarrassment of my audacity at even wanting to be in this room right now might disintegrate me. I stumble to take a seat at the head of the table where a pitcher of water and glass sits. The pristine leather doesn't make a sound as I slide into it and pour myself a glass, sipping slowly. As the liquid slides down, a hot indignation boils up to the surface, burning away my fear.

Roman fucking Wheatley. The man who drunkenly humiliated his fiancé before she dumped his ass is going to be directing my script. A romance. This had to be a joke. It would be if I wasn't about to watch my hard work go up in flames. What were they thinking? Wasn't the last thing he did a terrible, boring documentary of some kind? Didn't they have someone better to bring my story to life? This guy was going to take my dreams and shatter them into unrecognizable pieces.

I focus in and my resolve hardens. No. I wouldn't let him. Enough men had fucked me over for one lifetime. I wouldn't be intimidated and I sure as hell wouldn't settle for whatever Dreamaway thought they were cooking up. Nothing had been sold yet. I was still in control.

A figure fills the door, and my breath catches as I look up. He's gorgeous in that expensive way that makes you question your own worth when you see him. He's in a very dark gray suit; his cream shirt unbuttoned at the throat. There's a five o'clock shadow scuffing up his face, helping to relieve the sharp contrast of his jaw. His hair and eyes are dark, the pupils fading into the iris, so I can't quite tell what color they actually are. He fills out his suite nicely and I hate him all the more for it. Although I'll forget his features after I leave here, the thought of my attraction to him following me into the night makes my nerves wrap in knots. I pull myself together, eyes sharpening as I stand to greet him.

"Mr. Wheatly. Nice to meet you."

I reach out my hand to him. He looks at me quizzically before taking it. Instead of keeping his distance, he moves into my space, forcing me to give up ground, picking up my script as he does.

"Please, call me Roman." He eyes my title page before looking up at me. "And you are?"

My cheeks redden. *Who the hell does this guy think he is?* It's likely someone told him who he was meeting, and either I wasn't important enough to remember or he's playing that he forgot.

Either way, it burrows under my skin, and I can't help the words that pop out of my mouth, "On time, *Roman.*"

His nose furrows in surprise.

"I meant your name," he says, his own temper raising the thermostat a couple degrees.

I nod my head toward my title page.

"It's right in front of you, right under the title *Sailing Single*. Pencheske. You can call me Miss Pencheske if you'd like."

If he doesn't know my first name already, I don't want him to. I'd rather have the upper hand of him calling me by my proper name in any circumstance so that I don't confuse him with a friend. A small smile forms on his lips.

"What about V? That's also on your title page," he points out.

"V is hardly a name. I'd rather you just call me Miss Pencheske. To keep things professional."

He lets out a husky laugh, sending unwarranted goosebumps through my arms. I push down the lust and focus on my anger. I'm not sure what I've said that could be so funny.

"Come now, Five. We both know by now that I'm *hardly* professional."

His smile holds secrets. Inside jokes that I am very much on the outside of.

"Excuse me? Did you... Did you just call me Five?"

I've never been called a number. It's stripping, as if a name is too good for me, so I've been reduced down to a single digit. He laughs again.

"I did. If you won't give me your name in a friendly manner, and you apparently loathe to be called V, although I'd like to point out you've put it on your title page, I have no other choice than to make up some absurd nickname."

His shoulders shrug as if this is obvious and brilliant. Proud and sure. Condescending in a way he clearly finds funny.

"Fine." I grit my teeth, knowing arguing will only encourage him. "Five it is. Glad to see your reputation is spot on. And is that whiskey I smell, Mr. Wheatley?"

Two can play at his horrible game. If he wants to call me by a nickname, fine. It works in my favor, allowing me to never losing track of who he is when I can't remember his face. But that doesn't mean I can't mess with him the same way. He does smell of a night spent drowning in liquor. I pretend to have another sniff, as if I need it.

"Long night?"

I tag it on as if he's pitiful. I know I'm playing with fire, but the excitement of it pulls at my belly in anticipation.

His eyes narrow in challenge.

"Actually, yes, it was an exceedingly long night. A tiring night of rescuing helpless maidens and drinking away the pain of having to be here. Thank you so much for your concern."

He storms around me, stealing the seat at the head of the table.

"But you already know all about me and how my nights here in LA are spent. Let's talk about you and this script!"

His tone has changed from playful arrogance to mocking disregard. For the briefest second, I consider dumping the half full glass of water all over his lap, watching it soak him in fury. Thankfully, I pull myself together before I do anything rash. *The script, Victoria. Talk about the script. This will be great practice if nothing else.*

"Well, it's a modern romance taking place on a cruise. The title, *Single Sailing*, is only a placeholder. Basically, a twenty-something is roped into getting on this boat with her mom and her mom's friends..." The deepening of Roman's frown makes my words stumble one over another. "Uh... after a terrible break up, only to, ah, realize it's a singles cruise where she falls madly in love with the cruise director."

I'll admit, it isn't my best pitch. Being in this room with Roman, I can't seem to remember all the remarkable things I practiced saying a million times to sell this damn thing. My hands fidget and flutter, and I know I'm making a fool of myself. I hate the small voice inside of me that calls out in pain, wishing I could impress him. Impress *anyone*. It's clear he's disappointed. His hands steeple in what looks like a prayer, making my own sweat in anticipation of his rejection.

"Okkkk," he draws out the word, struggling. "Why?"

"What do you mean, *why?* Why do they go on the cruise? Well, because..."

"No, Five." He shakes his head, frustration marring his words and stinging my pride. "Why do I give a damn about this other than the fact that I have no choice?"

I reel back as if I've been slapped. He's still sorting through the pages, eyes skimming every word I wrote and finding them lacking. My confidence and resolve are slipping, but my anger is fresh. I grab onto it with both hands, shoving the rest aside.

"Well, maybe *you* don't!" I tremble out. "But another director might. One who is familiar with the concept of love, maybe? Of kindness and romance, and who didn't crash and burn their second chances to the ground?"

I am trying not to cry from the rage and injustice that fills my soul at being put to task. It's not that I don't know rejection, but there's something about *Roman* rejecting me, questioning me, for this, here and now, that is too personal and infuriating. I hate that my tears never come when they should, only when I am livid enough to hit something and can't. He finally glances up at me from the script, assessing the waterworks I am actively trying to maintain.

He sighs.

"Look, it isn't you that's the problem. I'm sure you're lovely enough..." I cut him off immediately.

"You vain prick. These tears are not for you! If it were socially acceptable to throw down right now, I would. I'm angry, not hurt. You already had it in your head before you walked through this door what kind of script this would be. You judged me and my work without even giving it a chance. *Nothing* I could have said would have changed that."

My voice is escalating, but I can't stop it.

"You're right!" His hands let my script slip to the table, matching me tone for tone. "I don't want to direct your silly little script. I'd say it was a good guess, but we're both very aware of how skilled you are in the art of judgment. You must have some connections because right now I don't have a choice. It's your 'romance' or I get sued. Every other script has passed or been passed on. And the documentary that may actually make a difference in the world has been axed. So, at the very least, you could work with me to make this something less than garbage! At least give me some sort of motivation... why the hell do you want to sell this script? *Why this one?*"

I'm taken aback by his words. Fury and hurt and confusion swirl into a mess of emotion I cannot begin to unravel in this room. I've had enough. I can't tell him this script was as easy to write as it is to breathe. That I wove pieces of myself into it, not even fully understanding what I'd done. I couldn't tell him it's the one that I chose not to work on my marriage, instead opting for a divorce, because it made me believe in my dream. He doesn't deserve those reasons, and I wouldn't lay my heart bare for this man. Not now. Not ever.

"The only garbage in this room, sir, is your attitude," I seethe.

Shoving back at the chair I'm sitting in, I accidentally catch my heel, almost slamming my face into the table. Roman's arm shoots out to land between my chest and the wood. A screech of embarrassment and annoyance escapes me.

"I've got it! I'm fine!"

He pulls his limbs away from me as I straighten up, looking terrified, as if he may lose one. Which I can't say is much of an overreaction.

"Have them call me when either you've found the *motivation* to take that stick out of your ass or they've found me a new director," I say over my shoulder as I exit the room.

Roman calls after me, *Five, wait,* but I'm already gone. I pass Davis, in his hand-me-down suit and balding head, as I glide down the stairs. He changes direction completely to follow me.

"Miss Pencheske! Miss Pencheske, wait, please!" He persists.

I finally slow my walk at the bottom of the stairs, but continue my way to the door.

"Did everything go well? Are we ready to make the next big hit?" he asks, hopeful.

I just barely hold in a watery laugh.

"Something like that." I stop in my tracks right outside the door, catching Davis off guard. "Is there any chance that my script will be given to a different director if you purchase it?"

Davis's smile dims a little.

"I know Roman can be... difficult. But I promise you he's brilliant. When he's not stressed and feeling trapped, he is a great guy. A brilliant director. He may not realize it yet, just like you don't, but I think the two of you will be great for each other and for the script! You just need to give him a chance."

His eyes plead, wanting me to see a possibility that just isn't there.

"Thank you for checking on me. We'll be in touch."

It's all I can say before walking toward the coffee shop, calling Monica to pick me up on the way.

SEVEN

Roman

THAT COULD NOT HAVE gone worse. My head throbs from the hangover I've been nursing all morning. I squeeze the bridge of my nose, trying to calm it along with my temper. I'd been short with everyone all day. The writer who I'd just left a meeting with before coming to this one had called me washed up and pretentious, so to say my fuse was short was an understatement. Davis warned me I was running out of time and options. That my next meeting had to be the one. Everyone else I had either passed on, or they refused to work with me.

But there was no way I could have guessed that it would be Victoria waiting for me, her normally long chestnut hair piled onto her head instead. She looked professional. Ready to take on the big, bad Roman Wheatley. And I wasn't at all ready for *her*. I was unprepared for the complete disdain her voice dripped when she said my name. I wanted the girl who smiled easily and gave me an open door to be friendly, even if I didn't deserve it. The only one I could smile at when she called me Captain. The one who gave me a chance, even when I put my foot in my mouth.

Instead, I got the one who thought she knew me with the same judgment that I got from every other person, and it gut punched me.

"How'd it go, Wheatley?" Beckson's voice echoes against the glass, and my eyes narrow in pain.

"Not great. Perhaps you should vet your writer's better," I jab. "Why did you think a romance would be good for me again?"

Beckson sighs in a way that tells me my ice is thinning.

"Look, Roman. I know we've let you run the show with the last two projects, but it's obvious we can't do that anymore." His hands are jammed into his pockets, and he teeters from heel to toe. "You're great at entertaining the masses. Truly, you could be one of the greatest if you got your head out of your ass and quit with this wanting to please your daddy crap. Until then, we just need some easy fluff pieces from you. Something that will make us all a few bucks. And this romance? It's not that bad. The price is right, and you can make it better. We know you can."

"Wanting to direct pieces that address real and impactful issues is not *please your daddy crap*, Beckson. The documentary I pitched addressing the hierarchal chain of hospitals throughout the US and the world is—"

"Honorable," Beckson cuts in. "But it isn't what you're good at. We tried it and you failed. It doesn't mean you can't try again; it just means you can't try again *right now*. And the word is that you were miserable on that shoot. You had no imagination. You moved through the motions and then got angry with everyone else when things didn't come together. When you were filming *Raining Daggers*, I've never seen anyone so happy. So, in their *element*. It was like you were born to it. You knew what needed to happen. You anticipated the audience. Then your father crushed it. And I know that's a low blow, but we need *that* you back."

He removes his hand from his pocket and drums his fingers on the table.

"We're running out of options. If you can't make this work, I'm not sure you'll be able to fulfill your contract, and we'll have to move on to other means of negotiation."

He stops short of saying *lawsuit*, but it lingers in the air as the threat it is. I stand from my seat, towering over Beckson before lowering myself to his eye level. I watch as the tint of pink fills his cheeks, and use the glare my family has perfected to remind him who the fuck I am.

"It will work."

My voice is steady. The voice of a Wheatley. I hold a second too long, then straighten and leave the room.

\#

By the time I get back to the condo, Thoren is stretched out on the couch, a bag of peas laid over his eyes like a douche. I toss my keys into the bowl with extra vigor just to make his ears ping, getting the slightest satisfaction when he shutters.

"Glad to see you're awake with the rest of us. Don't you have a proper ice bag, you heathen?" I call to him.

He waves a hand but doesn't respond any further. I head into the kitchen to grab a juice, hoping to shake off the rest of this headache and my afternoon in the office. I stand over the sink, chugging my drink, when Thoren appears, dripping pea bag water as he does. He throws the used bag back into the freezer.

"Dude. No. You can't just refreeze a bag of defrosted peas. Throw them out," I say.

He rolls his eyes but opens the freezer and tosses the bag in the garbage before sliding onto a barstool, dropping his head to the island.

"How'd work go? Did you find your redemption piece?"

His words are mumbled and liquid with sleep.

"Have I told you that you're disgusting when you have a hangover?"

I prop myself against the fridge and tell him the truth.

"It wasn't great, T. And now it looks like the only option the studio is giving me is a romance." I shudder in disbelief. "I don't know why they think that idea isn't going to crash and burn. The gossip rags will have a heyday with it."

Thoren's eye peaks up at me from the counter, judging me.

"If I wasn't so hungover, I'd laugh. Karma really has it out for you, big brother. You are putting out all the bad vibes." He sits up, chin in hand. "Want me to call a friend to give you a reading? Maybe she can remove whatever curse you're wrapped up in. I just went out with this gifted astrologist. She might be able to help."

I can't stop the snort that comes out.

"Thanks, but I think I'll take care of this one on my own."

Thoren can be a lot of fun, but he's never been the brother I run to for actual help. And at this point, I'm not sure there's much anyone can even do. I've begged and pleaded to all the powers that be and still have gotten no leeway. The studio has my entire future in their hands.

My mind drifts to Victoria and the ridiculous ways she keeps popping up. From a first-class upgrade to a celebrity plus one to a romance writer? A Jill of all trades. I wouldn't say she was great at any of them, except maybe the last one. She was a talented writer, even if parts that demanded soul sucking emotion were more detached that I knew they could be with my help. Something told me we'd work great together if we could get over our mutual irritation.

The script wasn't terrible—far from it. It was that it paralleled too closely to a reality I would never have. To a reality I had wanted. If I wasn't Roman Wheatley, master of the fuck up and yeah, maybe someone who wanted to make his father proud, it would be exactly the type of movie I'd want to make.

But I am my father's son, his voice thick in my head telling me this script is frivolous and a waste of my expensive education. It was more fodder for the terrible wheel that is celebrity gossip. *Dumped at the alter director takes on love in the movies instead,* they would say. They'd ask questions of Lauren and how I feel giving the world a happy ending that I was incapable of creating for myself. I would relive the humiliation all over again. My family would relive it. I couldn't allow that to happen.

I play with the phone in my hands, passing it back and forth until finally pulling up my contacts. Thoren must catch on to my thoughts, because he comes out of his fog long enough to warn me.

"Roman, hey, no. Don't do whatever it is that has you looking like that. No phone call you could make right now can fix this. It'll just cause more trouble. Just do the stupid movie and move on. It'll be fine," he says, scooting the barstool back as if to get up.

I set my phone between us and wave my hand at him to stay, pinning him in place.

"You know I can't."

For a million reasons, I don't have to explain. I want him to understand that I at least have to try. By the end of all of this, I want to look at myself in the mirror and know that I did all that I could to stop it. His head droops a bit before he slouches out of the room.

"Fine. But don't come yelling at me when shit hits the fan. I'm going to the pool. Tell dear ol' dad I said hello."

As soon as he's gone, I pick the phone back up and hit the call button by the name I've already pulled up before I can chicken out. The ring sounds like alarm bells in my ears and my finger itches to hang up. Before I can, the crisp click of the line being picked up echoes in my ear.

"Yes?" He says, greetings to me beneath him.

"Hello, Mr. Wheatley. Do you have a moment?"

I pace the floor, hoping he'll at least hear me out. I feel like a child again, under his ever-scrutinizing gaze, even if he is thousands of miles away.

"What do you need, Roman?"

"I received a final option for a film today," he scoffs at the word *film*, clearly displeased with this conversation, but I continue, "however, I think it would be in our best interest to push back. It's a romance…"

Before I can finish my pitch, he interrupts me.

"Roman," he snaps. "What would have been in our best interest is you going into law like your predecessors or medicine like your uncle. Hell, you could have gone into banking or bought a company like your brother. All would have been preferable to… *this.*"

His tone is disgusted, unable to even say director in case the word itself was contagious.

"But you didn't. This is what you chose." He pauses, but I know better than to think he's done. "We live in our choices, son. You wanted to live a dream that was beneath your value. Tell me, was it worth it?" He asks rhetorically, and I know better than to even try to answer. "Do the movie or lose your inheritance."

"Father, can I…" I try one more time to sway him, hoping I can unlock the debate he loves so much. But it is all for nothing.

"Do not call me again."

The phone clicks once more, then dead air before the incessant beeping of being hung up on begins.

I stare at the screen. An old picture of me on the set of my first movie stares up at me, his words echoing in my head. I wonder which choices he blames for having a son like me and what choices he'll make to try to rectify it? He wants me to shoulder this embarrassment; family name be damned.

Don't call me again.

It could mean about this or until I'm no longer a director or ever. With my father, you never really knew. He's always been unreachable, but the older I get, the further away he seems to be. I'm disgusted. With him for treating us like this and at myself for still wanting to make him proud.

I throw my phone against the wall and watch as the screen shatters, an odd sense of achievement swelling my chest. My past attaches to that small device and I have no problem sweeping it up and putting it in the bin. My father wants to condemn me to my passion? Fine. If I'm going to do this, I'm going to be good at it. And *that* is a choice I'll happily live with.

EIGHT

Victoria / Roman

FROM HERE I CAN practically see the world, even if I can't enjoy it. Lights from the streets and neighboring buildings are just starting to glow in the twilight. My head's too full of sugar and worry to add alcohol to the mix, so I sip on a Shirley Temple while my "date" sits next to me, texting on his phone. My thoughts drift to the last few days and the craziness my life has become, feeling the dips and pulls of too much happening all at once.

After Monica picked me up, she listened. She let me cry and purchased a god-awful amount of candy, making me sick, and snotty, and loved. I didn't want to talk about the way I was questioning, leaving my whole life behind just to be a last resort. That my pros and cons list for this adventure looked more like a hail Mary than a rational adult choice. On that car ride home, I really just didn't want to be *me*.

Thankfully, Monica never needed explanations or demanded feelings.

Instead, she hugged me and distracted me with a *Blade* movie marathon, my favorite non-romcom movie, to get my mind off my script. We talked about vampires and the apocalypse, giving me a target for my rage as we argued about the minutia of supernatural politics, theory, and mythology. Monica usually hates my tangents, but she participated all the same. Familiar eye rolls not excluded. And when the last movie ended, she turned to me and delivered the crushing truth; *you know you have to work with Roman right? If you don't sell to Dreamaway, they'll blacklist you as difficult to work with. It isn't fair, and it isn't right, but that's the industry. Can you really afford to take that chance?*

The thrum from the DJ pulses through my thoughts and lulls me back into my body. Tonight, I feel reckless. Wild. A sense of nothing to lose and everything to gain. Anything to shake the feeling of being trapped in a life that isn't mine once again. It takes every bit of restraint I have not to smash the glass in my hands into a million pieces, remembering.

She's right. I shouldn't blame the messenger, but it doesn't stop me from making her the villain, anyway. Monica is an easy scapegoat. If she hadn't offered me as a plus one, I would be... probably getting a million rejections from every studio in town. Even inside my own feelings, the logic of her words crushes down on me. I roll my eyes at the entire cityscape.

"You having a rough night too?"

Nick, my plus one assignment for the evening, asks in his perfect British accent.

He's handsome, but in a wildly average way. So much so that I'm terrified of leaving his side at the risk of never finding him again. Light brown eyes that match his hair, almost to the shade. He's got a slim, fine nose that covers lips I'm sure many women have used to show their plastic surgeons.

He's been scrolling endlessly on his phone, creeping on the minute-by-minute update his ex is providing on her feed. Apparently, they broke up three days ago and he's heartbroken. Per Beckson's instructions, I'm not supposed to give too many personal details about myself to the clients. He doesn't want me to appear as a social climber, which is insulting to say the least, being that this whole town has been built into a ladder. Not that my personal life would get me far, anyway. Beckson is a wolf in expensive suits, no matter how friendly he talks.

"Just work stuff. Nothing worth talking about."

I shrug, hoping my answer is vague enough to keep him scrolling. Instead, he puts his phone down completely.

"Is it me? Am I the work stuff?" His voice cracking. "Selena says that I can be such a bore when I'm sad. Selena said. Ugh, she used to say."

I rush to comfort him, alarmed at the climbing emotion.

"No, no! It's not you. I meant my *other* work. I'm not a professional plus one. I'm technically a writer, I guess."

He nods his head in acceptance, sniffling back the emotion swelling in his face. I'm worried I've overstepped but suck in a sigh of relief as he refreshes the feed in his phone.

I think I've escaped when his nose scrunches up before asking, "What do you write?"

My brain fogs in panic and I consider lying to him, but I have a rule: no colossal lies. Lying provides a complicated problem for me. It's infinitely harder to do well when I can't remember who I've told what to, a lesson I learned the hard way.

Just ask Trent's parents. The last time I tried to pull off a lie was after Trent had proposed. He had wanted to be the one to tell his family in person, only no one had let me know they were going to be in town. I didn't expect my excitement at showing the ring to my neighbors would end in a spoiled surprise. Nor did I expect the fight, the tears, and the apologies that came too soon after the enthusiastic yes.

So, as a rule, I don't try that anymore. Hesitantly, I answer.

"Romance. I write romance."

His face swells again as he looks into the pit of my soul.

"Ah. I see. Another romantic," he whispers.

Fuck, this is going to be a long night.

I put my hand on his and look him dead on. "Nick, it's going to be okay. I know you don't feel like it now, but either way, you're strong enough to make it."

As much as I want to escape from this party and his company, my heart still tugs for him. I know what it's like to feel abandoned by the person you hoped knew you best. Even if it isn't right. It still feels like your heart is being ripped out and steam rolled when what you thought was happiness is unmasked.

He needs good friends who care enough to feed him carbonara and garlic bread, with a bad movie rolling in the background, and the entire night to just cry. Instead, his manager said he needed to be here, for the sake of his career, as if this one party determined his entire future. Which I highly doubt, seeing that we've sat here for two hours while an entire party has avoided us like the plague. He nods his head in agreement, but his face tells me he thinks I'm full of shit.

"I need some water," I tell him.

At this point, risking losing him and hearing about it from Monica is better than sitting here making small talk. Unfortunately, Nick doesn't agree. His eyes widen and he looks around, panicked at the prospect of being alone.

"Perfect, I could use a drink myself. I'll go with you."

He stands from the couch, offering me his hand. Inwardly, I let out a shriek before putting all my weight into him and letting him haul me up.

I walk away from the beautiful cityscape into the covered building where the bar is. A few people smile and nod in my direction as I pass. I have no idea who they are, or if it's me they're nodding to, but I reciprocate all the same, my body on autopilot. When everyone's a stranger, you make a choice whether to accept embarrassment from being wrong or isolation from never trying. In a room like this, with the fear of missing out thrumming through my veins, embarrassment wins out.

The bar area is packed. Tiny booths sit in relative shadow off to the far wall, which I scan for the improbable empty seat. My eyes catch on dark brows that are narrowed in my direction. His hand comes up for a moment as if to call me over, and I start trying to put together any pieces in my memory that will help tell me if I know him.

I stop my mad dash to sort through my list of possibilities as it slips into his hair, sliding through with ease. He ducks his chin in acknowledgement of his tablemate. Even as the guy next to him gestures on, talking to him, his attention on me doesn't waver. *Not someone you know, just a handsome man looking this way. You don't even know it's you he's staring at.* A smirk tilts up just the side of his face, and it zips through me.

Every nerve in my body is called to his table. I may not know this man, but I want to. I realize I want to tell the biggest lie I ever have tonight, and I want to tell it to myself. That I'm not worried about my future. That I don't doubt who I am and if I'm good enough to have my dreams. I want to wrap myself in the confidence of that man's smile. I want to be the woman who isn't trapped, who doesn't have her story told, but who writes it herself.

And a story like that can only be written with unbridled passion and courage. It can only be *felt*. I want to be the adult version of Victoria that I always see myself as in the best of my fantasies. The one that was possible before responsibility weighed her down and fear took away her motivation to try.

Nick's hand rests lightly on my lower back, breaking the moment and expertly guiding me away from the booths to the bar. It isn't the lingering touch of a lover, a more gentle nudge of a friend, but it sharpens my senses all the same. It burns into the fabric of my dress, scorching on my skin, and I find myself wishing it was someone else's hand. Someone who could do more. Not the safe, predictable choice.

More like the guy in the booth.

Heat rises to my face. I haven't felt genuine passion in months, probably longer. The frustration and rage and (begrudgingly) attraction I was hit with from Roman begs for an outlet and, for once, I want to let go. Maybe tonight I can lean into it all and forget about my script, my ex-husband, my day-to-day life. There are certainly enough strangers here to have a wild night of fun. Even if my mind keeps drifting to only one.

We finally shimmy up to the bar, Nick ordering a Gin & Tonic and me a sparkling water with lemon. My chest is pushed tightly to Nick's, the crowd not allowing me to give him space. His arm is still wrapped around my back. I let my mind wonder about what this would be like. If it wasn't him, but someone else holding me like this at a party. Someone who wanted me. Someone who wasn't Trent. The thought causes my anxious grief and excited need to go to war deep within my belly.

The image is shattered as Nick's other hand starts his doom scrolling all over again while we wait. I itch to grab my phone, even though it is once again tucked safely away with Stan. My fingers drum against my arm as I try to occupy myself. The crowd drowns out any need to talk and I relax into the chaos until Nick's attention is suddenly taken away as someone slides up beside him. I brace myself for the worst, Nick's own nerves rubbing off on me.

"Can I borrow him for a minute, honey?" the man asks.

Nick is already leaning toward the man, almost eager to go, so I'm confident when I say, "Of course."

"Be back in a few," Nick tells me. "You should mingle or dance. I'll grab the drinks when they're ready and come find you. You deserve to cause some trouble in that dress."

He smiles like he means it before stepping away.

His eyes float from his phone to the man, only half paying attention to him, which is more than he's done for anyone else this evening. My heart flutters a bit as his hand gestures show genuine excitement. Nick appears to be a good egg and I'm happy he's finding something worthwhile in his night.

My eyes drift from him to the people bobbing to the music. *A dance might do me some good.* I move through the throng of people and onto the makeshift dance floor between the bar and the booths. The sunlight has faded to a glimmer, but the lights inside haven't been completely turned on yet, causing shadows to dip in and out of the room.

The beat pulses through me and I let myself go, swaying into the rhythm without thought. I close my eyes to a stray sun ray, dipping my head back as I do, my hair falling down the open back of my dress. I shed my stress like a physical thing and my whole body lightens. A shadow moves over me and my eyes pop open, only to stare directly into dark brows again.

He's sitting at the same booth, only now he's alone. His smirk is gone, but as I instinctively take a step toward him, it returns. This is absolutely the come-hither scene in any romance script I've ever written and right now I have the choice to ignore it or give in. I breathe deep, a smile taking over my exhale and move toward him.

Fuck it.

If I have to work with Roman fucking Wheatley on a romance script, I'm at least going to understand what I'm talking about.

My feet are steady and sure as I sashay my way to him. The closer I get, the more my breath catches. His shirt sleeves are rolled up, the top two chest buttons undone, hair already mussed from his hands running through it. I stumble in these traitorous heels, my teeth worrying at my bottom lip, trying not to think how I might not look as flawless as I imagine.

This is a mistake.

I'm out of practice and out of character, but I'm already in front of him. Unable to back out now, I do what I always do when fear threatens to overwhelm me; I jump in.

"Married?" I ask.

If he's startled by my question, he doesn't act it.

"No," he says, not missing a beat.

"Attached of any kind?" I verify.

Again, he's quick and to the point.

"Not in the slightest."

His voice is the baseline of the noise around us, and I lock onto it with everything I have.

"Good," I say as I put my knee into the booth, awkwardly crawling my way toward him.

I guarantee this doesn't look as sexy as I expected. My dress sticks and I can feel it ruching up from the vinyl with every move, exposing the skin on my thighs. Thoughts of straddling him flash but I chicken out at the last second, my legs sweeping out from beneath me, instead. My butt flops onto the seat while my knee clangs hard against him.

"Ouch!" I squeal.

I rub my knee under the table, accidentally grazing his leg, and he stiffens. This is a fucking disaster. But I've come too far. I pull my hands from under the table, placing them on each of his shoulders, and stare into pools of shadow.

"I'm going to kiss you now."

God, I am painfully awkward, but I lean in slowly, anyway. To what is probably both of our surprise, he doesn't pull back. He waits for me to move all the way in, my lips pressing close to his. He smells of cinnamon mint gum and vetiver, and I wonder if he'll taste the same. His stumble runs against the soft tilt of my nose and a spark of desire lights.

I need to know how this feels.

This could be the worst kiss of my life... or the best. I've lived all my favorite moments only in my script. For once, I want it to be real. To be a memory and not just a fantasy. I'm already more alive than I have been in years, and I'm drunk on it. I need more. My hands move onto his neck, pressing, begging him to give me something. Finally, and all at once, he tilts his jaw, opening his mouth to me, trapping my bottom lip in his teeth. His large hands cup roughly at my cheeks, tipping me back more.

All my rage, all my attraction, turns into a puddle of need. My body rotates into his as my back presses into the dulled edge of the table. His fingers bite against my skin, making me forget where I am entirely. Time has stopped for us, allowing this moment to be infinite. Nothing else existing but us.

\#

Her tongue dances lightly across my lip, a question to explore more, even as my control has slipped. I'm rough and desperate and more passionate than I thought I was capable of. I want to say yes, am dying to whisper her name and see the anger and frustration our words started earlier turn into one our bodies want to finish. Instead, I hear the shocked laugh of Thoren.

"Ro..." He starts and I rip my face and hands away from Victoria's in a way unbefitting of what she deserves. What this moment deserves.

Even if Victoria is a mess and probably hates me right now, a wave of protection and attraction flows over me. I had wanted to call her over earlier, apologize for the meeting and call a truce, but once her eyes fell on me, I couldn't. The flash of concern that swept over her made me stop and the flirty smile she gave me decided the rest for me. I wouldn't win her over as Roman. Not tonight.

Now, somewhere in the back of my head, there's a voice trying to convince me that if she knew the real me before she knew the name I was attached to, we could be something different. Something better. Five more minutes and I would've had that. Instead, Thoren had to interrupt and there's no salvaging this now.

My glare cuts him off completely and I shake my head in a language only brothers speak. *Don't you fucking dare*, it says. He may not know about Victoria, but he knows me.

Victoria is frozen, her gaze unfocused. Her lips are parted, slick from my tongue running across them. I can only imagine the *Oh* that could escape them if we did not have an audience, and I was left to finish what we started. Her cheeks are flushed and full. I want to wrap my hands back around them, capturing the heat as I press against her again.

I hate what Thoren's interrupted, even if I know he needed to. And I know I'm having trouble hiding how pissed I am by Thoren's chuckle.

"Well..." Thoren starts. "Do you at least want to introduce me to your friend?"

He's gesturing to Victoria, his eyes laughing openly. *No, I don't, you dick.* I try to telepath to him. His look tells me, *one way or another, you're not getting out of this.*

To my surprise, Victoria pipes in, "Actually, we're not friends."

She's already scooting away from me, my hands following her without thought. I move with her to the edge of the seat before she stands up, blocking me from moving any more without pushing my arousal directly into her.

"And honestly? I kind of want to keep it that way."

She grins flirtatiously at Thoren and it's a knife in my side. *She doesn't know it's you, Roman,* I remind myself. *But then why is she going around kissing strangers? And why does that make me want to throw her over my shoulder again and throttle whoever she would've kissed if it wasn't me?* I want to let her know we do know each other from the last plus one party, to show her we're drawn to each other, even if it's only as Captain. Before I can interject though Nick LeMay walks up to the table.

"There you are! I've been looking everywhere for you!"

He's smiling at Victoria, obviously her plus one date for the night. He looks back and forth from Thoren to me, dismissing us both as the strangers we are. Sure, we each know the other's name, but we don't run in the same circles. Even before I left.

He offers Victoria his arm.

"You ready to get out of here? I think I've fulfilled my obligations for the evening and I'm ready to go home."

Victoria nods, stepping up to take his arm, but he stops her.

"Let me just take one selfie," he says, holding his phone high above them, leaning into Victoria's space. At the last moment, he brushes a kiss across her cheek before snapping the photo.

She laughs. "Oh, you're sneaky!"

His cheeks blush in the dim light as he shrugs. "It's for the 'gram. What's your handle? Selena isn't the only one scoring tonight. Even if my score was a new movie opportunity, she doesn't need to know that."

Victoria beams up at him, her hand still resting on his arm. A dark unfurling is happening in my chest that I'm not sure what to do with. I know my face must look like I'm about to commit a murder.

"Good for you, Nick. But do not tag me in that. I don't need to read those comments."

They're already walking away from us. Both Thoren and I are dumbstruck at what the hell just happened. I'm confused at both what Victoria is thinking, and what it is I'm currently feeling. The awkward, funny pain in the ass I've been constantly running into just turned into a hell of a lot more than *some girl* within the span of fifteen minutes.

Before she gets too far, she turns back, her face thrown over her shoulder, "thanks. It was fun."

She tries to do a sexy wave but loses her balance and stumbles into Nick, who catches her. Her face is elated, flushed by whatever we just did. She giggles and stumbles off as they continue to the elevator. The same voice in my head tells me to follow her, that we're not quite done yet. I fight it, knowing I need to let her go and instead turn to Thoren, unsure what to even say. I shake out my limbs from the tension Victoria's presence has caused and wait for the hammer to drop. His good-natured smile is back in place, but there's a steeliness to it that suggests I'm in deep shit.

"Spill, brother." He drums his fingers on his crossed bicep. "Now."

Fuck.

NINE

Victoria

THE BRIGHT CALIFORNIA SUN spills onto my laptop in the living room of Monica's apartment. I'm using the desk she so graciously pinned up to the window to edit pieces of my script, jotting down ideas in my notebook as they come, determined to stay focused. Last night's exploit had me waking up this morning renewed and ready to tackle what Roman so lovingly referred to as 'garbage'. Even that asshole can't get to me right now.

The scene I'm writing is particularly spicy, a conga line gone X-rated, with my main character and her cruise directing hunk leading the charge. He's getting handsy with the bareness of her skin, guiding her along to get her alone. I can't help but pull pieces of their moment from last night, giving them both a wildness they didn't have before.

To say kissing a stranger was inspirational is an understatement. Sure, there are definitely parts I'll leave out in my memoirs, but most of it wasn't half bad. I'm daydreaming about those good parts, my mind already sugarcoating the memory, when my phone blasts at top volume, the caller ID showing a number I don't recognize.

"Hello?" I answer.

Normally, I'd let a call like this go to voicemail, but with my new gig and current script negotiation, it might be the studio, and I can't risk missing that call. My blood runs cold at the voice on the other end.

"Morning, Five."

His tone calls to me, fighting with what I know to be true versus what it promises.

"Roman," I say clipped.

I let the silence hang. *He* called *me*. I'll be damned if I am going to hold up this conversation. If he has something to say, he can damn well just say it.

"I know some things were said." He sighs and I can hear the scratch of the mic as something rubs against him. "Look, I'm not great at this part. I know how to mess up, as you well know, but I'm not as great at making amends. Which I'd like to."

He sounds forlorn, almost as if he truly wants to mend the rift.

"Well, an apology would be a great start."

My words are still pointed, but I'm opening the door. All he needs is to walk through it. The line is silent for too many heartbeats, and I worry that he may have hung up.

"You're right. I'm sorry I called your script garbage. It isn't garbage, it just... it isn't what I was expecting to be given for this film. My frustration was with myself and the studio, but I took it out on you. For that, I *am* sorry."

At the very least, he sounds sincere. Even if it is a shit apology.

"OK," I say.

"OK?" he asks in disbelief.

"Yeah. That was a shit apology, but we both know we're kind of stuck in this. So, I accept," I say, trying to be done with this conversation.

"Can I ask why?"

"Why what? Why do I accept? Did no one ever tell you not to look a gift horse in the mouth?"

"No, I meant, why was it a shit apology? I meant it—"

I interrupt, "it isn't about whether or not you meant it. It's about what it *means*. You addressed what you did and why you did it, which are both starting points, I suppose. But to me, the only thing about an apology that matters is what you're going to do in the future. Saying you're sorry to placate some absurd polite societal construct is just garbage. So, next time you apologize, leave out the excuses and let the person know how you're going to fix it."

I can practically feel Roman turning my words over in his head through the phone, the quiet of his breathing weighted. I let him hang on to my words for a few more moments before releasing it, ready to move on.

"Sooooo. What now?" I ask.

"Well, we might as well get to work. Do you have some time today to go over potential edits? I'd like to get this wrapped up in the next few weeks so I can get on the same page with the casting director. We rarely work before a script is officially purchased, but we're kind of on a tight deadline."

"Sure. I'm free in about an hour. Would that work?"

"Perfect. Let's meet at the office. Do you remember where it is, or do you need a ride?"

I can just imagine Roman picking me up and the torture of being crammed into a tiny steel box with him. The thought is unbearable.

"No, I've got it. Can you just text me the address?"

"Sure. See you in an hour."

Before I can say goodbye, he's already gone. Then seconds later my phone dings with a new message. It's the office address quickly followed by another that says, *this is Roman*. I laugh at the stupidity of it. I quickly save the address and his phone number. He won't be able to catch me off guard again. I definitely want to be able to screen his calls.

By the time I get to the studio, I'm already six minutes late. I quickly tip the Uber driver and sprint into the building; thankful I opted for my Chucks with this sundress instead of heels. I figured this is a working meeting and decided to dress down. Besides, after so many nights in heels and the damage to my feet, I wasn't sure I'd be able to handle another day in them. I give the receptionist my name. She escorts me up the stairs and we end up in the same conference room as before, except this time, Roman has apparently beaten me to it.

"Mr. Wheatley, your appointment is here," the receptionist says after lightly rapping on the outside of the door. She leaves us as I step fully inside.

"Would you mind closing the door?" Roman asks.

A chill runs up my spine at the thought of being in a closed room with him, but I don't want to show fear now. I nod, closing it behind me.

My first full glimpse of him has his features rushing to me like open water from a dam. I try to line up the feelings I remember with the man standing before me, and I'm failing. In my mind he's been earmarked as tall, dark, and handsome (a classic standby), and even though he still fits that description, he feels... lighter. As if a weight is lifting. His smirk still makes me feel like he's conspiring, but today it doesn't feel like it's *against me.*

My stomach does a tiny flip at the change in mood, my energy begging me to match his. A small paranoid part of my brain asks if this is even the same guy. Déjà vu filters through me, and I bash it away. Being faceblind makes everything less trustworthy, but I know this is Roman, and I remember too well the few, if only brief, interactions we've had. Before I can ponder anymore, he cuts into my thoughts.

"Five. Good to see you. Looks like you had a little trouble today being... on time, was it?"

He's smiling. I can feel the tease down to my toes. Either he's trying to throw me off my game or he's had a personality transplant. My money's on the former.

"At least one of was," I shrug my shoulders before sitting down at the same end of the table. "Let's talk edits."

I don't know if I imagine the brief look of disappointment, but if it ever was there, it's gone before I can blink.

"Right," he says before diving into the script.

He's flying through pages, providing me note after note. He's marked up the entire draft, black scribbles filling the margins and spaces. Basically, any blank space left on the paper. I mark thoughts and ideas into my copy, forgoing about every third one. I hate to admit it, but he's good at this and I'm seeing my writing from a completely new perspective. He's pulling out weaknesses and shining lights on what can make the good parts stronger.

I hate when an arrogant bastard is right.

We're onto the inciting incident, where the main character, amid her heartbreak, agrees to go on the cruise, when I slam my foot on the brakes of his diatribe.

"*Excuse me?* It sounds like you want to make Jo, our all-around bad ass, a sniveling weakling. You can't just change everything she is…"

Roman leans back in his chair.

"That's exactly what heartbreak does. On a fundamental level, it should rip you apart. Tear you down to the basics of what you know. Of what you *are*."

His pen is dangling from his fingers, the tip just breaths from his lips. I want so badly to shove it up his nose.

"What are you… What the hell are you talking about? She's obviously heartbroken. She's at the end of her rope! She goes to her mother, who you can see she has an exceedingly difficult relationship with and AGREES to go on a cruise for singles. WITH HER MOTHER. What about that doesn't scream heartbreak?"

I'm standing at this point. Roman stares at me, my chest bobbing up and down from exertion. He tilts forward on his elbows, pinning me with his gaze.

"Mental breakdown, maybe, but if you think this is heartbreak, Five, it's painfully clear you've never really felt it."

He sighs, then stands up, pacing next to me.

"True heartbreak, the kind that comes from someone who knows you, who *sacrificed* for you and you for them, that burrows into your self-worth. It drags into your chest to where you're not even sure how to breathe anymore. It drowns you under the weight of your love. You can't make *decisions*. Trivial things like showering are impossible. You can't immediately just mend another relationship and jump on a cruise."

He halts in front of me, his arms reaching for my shoulders before dropping without contact to his sides.

"Either she loves him this deeply and you change how she gets to this point, or she only ever loved the idea of him."

I can't get a word out. My voice feels like it's squeaky and thin. Like it'll break at just the thought of being used and I can't begin to understand why. Roman's face scrunches up in confusion as he takes another step towards me.

"Victoria," he whispers softly, "are you okay?"

I'm not sure why he's lost the edge to his words until I touch the mist on my cheeks. I wipe at them furiously, unsure why I'm suddenly falling apart. Empty moments of my past assault me, blank faces I can't place with names I'll never forget. I want to lash out in defense, explain that she could have loved him, or that she tried to, but my throat is too thick. Besides, something tells me right now if I defend my Jo, I know it'll leave me vulnerable somehow, and I can't have that.

"I'm fine. It's fine."

I just need him to back up, to look away. I can't take the pity that clouds his face. He's reaching for me, a *sorry* brushing across his lips. He's leaning like he might hug me, and I desperately want him to go back to ripping my script to shreds instead. Before I can tell him to fuck off or something else wildly inappropriate, an ear bursting alarm rings, making both of us hunch to cover our ears.

My tears dry up in surprise and confusion.

"WHAT IS THAT?" I yell.

"FIRE ALARM," he mouths.

I follow him out of the conference room and the building, sure to grab our work in case this is more than just a drill. The parking lot fills with studio employees, my ears still ringing as I try to balance myself from the abrupt change of environment and mood.

"What happened?" Roman asks someone in the crowd.

"Bill burned the popcorn again. Now we have to wait for the fire department to show to give us the all clear," they say.

"Great," I mumble.

I couldn't be happier that the alarm saved me from an embarrassing explanation to Roman, but before that, we were on a roll. Still, I am ready to be done. I don't want to prolong our meetings any further than I have to. He's seen enough of my turmoil and is pulling a thread that I am desperately trying to bury. Not to mention ignoring the fire I feel when he's not pulling his punches and how my heart snapped tight when he softened.

I regret having so many pieces of myself wrapped in this script that allow him to put me together in ways I'm not ready for. It makes me wary of him, and myself, all the more. Roman must see my frustration, and he waves me further into the parking lot to get away from the noise and the others.

"I know it isn't ideal, but I think we've gained some good momentum, and we should capitalize on that," he says, hands folding into his pockets.

He looks unsure of what he's about to suggest, but knows there are no other options.

"We could try a coffee shop. There's a cafe not too far from here, near the beach. It used to be fairly calm during this time of day, from what I remember. I did a lot of edit notes there while working on my first movie."

He's uncomfortable. I'm sure he doesn't want to be trapped with an emotional mess like me any more than I want to be trapped with an asshole like him, but he has a point. Still, I'd rather not be in the small space of a vehicle with his ego and my emotions right now.

"Couldn't we just wait? I can see the fire trucks now."

The dour line of stubbornness cuts across his lips, and I'm shocked to realize I know this means he won't let us.

"It could take *hours*. Do you really want to be here with me that long? We could halfway through our edits by then if we just go to the coffee shop."

I fold my arms across me, looking back and forth from the roadway where the flashing lights are getting closer and the building that's clearly not on fire.

"C'mon, Five. Where's your sense of adventure?"

He's got that smirk that sends my blood soaring and makes me step close in challenge.

"Fine. Let's get out of here," I say.

In response, he turns and starts walking, checking over his shoulder to verify I'm still behind him. He steps up to a boxy, green Mercedes SUV, so unlike the sports car I expected. Its freshly polished paint reflects my face back at me, the emblems and wheels such a flat black that the contrast throws me. It looks like you could take it anywhere, if you didn't mind dirtying up a six-figure car, that is. He gestures to it like he knows I'm already judging.

"It's my baby brother Thoren's. Can you tell he didn't get enough love as a child?"

I laugh despite myself. "If this is what he got, maybe I should have been loved a little less."

His face brightens at the response, and for the first time, I think we're actually smiling at each other. That's until I realize what's happening and quickly get my face under control. He pushes at the keys as soon as my lips fall, the car clicking as it unlocks. I pull open the passenger door, breaking contact with Roman as he gets in on the other side.

We are cruising, traffic not nearly as bad today as it has been. The AC is on but still I roll down my window, hoping the wind will take the place of any meaningful conversation. My hair whips out of my ponytail, curls of honey-slicked brown kicking up, and I relax back into my seat.

I expect Roman to ask me to roll it up, worried he'll ruin his perfectly groomed coif, but he matches me. He pulls out a classic pair of Ray Bans from his visor and slides them on like he's a model in a tourism commercial. I roll my eyes at his cool guy attempt, then flip his radio on and blast the volume. I laugh hysterically when the Pop Divas 100 playlist fills the screen. Roman just shrugs.

"I TOLD YOU. THOREN," he yells over the wind and the music in a way that feels conspiratorial, eyes rolling back at me.

As if I know Thoren and that's enough of an explanation. My stomach flips. I like the feeling that Roman and I could share more than disdain. That the tables are flipped and for once I could be in on something so personal. I quickly slap the shit out of myself mentally. *You are hopeless,* I tell my stupid romantic heart.

"RIGHT," I yell back, mouthing Thoren's name more than saying it, before turning my attention out the window to watch the world fly by.

I hide from Roman the glimpses I keep catching of him as we go. His fingers tap to the beat on the steering wheel perfectly in time. His mouth lip syncing ever so slightly. The delicate brush of air ruffling his hair. I tell myself these are notes for my next script—a romantic notion in motion. I don't notice him because I want to. I notice him because my craft demands it. *Yeah, right.*

By the time we get to the cafe I've gone too far into inspiration and am now thoroughly in my head with all the things I want to do to Roman Wheatley and all the reasons I can't. Most notably, he's digging up a whole shitload of personal emotions I don't want to explore. Making me distrust the stories I've told myself and if I've been ignoring the truth.

This has to be the worst case of Stockholm syndrome of coworkers anyone has ever seen.

I slide out of the car and follow Roman inside. My voice is cracked from belting, *Man, I Feel Like a Woman,* and I know I need something to drink in short order. The cafe is sparse and beach themed. It has a cheap tiki bar set up that looks like it serves both coffee and alcohol depending on what time of day you happen to arrive, or if you know the person on staff who will slide you whatever you need. There are only a couple of people milling about working on cheap college laptops and about a half dozen tables are occupied.

For a million reasons, from decor to clientele, I cannot see this being the office of choice for my companion. I try desperately to see the appeal he sees in this little shack but come up empty-handed. The squeaky floors, ranging from blue to brown from age, aren't exactly clean. There's a dead karaoke machine in the corner, a half-assed hung projector screen just a slice above it, dangling from a worn surfboard. It's just the sort of place I would love to come across. Quirky, messy, fun. Always some new detail to see and questionable drink to try. But I'm not exactly Roman's type.

He interrupts my chain of thought.

"We can take one of the tables on the patio if you don't mind and I'll get us drinks." A look of panic must take over my face because he quickly follows up with, "on the studio."

Immediately, I breathe out a sigh of relief.

"I'll take an iced green tea, please. Any flavor or variety will be fine."

Roman nods his head, then makes his way up to the bar as I scope out the tables outside. I snag one still covered from the afternoon sun, the shutters on the window thrown open so I have a view directly inside.

I catch him smiled at the barista while she starts on his order, his hands drumming on the counter unwilling to stand still. He's wearing navy blue slacks and a dove gray t-shirt, making him business casual but not casual enough to fit in here. His eyes lazily stretch from one item hanging on the wall to another, eyes brightening as he reaches the dusty singing machine. A small jolt of hope shoots through me, raising the tiny hairs on my arms. *Maybe we're not so different after all.*

It feels like ages before Roman joins me out at the table. Both of his hands are full, along with two muffins tucked into the crook of his arm. He sets my green tea in front of me, an orange twist of fruit floating between the ice.

"They said it was a peach green tea, so I hope you don't mind."

He sets both muffins down between us before sliding into his own seat.

"I also got two muffins since it was all the baked goods they had left. One is a lemon poppy seed, and the other is chocolate chip. You can have first pick."

I slide the poppy seed flecked bread my way and hear Roman's hum of approval. My brows slide into a question, and he huffs out a tiny laugh in response.

"I have a bit of a soft spot for chocolate," he says, sounding completely casual and so unlike himself.

My face softens into a smile. I unwrap the plastic around my muffin and wait patiently for Roman to do the same before I hold it in the air for a toast. Roman quirks his lips in amusement but lifts his as well.

"To a successful, if not completely inconvenient and messy, partnership."

I tilt my muffin into his before taking a large bite and setting it back on the table.

Roman takes a much smaller bite before setting his down as well. He flips into his copy of the script, no doubt finding the last point of our conversation before my embarrassing tears and the fire alarm saving me. I quickly rush to swallow, gulping down part of my drink and stuffing the remaining crumbs into my cheeks.

"How about we start after she's already on the boat," I plead, straightening myself to hide the desperation I have at not revisiting the heartbreak scene.

Thankfully, Roman agrees. An ease takes over and I can feel things shifting between us as I realize he isn't going to bring it up. *Maybe, he isn't so bad after all.*

He flips a couple of pages ahead to the first scene where Jo is on the boat and starts in. We work that way for a couple of hours, getting almost three quarters of the way through, before the cafe turns into happy hour and the rowdy beach goers crowd in. Time flies by until an overzealous twenty-something nearly spills her drink all over our table from the open window that's beside us, making Roman finally call it a day.

We walk back to the car in companionable silence. After accomplishing so many edits and seeing the story getting stronger with every note, I feel lighter walking away from the cafe than I was walking to it. We're finding a truce, and I think I might enjoy spending time with Roman. As much as he can piss me off, he makes my writing better. Not that I'll ever admit that to his smug ass face.

TEN

Victoria

"We're going where? When?" Monica screeches.

I sigh, digging deep for as much patience as I have.

"Monica. I'm only saying this one more time. We're going roller skating for Jessica in HR's birthday party. She's rented the whole place out and has *personally* invited us. I've told you this for the last few days. You knew it was coming up tonight, so suck it up buttercup, because we're going."

After Roman dropped me back off at the office, I noticed I needed to run in and grab a book I had left in our rush to get away from the fire alarm. Unlucky for both Monica and me, Jessica, whom I was pretty sure I'd never met before, was lying in wait. She cornered me, begging that I bring myself and Monica to her big birthday bash at the roller rink she rented. She shoved a funky 80s themed flyer in my hand and sent me on my way, nodding in agreement. I'm pretty sure Monica believed that this act alone made us even for all previous discretions.

"Never talk to strangers, Vip. How many times have we gone over this? You never know what kind of crazy, stupid ass shit they'll rope you into. A WORK PARTY? I have managed to avoid every single birthday, anniversary, engagement, retirement party from work for the last three years. You're here less than a month and that's just gone. Out the window," her hands flutter like a bird flying the coop. "You don't even care about the damage you've done. Now I'll be expected to participate, *Victoria*. I... I cannot even explain to you the depths of my despair right now."

She walks from the room, huffing out her frustration.

"Sorry Mon!" I call, though we both know I'm not really. Getting out will be good for her and even if I'm not ecstatic to get on a pair of skates and break something, I know we'll figure out a way to have a blast. Even with her poor attitude and her penchant for work parties, Monica loves a theme.

And as expected, within hours, she has outdone herself. We're both dressed up in our finest 80s party wear, though I'm surprised at the selection she just had lying around in her closet. I'm rocking the classic denim jacket, my hair pin curled into fine springs, giving me more volume than I've ever had. We're both wearing black fishnets. Mine are crafted into a sensible top with a black bralette that peaks through along with black leggings. Monica has opted for hers to be a bodycon mini dress with a lace bralette in highlighter pink that matches her leggings.

For someone who wanted to fly under the radar, she's going to, quite literally, glow all night.

A few people idle outside of the door to the skating rink and Monica homes in on one of them immediately.

"Jessica is greeting people *at the door*. I swear that bitch is trying to trap me. There's no hope of getting out of tonight without talking to her, is there?"

My shoulders shake from my suppressed giggle as I pat her shoulder.

"There, there. It'll be alright. You'll see."

She swats at my hands, almost missing the turn she started to take into the parking spot but rights herself before clipping the car next to us.

"Do not kill us just so you can skip a party, Mon."

"You mean there is a way," she says, eyes sparkling.

I roll my eyes and push at her shoulder as I hop out of the door. Monica beats me around the car, rushing toward her fate. A girl who I assume to be Jessica gasps so loudly I turn to see who's behind us.

"As I live and breathe, that couldn't possibly be Monica Wilson walking into a party for me!"

Her voice has found an accent that isn't hers, and her eyelashes dance wildly for attention. The guy standing beside her coughs out a laugh into his hand. Monica just sighs, holding out a card for the birthday girl.

"Happy Birthday, Jessica."

There's no fanfare or excitement and as soon as Jessica's finger touches the card, Monica is through the door, disappearing into the crowd. I stand there stunned before quickly recovering.

"Yeah, Happy birthday! We appreciate you inviting us both. I think she needed to use the lady's room. We'll see you in there, though!"

I make my escape in the same fashion, scanning everyone for the highlighter pink of my friend.

The crowd is a decent size, with about half showing up in theme while the other half are casual partygoers. I give up on finding Monica, knowing eventually she'll find me or a black light. Either will work. I make my way to the rental counter to get a pair of roller skates determined to take my moves out on the floor.

I used to love skating as a kid, even though I wasn't any good at it. When you're from a small town, though, any activity with loud music and lots of other kids seems worth it. All four of us would beg a parent or sibling to take us and then spend all night on the floor. And despite what Monica says, she was actually pretty good. A dull pain shoots through me at the memory, and I realize I wish Cherie and Katie could be here, too. I snap a few photos, sending them off in our group chat the caption reading: wish you were here. I tuck my phone away again, promising myself that I'll force Monica to take a few once we find each other.

The counter is empty. Most everyone is skating or decidedly not taking part and chatting with the other party-poopers. The smell of musty crowds and sweat heats my cheeks and I can feel the strobe lights already creating a pulsing in my brain that I'll regret come morning. But right now, I feel a million miles away and a lifetime of adulthood lighter.

The acne-pocked teenager hands over my cardboard brown skates and I hurry to lace them up at the nearest bench, suddenly very glad for the legwarmers and thick socks protecting me against the tall, gritty boot top. The wheels wobble beneath me. I take baby steps until I can remember the balance I need to roll a few feet without falling. My arms slice out at my sides like I'm an airplane or a toddler looking for purchase.

When I can finally place my arms down without slipping forward or back, I know it's time to leave the blanket of the carpet and hit the hardwood. A poppy, upbeat song I don't know pumps through the speakers, and I can feel the other skater's wheels pounding the wood as soon as I step on. A few eager ones spin around me easily as I make my way toward the inner ring, away from the rail holders and speed skaters. The lights turn down, black light and a sparkling disco ball bouncing off shoulders instead.

The song ends, another one picking right up, mashing into the first. This one I've heard on the radio, and I watch as several people get excited, hips and arms swinging every which way to the beat. I decide to join in, testing my balance with every roll of my hips. I fling out an arm, lashing my hair out as I do, only to hit something solid and human with the back of my hand. A soft *oof* whisper above me and I look up to see a man.

"I am so sorry!" I squeal, pulling back all my limbs while trying to keep all eight wheels on the ground and not fall on my ass.

He's got a hand over his chest where I must have hit him, but he doesn't look upset as he looks me over.

He catches me in his gaze, a smirk pulling at his lips.

"No need to resort to violence, Five."

Roman. I'm starting to like the nickname and how somehow he knows I need him to use it to recognize him. My eyes scan from head to toe. He isn't dressed up like me, opting instead for the safer choice of a green polo and dark wash jeans. His hair is wet, and I wonder if it's from sweat or a shower. My thoughts catch on that image for a moment before shaking it away. By the playful way his brow is cocked, it wouldn't surprise me if, somehow, he knew what I was thinking, anyway.

"What are you doing here?" I blurt.

His hands pull at the back of his neck before answering.

"I was invited. The entire office was, apparently."

"You just don't strike me as the type of guy who comes to this stuff."

I know I'm being rude and picking at the delicate truce we've reached, but something about him being here looking like a J. Crew model while I'm in fishnets and leggings throws me.

"Normally, you'd be right. But Thoren caught wind of it and pulled out the big guns to get me here," he says gruffly. The sharpness of his tone soothes something in me.

"Ah, I see. And Thoren's here? Because I'm starting to suspect he doesn't actually exist, and you just use the name to blame things you're embarrassed about on."

Roman's cheeks tint pink, and I try to get my fluttering heart under control.

"I promise he's here." His eyes flash around until he finally sees what he's searching for. "There! He's got the pink and blue leopard print shirt on."

He's pointing to a tall man zooming in and out of people on rollerblades.

"I can introduce you later if you'd like. Anything to clear my name of the accusations you've laid," he says jokingly.

"Alright, alright. I believe you. At least one of you came here on theme," I jab.

"Hey!" He points to his shirt. "I'll have you know this was *very* popular in the 80s. Green and beige preppy golf shirt? I absolutely saw my dad wear this. You don't think I actually dress like this, right?"

I smile.

"Nice try, sparky, but that's just a regular shirt. And don't get testy with me because you don't like your closet. I only think you'd wear what you actually wear. That's a conversation between you and whoever buys your clothes."

"I'll have you know I'm a big boy and buy my own clothes, thank you! Your opinion is even lower than I thought! And here I was sure we were starting to get along."

He's smiling, but there's a question in his words. An underlining truth he wants to sus out.

"We are. Sometimes. But that doesn't change the fact that you are claiming you are on theme. Look at me! I cannot give you credit when I look like this, and you look like that!"

My laugh echoes in the suddenly quiet space, the music being cut out while the DJ comes over the speakers.

"Our next song goes out to all the twosomes, threesomes, and more. We're doing a couples only skate by request. So, find someone, take them by the hand, and share a skate on Bonnie Tyler!"

Total Eclipse of the Heart blasts into every corner of the rink. People around us link up and I realize that both Roman and I have come to a complete stop in the middle of the floor. My hands sweat and I feel myself begin to panic, unsure of what to do. Before I can put together a coherent thought or skate off, he makes a choice for both of us. I watch as he offers me his hand, palm upright, in the middle of the skating rink floor.

"Want to skate?"

It's so simple, casual. There are no implications that it's anything more than it is, but my skin ignites anyway. I rub my palm against my legging trying to dry the nervous sweat away before setting it in his. He's warm, palms dry and all I can think about is how gross I must feel, but I don't pull away and neither does he. We push off together to join the other couples skating around the circle, careful not to tangle up our wheels as we do.

The song swells between us. I don't know what to say when I'm holding hands with Roman, so I stay quiet and just enjoy the nostalgia of being thirteen, couple skating with a boy, again. And just like then, I cannot wait to scream about this with my friends. Roman must be lost in his own thoughts, too, as he isn't in a hurry to make conversation either. We bob and pull against each other as we roll around people to the song.

"Hey Ca—" Calls from behind us.

Roman turns just his head, trying to see the commotion. Neither of us are good enough skaters to do much more. Thankfully, there's no need. Another voice pipes up right next to me.

"Calvin! Buddy. Don't you see these lovely people are sharing a skate? Don't be rude and interrupt them, ok?"

He winks at me, his pink and blue button down, giving him away before Roman says anything. His arm is wrapped tightly around the shoulders of another man, pulling him away from us.

"Hey T," Roman says to Thoren, completely ignoring poor Calvin.

I tug on his hand to get his attention.

"If you need to, ya know, talk to that guy..." I nod my head in Calvin's direction, letting him know I understand. He just shrugs.

"Nope, I don't. It always happens at these types of things; someone has an idea or a friend or something they want to run past me. But all of that can wait until I'm in the office."

He shrugs, used to people using his connection.

"And Thoren plays interference?" I ask. That gets me a grin.

"Yeah. Thoren likes to bounce people, and I like them bounced, so it works for us."

The songs dying down, our interlaced hands still swinging between us. I don't want to let go but it would be odd to continue. I loosen my grip reluctantly and our hands hang lonely back at our sides.

"And we're back to an all-skate! Everyone get on the floor!" The DJ coos.

Another smash 80s pop song plays on, but I'm no longer in the moment. Now, slowly rolling here with Roman is awkward. From the corner of my eye, I catch a neon pink bra with matching leggings and I'm pretty sure I've found my out. If it isn't Monica, at least I'll have an excuse why I thought it might be.

"Thank you. For the skate." I smile, then nod my head toward who I hope is Monica. "I think I just found my lost friend and I want to snag her before she disappears again."

Before I can leave, he says, "we'll need to continue editing. Does tomorrow at the office work?"

"Yeah. I'll need some extra sleep, I'm sure, after the inhalation of all this fog. Can I text a time tomorrow?" I ask.

"Of course. See ya later Five."

He gives a flick of his fingers in send off.

I push away from him and head straight for the benches where Monica is lounging. She's typing furiously into her phone, which is forgotten the moment I roll up to her.

"You and Roman looked awfully cozy couple skating out there," she smirks.

The nostalgic feeling of roller rinks and schoolgirl giggles fades, and I don't want to tell her shit. Instead, I try to distract her with what I know she desperately wants.

"Let's get out of here!"

She narrows her eyes, aware of what I'm doing but cannot ignore the call of getting away from her coworkers.

"Fine. But you can't hide from me forever, Vip."

No, I think. *Just long enough to get the script done.* Good thing I'm excellent at masking feelings, even from myself.

ELEVEN

Victoria

FOR THE LAST THREE script meetings we've had since the skating party, Roman and I have almost found a truce. A rhythm. There are still so many moments I want to grab him by the face and scream, but now there are moments where I don't. Ones where I want to spill my secrets and tell him about Trent. About all the reasons I wrote this script. Something tells me my feelings would be safe with him. That he wouldn't demand their depths or skim over their surfaces. He would be steadfast and challenging and, in the end, I might be better for it, too.

Not to mention the thoughts I've had of doing other things to his face, particularly his mouth, but I'm not ready to dive into what exactly that means yet either.

Currently, we're sitting in the conference room staring at the window, careful to avoid each other. The warm glow from outside floats down across the floor, casting a tangerine light to reflect on every surface. We've just had another disagreement on the viability of falling in love over the span of a two-week cruise for Jo and her cruise director, Xavier, and neither one of us is budging.

I, of course, believe it can happen. Attraction and energy don't need a long timeline to form. My heart demands that I live in a world where the possibility to just *know* is out there. Roman disagrees. He argues their friendship is more important than their chemistry and that I can't just fill every other page with lust and sex, and call it love. He thinks they need change instead of just attraction.

The feminist in me applauds the sides we've both ended up on. The romantic in me worries for his emotional state if he thinks love doesn't start as chemistry, which then doesn't lead to sex. Sometimes attraction *is* the change and feelings this big are brand new. I take an enormous sigh, still skirting his side of the room with my eyes as I adjust.

In truth, it might be time for a break. My head keeps turning to the sun, my body demanding to get some vitamin D and beach time. But I'll be damned if I'm the first to suggest we quit early. Especially after a disagreement. Roman has taught me that, with the right circumstances, fighting is worth it. So, instead, I sigh.

Roman must be reading my mind when he says, "How about a change in scenery?"

I immediately perk up, excited about the compromise and feeling like the tide has turned in my favor.

"What do you have in mind?"

"The cafe?" he asks, hopefully.

I let the word sit between us for a moment too long as his eyes fall back to the desk.

"We can stay here, it was only—"

"Let's get out of here!" I interrupt, not willing to let him take it back.

Without another word, he grabs up his papers and heads to the door.

As soon as we hit the cafe, the day picks up. As per our unspoken agreement, the last time we were here not to bring up the disagreements of the office, we start in a new spot and continue with our edits. Roman retrieves both our beverages of choice: medium black iced coffee with a splash of hazel nut for him, peach iced green tea for me. I can also see the crispy golden tops of muffins poking out; poppyseed and chocolate. The routine feels normal. *Right.* I realize I don't feel trapped or discarded. I actually feel excited. Even if circumstances forced us together, we're good at this.

My thoughts immediately turn our disagreement over, ready to volley our points and open myself back up to the process, and in turn, to Roman. He must feel the shift in my energy, too, as pieces start falling quickly into place for our couple, and after only one iced green tea in, we decide to call it a day.

"So," I start on our way back to the car. "What does Roman Wheatley do when he's not tearing apart people's dreams at work?" I ask.

There's a playfulness in my voice that I tell he picks up on by the half smile he throws me. I feel light at our progress, as if we're not only changing my characters, but me, too. He pauses too long, and I can't take his contemplation any longer.

"Roman Wheatley..." I start for him.

He rolls his eyes at my use of his full name.

"Goes home and studies the script more," he sighs deep before adding, "and hopes that people leave him be."

There's a sadness to his voice that pops my elation. A truth to be left alone but also a real cavern of loneliness. A man this young, this good looking, this *successful*, shouldn't be living a life so devoid of fun.

"What I'm hearing you say is you have no plans?"

I make a split-second decision before I can regret my choices.

"That's—" he starts before I cut in.

"Great! I know just the thing."

I snag his hand and pull him back toward the cafe. He allows me to lead him and, to his credit, doesn't question where we're going. I pass the cafe and continue toward the boardwalk. Venice is picking up, people taking advantage of the sun and the lackadaisical whim to the day. I drop his hand, sure he'll follow, as we dive into a street filled with shops.

After searching the signs and windows, I finally lay eyes on what I've been looking for. I skip around a rollerblader, nearly knocking us both down in the process before finally stepping into the shop. My hand snags a few snacks, then I find some cheap boxed wine, which I immediately scoop up. Looking back I see Roman standing in the door, a smirk all the validation I need as I pay for my finds.

Roman holds the door open for me, saying nothing as I continue hiking down the boardwalk. I like the way he trusts me, letting me surprise him, even if it isn't truly a surprise. The smell of the ocean washes over me as the wind picks up the closer to the sand we get. That childlike emotion overtaking me. I hand the boxed wine to Roman, linking our now free hands and taking off into a sprint.

He doesn't hesitate. He doesn't hold me back. His own feet keep pace, letting my shoes sink into the sand as we race to the ocean. Most of the people have thinned out around us, only a young family and their dog running around to our left. I figure this is as good of a place as any and plop my butt into the sand.

Roman stumbles at the drastic change in pace before sitting down beside me. He undoes a few buttons on his shirt before rolling up the sleeves to match. Then, without prompting, he takes off his socks and shoes, burying his toes deep into the sand. My mouth falls open in surprise and then I do the same. He methodically unwraps the boxed wine, handing one to me when I finish.

I take a swig. It's too sweet. Too cheap. A taste that reminds me of being twenty behind the Cash N Gas with Cherie, thinking we were infinite when really, we were toes deep in cigarette smoke and the stench from the garbage can two feet away. Somehow, it is completely perfect as I stare into the sea.

I sigh happily, letting the stress and emotion of the last few weeks drift off with the tide. I swear I can feel Roman's stare, but instead of it being suffocating, comfort wraps around me. Like he gets what we're doing and why, even if I'm not quite sure myself.

When I finally look at him, his eyes are on the horizon. There's a soft tilt to his lips. A lightness in his shoulders, like a weight has been lifted from him, too. I want to know what memory the taste of *86 prosecco* from a beach side tent brings him. Who the people he loves are. What dreams plague his days?

With what I do know about him, the failure of his movie, the breakoff of his engagement—I realize I don't have any of his shiny moments. The ones that draw the silver lining when someone is hard to bear. What must that be like, being mostly known by your failures? I never considered what that could be doing to him. Who that made him.

What if he's as lost as I am?

"This is probably my favorite place in the city." Roman's honey voice drags my thoughts to here and now, but he doesn't take his eyes from the water. "A perfect beach day in California is hard to trade up for in Connecticut. Although a good thunderstorm is a remarkably close second."

I can see Roman now, standing on some wrap-around porch while the eastern sky lights up around him. That same peaceful smile he's got on right now, lighting up with the world around him. My heart leaps and I find myself needing more of him. More memories, more favorites, more history. I'm desperate for him like this, open and soft. As if we could live in another life.

"Both somehow suit you," I say. His smile widens. "So, Connecticut is where you call home?"

I am trying to grab pieces of him with whatever bait he tosses my way. Somehow, this is the wrong thing to say. His eyes dim, shoulders sag with weight once again.

"Yeah. Or at least something like it. Minimally, it's where the Wheatley name has called home long before me," he answers.

I'm losing him to his past. It's dragging him under and my mind scrambles for purchase to bring us both back to the present, or the future that could be.

"Funny. From what little I know of Thoren, which is to say he drives an expensive SUV, listens to top 100 divas, wears brilliantly themed attire, is the baby of your family, and is obviously your favorite sibling, I couldn't imagine him anywhere but California. It's like he was made from cocktail parties and celebrity dreams."

Roman laughs, the light coming back to his face.

"Yeah. Thoren... well, he's excellent at adapting. But this time, I think he likes where he's at. At least, for now." His shoulders shrug and I laugh.

"Oh! My best friend, Cherie, is just like that. Always dashing to the next thing. I love her, but she enjoys *options.*"

I try my best to wiggle my eyebrows, bringing out a deep husk that I feel through trailing down my spine.

"Do you and Cherie share that in common?"

He's looking at me now, the sunset forgotten. I shake my head and look at the sand shifting from one of my hands into the other.

"Nah, we don't. I over commit. It's like when I find something that works well enough, that I've put time into... I don't know. I just can't seem to let go. Even if I know I should. Monica used to say it was that good money mentality."

"Good money mentality?" he asks.

"Yeah, you know... *I spent good money*."

It's clear by Roman's face that he has no idea what I'm talking about. I sigh and turn toward him.

"My mom used to buy all these art kits that she would never actually use. They'd be scattered around the house, and it drove my father mad. But every time he would go to donate or throw them out, my mom would always say, *but I spent good money on that, Nick!*"

I look at Roman, still lost but nodding eagerly for me to continue, so I do.

"She was basically saying that she made a choice. She invested something no matter how small into it, and now she was stuck with it. And while she knew she could just buy another one if she ever wanted it, she just couldn't face the fact that she would lose what she already put in."

The familiarness of my mother in this moment slips through my skin like paper. I think about what she would think about how different our relationships were. How much of a failure I turned out to be. Something about hearing their voices in my head made me want to tell Roman everything, like how that good money mentality ended with me losing everything from holding to the wrong things too tightly. I don't want their loss and my past clouding this moment. Roman, blissfully, pulls me from my thoughts before the tears pricking my eyes can take shape.

"I get that. No one likes to lose. Especially if they aren't sure they'll ever get it back." He thinks for a moment before adding, "but I've never heard that expression. Sounds like something you saw in a movie and just took on yourself... HEY!"

He laughs as I throw sand at him for his accusations, dusting his pants with fistfuls.

Roman starts pushing sand over my feet and legs in retaliation and before I know what is happening, we're both laughing and dirty, our legs intertwined with each other. My body moves with him as if familiar, my hands finding purchase on his shoulders. I think I mean to get up and instead my chest tilts further toward him.

Our breaths are ragged, and I can smell the fruit from the wine on his exhale. Neither one of us is laughing now, the smiles slipping into something deeper. Something wild. His eyes dare me to give in. He's on the edge of saying something when a neon yellow ball falls between us. I just catch the tail end of someone's yell before the wind is knocked out of me, a golden pile of fur blocking my vision. A rough, thick tongue licks at my face before snatching up the tennis ball and bounding off as fast as he came.

"SORRY!"

The kid yells are he snags the collar of his pup, wandering off in the opposite direction, lovingly scolding him. I pick myself off the sand, dazed as I try to catch my breath.

"Are you okay?" Roman asks.

Whatever the moment was between us, it's gone. His brow bends in worry, as he looks over my features for any cuts or scrapes.

"I'm okay! That just... I wasn't expecting that." I breathe out a tiny laugh, my hands still shaking from the adrenaline and odd turn of events.

"I should probably get you back. Wouldn't want you to be the first writer mauled by an overzealous game of fetch on my watch, now, would I?"

Before I can protest, he's standing and offering me his hand. Even though I want to stay, want to go back to when I thought he might kiss me, I take it and get to my feet.

TWELVE

Roman

The first thing I feel when I wake up is excitement. It's been so long that my heart's quick beats terrify me, and it takes me an embarrassing amount of time to realize what it means. I look at my phone and realize that, for once, I'm up early enough to shower, grab a coffee and eat breakfast while still being on time to meet Victoria at the studio. I rinse off then head to the kitchen where Thoren is already waiting.

"You look dangerous," I tell him. "Dressed to take someone's money today, little brother?"

He laughs, a deep bass that warms my heart more.

"Actually, yes. I'm meeting with a few capital investors today to go over a new portfolio option."

It's easy to forget that underneath his goofball nature and little brother's annoyance, he's sharp and brilliant with numbers. There's a reason he's been managing our play funds since he was fifteen. Dressed in an expensive suit, he looks so much like our father that I need to remind myself not to be angry with him. I can feel the frown pulling on my cheeks and lips. He breaks up my perusal and the dark thoughts clouding my mind.

"You look... happy," he tries. "At least, until just now, when you saw me. But before that, I'd say you were downright chipper."

He's smirking, hip kicked up against the island while he sips at his coffee. To hell with not being irritated with him.

"No happier than usual."

I try to play it off, hating that he's sniffing where he doesn't belong.

"You sure? I don't remember what 'usual' happiness looks like for you," he shrugs. "No, I would go so far as to guess there's an unbelievably beautiful woman you are seeing today. Victoria, is it? Or are we calling her Five in passing?"

I could easily break his nose. One quick jab and his suit would be ruined. I exhale heavily, determined to not let him goad me into ruining my morning. I slide around him and make my coffee while a piece of sourdough toasts.

"You are calling her nothing. As a matter of fact, we're *never* talking about her again. Do you hear me? I wouldn't have told you about it in the first place if... circumstances wouldn't have required it," I say.

Thoren laughs.

"Circumstances. Right. That's what the kids are calling it these days." He's practically snorting out coffee through his nose. He pulls himself together. "Look, all teasing aside. It's good to see you happy. It's been a while."

He pats me on the shoulder, dancing away before I can snag him in a headlock. I hate that he can read me so easily after a lifetime of learning how, but he's hard to stay truly mad at.

"Tell her I say hello and that she's currently my favorite person in the world," he calls from the door before he's gone, and the condo is quiet.

By the time I get to the office, my heart is doing backflips in my chest at the anticipation of seeing Victoria after our day at the beach. I replay the moment I almost lost myself entirely and kissed her. That is until the dog made his move first. I wonder if she'd recognize me then. Would she know that it wasn't our first kiss? That I was the stranger at the party, and several other run-ins before that?

I had done some online searching to understand what faceblindness meant, but there were so many variations and levels to it that it left me with more questions than answers. But I knew in my gut that I would need to tell her soon.

It was only a matter of time before someone called me out or she figured it out on her own. The closer we got, the more details I would inevitably let slip. Besides, we had gotten past my shitty reputation, hadn't we? Yesterday's outing proved that.

As much as I hated what happened with Lauren, I had learned from it. Lying when it came to other people's feelings only led to guilt and pain. I didn't want to jeopardize what Victoria and I have, even if I'm still not sure what exactly that is.

I settled with myself that if today went as good or better than yesterday, I would tell her tomorrow night at the awards show. Assuming she would attend again as a plus one. The thought of her face flashing with the betrayal, made my stomach clench in fear. Neither one of our careers could handle the paparazzi getting their hands on something like this and Victoria at least deserved a chance to make it in this industry without my history weighing her down.

Maybe not *at* the show, I reasoned. But definitely after. I'd call her if I had to.

Walking toward the conference room, my heart stops as I catch golden brown hair through the window. Victoria is already seated at the head of the table that we've been fighting over. I can't help the chuckle that escapes at her competitiveness to be early. How long has she been waiting? Her head pops up from writing notes into her book as I step through the door.

"Here's a riddle. Are you still late even if you show up on time, but I've been waiting for you?" She teases.

My breath catches. *What if I've been the one waiting for you?* I think this romance script has gotten a little too far in my head. I couldn't remember ever being this nervous to like a woman, nor this excited to talk to one. Lauren had been a comfort, something to link me to who I've always been. But Victoria, she was the possibility of who I could be, and I couldn't get enough of the taste of that freedom. I shake out the sappy feelings, pushing them back into a controllable box, only to be looked at for the story. Not for me to say something incredibly stupid and embarrassing.

"Never," I shake my head. "Your delusions of time, Five, shouldn't penalize me."

She laughs like my favorite song blasting from a radio, warming me from tip to taint. Her chest heaving at the sound of her nickname, solidifying it for the rest of our lives.

"How'd the rest of your night go?" I ask.

Her head tilts forward, causing a curtain of hair to fall over her cheeks. She blushes as she answers.

"Good. I wrote until one in the morning. The beach was inspiring."

I stop at the chair across from her, my hand gripping its back as I lean in.

"Oh yeah? A new script idea?"

I'm desperate to know what she's written. If it's another romance that stars the two of us. If, in her version the dog didn't interrupt, and instead other steamy words filled in the blanks. If I'm the same man on and off the page. But she doesn't elaborate. She simply nods, a small smile still resting on her lips, then fiddles with her notebook. Teasing out all her secrets is the only motivation I will ever need.

I let the silence hang in the air only long enough to take my seat. Then, pulling out my heavily edited copy of her script, I release her from the awkwardness.

"Well, while you moved on to a new idea, I spent a couple of hours going back through the entire script and jotted down some more notes based on what we talked about yesterday. We may need to go back and adjust the beginning to match what we've changed in the middle."

I open the script up, flipping to a few pages before the heartbreak conversation we had yesterday. Looking over, I see Victoria doing the same. She has new tiny blue notes scribbled in the margins.

"I actually thought about what you said yesterday, you know, before the fire alarm." Her fingers curl up the edges of her paper. "You were right. It didn't fit emotionally with what I was trying to show about the character. Instead of being heartbroken over losing a boy, I think she needs to be heartbroken over losing herself."

Her words are hushed but firm, sincerity clear. If she knew me now like I know her, I would wrap my arms around her. Let her know I understand. But she doesn't. The lie settles between us like a canyon that, no matter how much

I want to, I cannot cross. Guilt and fear well up inside me, but I cannot slam down my emotional walls now that she's finally opening up. Instead, I do what any good director does and orchestrate her words into action.

"Mmm," I hum, nodding my head. "That works well, actually. It's believable. It's relatable. How can we show that in her decision to go on the cruise?"

"I have no idea yet." She smiles, her shoulders reaching for her ears. "But I figure we can circle back after the edits are complete. Maybe you have some ideas? I think a lot of it can come from the actress' expressions. Her wild and uncharacteristic actions. I'm not sold that it has to be said. Maybe she doesn't even know it herself yet."

I want to pry. To dig. She holds her emotions close to the chest, and I want to know every memory that is building this character in her head. Even if it means she has to get close to me, too. I gently nudge at the idea, suddenly less interested in the script.

"What would you do?"

I lean back in my chair, giving her space to answer. The quiet burns my ego and I worry that I've overstepped a line in the friendship we've just drawn.

"Well, I would probably move to California to try to find myself again. Maybe meet someone different. Someone who challenges who I thought I was. Who doesn't let me hide behind easy."

This time, instead of looking away embarrassed, she looks directly at me. I don't shy away either.

"Sounds like this is personal," I muse.

"I didn't think it was when I wrote it two years ago. But now? I guess it kind of is."

"What changed?"

I know I'm pushing my luck, but I can't stop the words from escaping.

"I did."

She holds eye contact for another moment before looking away.

There are a million questions shooting through my mind: *Who was he* and *how did you change?* But I refrain. This is as far as we're going to get, and I know better than to tip the boat over into freezing waters. Ghosts of exes are circling our very tender truce, and the last thing I want is to let them in.

"Well then, I don't think you'll have any trouble making the edits. But let me know if you need to brainstorm." Then I have the audacity to add on, "or if you just need to talk."

"That sounds... nice." Her blush deepens. "If you're in such a sharing mood, what would you do?" she asks.

Normally, with a question like this, I would think. I would hold the words in my hands and rearrange them until they were confident and sure. Not too revealing or vulnerable. But when Victoria asks me, my ability to filter breaks loose.

"I would mourn and hide hoping I'd be forgotten."

She's looking at me now, mouth barely agape.

"Or, at least, where I could meet someone that knew nothing of my past. Who could see me for who I am and not just my reputation."

Sympathy fills her eyes, her hand inching towards me and I know I'm in trouble of forgetting myself entirely if I don't change the subject, so I do.

"Let's move on to the next scene," I say as I flip through my page to more notes I'd found about Jo and her relationship with Xavier.

Thankfully, she lets me go and we continue through the notes we've both made, careful to stay on topic but finding it incredibly difficult. Her eyes keep finding mine, while her hands find gentle ways to bring me back into my body. A forearm touch. A shoulder shove. We've found a rhythm of friendship I haven't had with a woman since Lauren. If only friendship was all I was feeling.

My mind keeps drifting to her lips, the feel of her knee between my legs, her hand at my nape. Thoughts entirely inappropriate for a business meeting. Thankfully, if Victoria notices, she doesn't let on. She just lets the banter continue, the energy in the air build. A piece of myself I'd almost forgotten slips back into place, and I can't ignore what I want any longer. I decide to hell with it. If it's going to blow up in my face, it might as well be now. I interrupt our silent reading of one of the ending chapters, taking advantage of the lull in conversation.

"So, Five, I wonder what a girl like you does on a Saturday night? Meet up with a friend, perhaps?"

My eyes are still scanning the page in front of me, trying to continue to play casual. I didn't plan for this. Know that I might be pushing things too soon. But my heart and mouth have a mind of their own, and even with the genuine concerns I have between us, they're screaming, *now, now, now* and *more, more, more.*

"A girl like me?" She asks, laughing.

"I mean, I told you what I do..." I push.

"Well, I guess it all depends on what my options are and who the friend might be."

Apparently, she isn't going to let me off easy. I love it.

"Anything you want with me," I add, chancing a glance. My voice has gone deeper, falling into a flirty tone I don't quite remember ever using. Her chin is propped up in her hand, looking at me.

A soft sigh escapes her, her hips shifting in the chair. She makes to uncross and recross her legs, the tip of her toe glancing across my pant but her knee slams into a part underneath the table and her sexy attempt has been extinguished. Yipping in pain, she grabs for her knee, clearly embarrassed at her botched attempt. If only she knew wanting to kiss her better is the only thing her clumsiness has accomplished. My hand reaches underneath the table, falling on top of hers at her knee.

"You okay?" I ask, voice husky and quiet. Her eyes look from my hand, then trail up into my face, her confidence returning.

"I suppose all *friendly* Saturday nights start with dinner," she says, giving me the opening I so desperately need.

"Seven?" I ask, my breath holding, praying I haven't completely misread this situation.

"Seven," her phone rings, breaking whatever bubble we've been in and she pushes away from me as if caught red-handed. "Shit. That's Monica, my ride," she says, glancing at her still ringing phone. She picks it up from the table. "I'll text you my address."

Before I can respond, she's picked up her phone and is skipping out the door. I watch her all the way into the lobby before what's happened catches up with me. The misnomer of this being a hangout was provided, but it felt like a date. That means I have until Saturday at seven to tell her the truth and make her not hate me or else our friendship, let alone anything more, could be over before it even starts. My head falls into my hands. No pressure.

THIRTEEN

Victoria

"So, WHAT, YOU GO from him being the biggest dick you know to dating him in five point five seconds?" Monica spits out.

She's been asking me the same question in different colorful language since I told her about Saturday's plans on the car ride home. I roll my eyes to her reflection as I continue putting on my fire red lipstick named appropriately, *seduction*.

"Like I told you, we're not dating. It's dinner. With a friend. And he's still a dick, but..." I put the lipstick down as I reach for the words to explain my change of heart. "It's different. His reputation seems harsher than the reality. And he's making me a better writer. We're stuck together whether we like it or not. I'd be crazy not to make the most of it."

The half-truths pour from my mouth like drool during a good sleep. After the beach, my heart was a mess. I wondered if I've been jumping to conclusions. All week I had been replaying our encounters as I would a favorite movie, and while the beginning was certainly rocky, his feedback had been valid. His ideas improved my story, my writing. They made *me* better.

Even when we fought, I was still an equal partner, and my story was coming to life in our hands. Roman made me feel seen, like everything I strived to accomplish mattered, and it was well within my grasp. Even as he was ripping my writing apart, asking me questions that *hurt* it was in a way that said everything I am, even with the mess of emotions, was worth something. His presence now oozed safety, and I wanted to spend more time with him. I'd never felt this way before, and I didn't want to lose whatever was blooming between us.

"Well, just remember, if you make the most of his bod to use protection! Who knows where a guy like that has been while he's out hiding from the spotlight," Cherie chirps in from the speakerphone Monica is holding. "Although, I will say that man is an upgrade if there ever was one. Perfect rebound too. Never mind, Monica! I'm team Roman."

Katie hushes Cherie on the other side of the speaker. Monica looks appalled, and I can't help the bubble of laughter that rises from me.

"Ladies! There are no *teams*. We're not dating!" I groan, but no one is listening to me at this point. Thankfully, Katie changes the subject.

"Monica, please do not forget to leave the key with the doorman! Cherie and I are going to be there tonight at eight, but we'll need to drop our stuff before meeting you both at the after party. Is the air mattress out and filled?"

"Yes, yes, and YES!" Monica grumbles.

"I still can't believe you two are flying down here for the weekend. I haven't even been gone that long!" I say.

"Hey! We can miss you during any amount of absence, OK? Besides, the tickets were highly discounted from work. If this isn't the time to use my being a travel agent to my advantage, I don't know when is! Besides, we all know Katie needs a break from her beautiful, loving, vomit-inducingly perfect family." Cherie says, a fake hurling noise traveling through the phone.

"STOP, CHERIE! That sound is going to make me actually vomit!" Monica squeals, her face already turning green, while Cherie cackles into the phone.

"Sorry, Mon!" She coos. "Alright, well, we've got to shake. See you both soon!"

The line goes dead as Monica and I lock eyes in the mirror.

"Monica," I say seriously, "you have to *promise* me you'll keep Cherie away from Roman. Those two... I really, really doubt will get along and I cannot have her embarrassing me. Or should I say *us*."

Her small, perfectly white teeth peak through burgundy lips, her head tilting in the smallest nod. "Of course, Vip. I've got you."

Butterflies erupt in my stomach. For the first time since Bobby Jay wiped peanut butter on Katie's seat at lunch on the second day of eight grade, us vowing to get revenge on him, Monica and I share a common goal. There is nobody better to have on your side when it comes to espionage, revenge, or distraction. Before I can ruin it by saying something sappy, she breaks away and fumbles in her closet.

"Do you want to try this?" She holds up an emerald green gown with a slit clean up to the left thigh.

"Sure. I mean, if you think it'll pass the dress code."

The last thing my bank account needs is to splurge on a dress I'll never wear again. I mentally cross my fingers and toes that she has something that will work. The finalization of my script cannot come soon enough. The plus-one date money has been nice, but LA is expensive, and if I ever want to leave Monica's couch, I really need the contract signed and my divorce finalized.

"Yeah. It's dressy enough to not stand out in the crowd, but not too glam to take away from the actual stars. This isn't one of those big, televised awards shows, so no worries on the cameras, but it's still an awards show. You can't show up in jeans and a t-shirt," she tsks at me.

I just roll my eyes.

"Wouldn't dream of it," I mumble.

She tosses me the dress, and I slip it on. It falls over my curves gently, giving me enough shape to be seen, but not enough to be lustful. I point my leg out through the slit and smile when it falls perfectly to the side, revealing my newly shaved thigh.

"That'll do donkey, that'll do," I say to Monica. She curls her lip, sneering.

"Do not quote Shrek." She walks out before throwing over her shoulder, "besides! If I'm anyone, I would be Fiona. NOT DONKEY."

I chuckle, slip on my beloved heels, and follow her out. For the first time, I think tonight will be fun regardless of my date.

FOURTEEN

Victoria

THE DATE IS NOT going well.

It is always my luck that when I finally decide to let go, to decide that things are fun and exciting, everything goes to shit in a handbasket. Tonight's weird is a guy known only as Andrew. He looks normal enough, if not unique, with his tan skin and dusty red curls that stand about an inch from his head, making us roughly the same height when I'm in heels. He's got eyes the palest blue I've ever seen, and they look constantly terrified. Almost as if he's being hunted. His nerves have *me* looking over my shoulder every five minutes.

When we had arrived, Monica pulled me aside with what appeared to be Andrew's publicist, to give me a five-minute rundown of my night. The takeaway? He has deep-seated social anxiety, I'm not supposed to let him smoke any weed until the award is announced, and I'm here to play the buffer between him and... well, everyone else. This should have been a fucking preparation meeting *before* we walked the carpet. To say I'm irritated is an understatement.

Andrew awkwardly offers me an arm, not quite bent enough to take but also not stretched out enough to grab his hand, as the line to the tables moves forward. I cup my arm around his and before I can adjust, he slides it all the way up into his armpit, his hand tucked tightly into his pocket. The pinch of his suit is going to leave a mark, and the moistness of the fabric is already sticking to me.

Still, I try to put on a smile for Andrew. He's trying, at least. I cannot fault a man for that.

The hosts are sorting people through the door, staff leading each couple or group to their respective tables. When they finally get to us, they address Andrew, but look straight at me.

"Hello Mr. Andrew! We have you seated at table 33 as requested. Please follow Lisanne and she'll get you seated."

The woman hands us off to an identically dressed staff member who escorts us to a table on the outer edge of all the other diners, before rushing off to the next group. The table is smaller than the others, only four dinner sets laid out as opposed to eight. Andrew takes the seat that sits directly in front of the pillar, away from everyone else. I pull out the chair next to him and realize that I am, literally, a shield for him from the walkway. *As requested, indeed.*

"So, Andrew. What can I do to make tonight easier? Do you want to talk, or would you rather have the quiet?" I ask.

His eyes are darting, hands and feet tapping incessantly, making it obvious he's struggling. From what I've gathered, he's a composer of some sort and doesn't like or want fame in any way. He enjoys the work, not the recognition. This awards show is completely out of his comfort zone, and I'd bet he's regretting whatever movie he did that got him here tonight.

"Actually," his voice is mild with a lilting accent I cannot place, "talking is fine. With you. I mean, you're fine." His eyes close and he lays his hand flexed out on the table. "I'm sorry. What I meant to say is talking with just you is fine." He takes a deep breath before opening his eyes again. "This night has me so nervous. I hate these things."

"It's okay! It may not seem like it, but I get it. At least, some of it," I say, locking eyes briefly before giving him the space to shake out the nerves. "Being faceblind means that everyone at first is a stranger. Which can make me extremely anxious. You're probably the only person I'll recognize all evening."

Although there is flattery in my words, I'm not lying. With all his unique features, I should be able to pick him out in a crowd easily enough. My words help, at least a little, as his shoulders relax. He slumps even deeper into his seat before reaching into his pocket. He pulls out a handful of brightly colored, individually wrapped candies.

"Want one?" He holds out a neon green one to me.

"No thanks, I'm good."

He shrugs his shoulders. "Suit yourself."

He pops the candy open and downs it without a single chew.

"So, do you know who's sitting with us tonight? Are you allowed to tell me?" I ask.

"Yeah, I don't see why not." He wipes his nose on his suit sleeve before coughing a bit. "It's the actors who are in the movie I'm nominated for, *The Last Goodbye.* Have you seen it?"

Have I seen it? The whole fucking world has seen it. My jaw wants to drop to the floor but somehow, I keep it clenched in place. *I'm going to be sitting with Kimberly Fletch and Miah Omar.*

I manage to nod my head in a small up and down motion.

"Yes, I have. It was a great movie."

"Eh. I mean, it was good. But I'm not sure what the fuss is all about."

He doesn't sound like the fake modesty you often hear from people who do remarkable things. He genuinely believes he was just doing a job, apparently. I let it go. Getting into a compliment war with this man will do no one any favors.

"Agree to disagree," I say.

Andrew digs into his pocket again for another candy.

"You are going to ruin your appetite," I joke.

He laughs at the punchline a little too hard and I'm worried I missed something important.

"Sure. My appetite. Are you sure you don't want one? It always helps with my nerves."

"Nah. I've never really been one to take candy from strangers."

I wink for good measure, and he snorts before popping the candy in his mouth. I've heard of all sorts of tricks to help with anxiety, and hard candy is one of the least offensive. The mix of bitter and sweet drifts to my nose making me think of peach beer.

"Too bad. How do you ever get the good stuff, then?" He teases right back. "I would also like to point out that, at least for tonight, I am the least likely to be a stranger."

It feels good to joke with someone like this again. I've always tried to make being faceblind fun, like its something to enjoy instead of fear. Right now, my main priority is to make Andrew feel safe and calm, and if he wants to share one of his candies, it's the least I can do.

"You're right. Hand one over!"

He does, and I quickly pop it in my mouth. It's disgusting. The bitterness tasting only mildly of peach. I want to ask him what kind of garbage candy this is, but the host leads a couple to our table, dropping them off at the vacated seats, taking the chance away from me. My focus follows who I can only assume are Kim and Miah sitting directly opposite of Andrew and I.

"Hi there! Y'all, I am so glad we're at this smaller table. Andrew, you always have the best instincts!" Kim says, reaching her hand across the table to grab Andrew's.

He lets her, squeezing once before retreating back into his pocket. He doesn't say anything, just nods to both, taking out another candy discreetly behind the pillar. Kim isn't fazed as she turns to me.

"Hi, I'm Kim! You must be Andrew's date," she draws out the word date, leaving me to fill in the question she's asking without her having to actually ask anything.

"Yep! I'm Victoria. It's so nice to meet you!"

I put my hand out, and she takes it limply in hers before shooting her gaze to Miah.

"This is Miah. We're not really dating, but it's all about optics, honey. You know about that, I'm assuming?"

She's prying into Andrew's life and if I didn't know any better, I would think she might be *jealous* of me. Or should I say jealous that I'm here with Andrew. I want to tell her I'm a plus one and there's nothing to fear, but contractually can't. My suspicions only deepen as her eyes dart from me to Andrew.

"Victoria is a beautiful name. Does it run in the family?"

Miah reaches over to take my hand, obvious in his attempts to cover up whatever is happening with Kim. I am more than happy to let him.

"Actually, yes! Every third or so generation gets a Victoria. Good guess," I say nervously.

I try to smile but I know I'm showing too much teeth by the ache starting in my cheeks. Still, he returns my deranged one with one of his own, which unsurprisingly is perfect. His hand is still warm as it slips from mine.

The conversation lulls after that and a foggy, thick silence hangs in the air. I work to keep all the questions I want to ask in check for fear of fangirling too hard. Kim tries to catch Andrew's gaze, which he ignores. She decides this is my fault and narrows her gaze on me every few minutes that he doesn't respond. Miah has taken up his phone, apparently done playing referee. The house lights dim as servers put out the courses, and an announcer takes the stage.

"Welcome everyone to the third annual Film in Feelings Awards Banquet! We are excited to have you all to celebrate the most emotional, moody, and heart rendering films we've had the pleasure of watching this year."

The crowd erupts in applause, which I join in at half a beat behind. Someone sets a lovely bowl of soup in front of me, and my attention is taken completely from the stage. My first slurps are spectacular. Monica warned me to eat lightly today since the five-course meal tonight was prepared by James Beard award winning chefs I wouldn't want to miss, so I'm starving. After the first taste though, I am so glad I took her advice. My financial situation hadn't awarded me any excellent restaurant outings in LA yet, so I plan to eat every morsel on my plate this evening.

I look up at Andrew and see him pulling out another candy. Kim notices too, a puff of air escaping her as she sees what he has. Andrew's eyes flash to her and he offers her one. Her head shakes a laugh exploding out of her. Miah's head pops up from his phone.

"What did I miss?" he asks.

Kim looks like the cat who ate the canary.

"Oh, Andrew has brought some of his special treats. Miah, you want one?" she asks him, all wide-eyed and sweet.

Miah's eyes grow into saucers as a wicked grin lights his face, too.

"Yeah, actually. But only one. Last time I took two, I was high and unable to get off the couch for an entire day. I've got to get home tonight, Andrew."

He laughs while reaching his hand across the table to accept the treat.

I must be missing something important. Something that's sitting just on the edge of my thoughts, but I can't quite grasp. My face must give me away because Kim takes one look at me and laughs again, drawing eyes from a nearby table.

"Maybe talk your date into having one too, Andrew. It looks like she could loosen up a bit," she says.

Andrew doesn't hesitate as he offers me one again.

"She's already had one, but you're welcome to another. They really do help with these events. And don't listen to Miah, he's a bit of a lightweight and I think I've finally got the doses down."

"I'm lost. What exactly did you give me?" I ask, worry climbing in my pitch.

"The good stuff," he says, eyebrows wiggling.

"They're edibles, Victoria." Kim says, her satisfied smirk aimed at me. "I thought your publicist said no more 'wild nights' in public, Andrew."

"She did." I pipe in towards Kim, then turn to Andrew. "Hey, I thought you were supposed to wait until after the award was announced," my voice is full of concern because this was one of my three jobs for the evening and instead of stopping it, I've unwittingly joined in. Monica is going to be pissed. Andrew rolls his eyes, leaning back into the pillar.

"She's being dramatic. Trust me, a sober me at these events is much, *much* more embarrassing," he promises.

"Ah. I would disagree with you. Do you remember the last party on set where you were forced to attend? You, my friend, got a bit delusional and tried to drown one of the dummies because you swore it had begged you for a drink of water." Miah says. "How many have you had?"

Oh no. I am in so much trouble. *I* had one of these. He's had at least three. Maybe four? Fuck. Was it five? I start to panic.

"I don't know, man. A couple," Andrew says.

"I can't be high. *We* can't be high. What the hell, Andrew!" I yell.

Miah must see the look of terror I have and think it's well warranted. The servers come around to clear the soup course, taking my half-eaten bowl away. This just ignites my fear, turning it into anger. Miah pops up from his chair, coming around to Andrew's side and snagging him by the arm.

"I'm going to take him outside for a bit. Get some water and fresh air into his system. They're going to kick in any minute now, but after the first bit it should be fine," he says.

I glare at them both.

"His award is one of the first of the night! He has to be here in case he wins. You can't leave yet!"

My voice is rising. I quickly lower my tone, avoiding the glares from the table over. Miah just shrugs his shoulders.

"I'm sorry, love. But he cannot go up there like this. A lap or two. I promise we'll be back before the announcement. They're always running behind at these things. It'll be fine. You'll be fine. One shouldn't be too bad—just add a bit of calm for you. It'll be good. We'll be back."

With that, he drags Andrew into the darkened walkway and out of the banquet room.

Kim and I are now alone at the table. She's having a fit trying to keep herself from laughing in my face. I no longer think she's as beautiful or as talented as I did before she sat down at this table, and I can't help hoping she chokes on the small plates currently being served. I quickly pull out my phone and text Monica, *code red*, and hope she'll find me so I can explain what's happened.

We remain quiet as the plates are set and cleared, and the awards continue to be given away on stage, as if my universe isn't melting. My nerves are so bad that I can hardly eat any of the food put in front of me. My stomach churns in knots as the host announces the next award. The waft of what I now know is weed in my throat has me downing my glass of water.

"Now this next award is for the brilliance behind the music. All emotion, when summed up by song, can float across languages, ages, and cultures. It's these brilliant minds that truly catch the heart of a scene..."

Andrew and Miah are not back yet. The projector screen floats through the candidates and familiar dusty red curls appear in a candid photo. My stomach drops to my shoes. *Where the fuck are they?* I want to scream. I reach my hand across the table in instinct and grab onto Kim's arm.

"What do we do if his name is called?" I ask.

She turns to me, a cruel smile lifting her lips.

"What do you mean we? You're his date. You'll have to accept it on his behalf."

No. *No.* Absolutely fucking not. This is *not* happening. I can't stand up in front of all these people. I'm not prepared. There's fucking soup spilled on the front of my dress, for fuck's sake. I'm high on God only knows what! My hands begin to shake as the panic takes hold.

"Kim, can't you do it? You're much better suited. This is your movie too. You should do it. I... I can't." I stutter.

She shakes her head.

"Afraid not. I'm already up for my own nominations. Besides, with the rumors about Andrew and me, how would it look if I accepted an award on his behalf? Optics, Victoria," she tsks.

I could just leave. Stand up and walk away from this entire evening. I could wait outside for Monica and explain what happened. But then, what would Dreamaway say when I tell them why no one collected his award? Would I still get paid? Hell, would they still produce my script? Anxiety fights against the lag the candy is pulling me into.

The host is booming the winner's name into the mic and it's too late to decide anything when Andrew is announced. I barely hear it as the crowd turns to our table, every eye on me and Andrew's empty seat. Kim, poised as ever, stands up and hugs me, pulling me up with her and gently pushes me toward the stage. My feet betray me as they move, shaking with every step.

I walk carefully around the table sitting closest to the stage to get to the stairs. Before I can even take the first step, that beautiful, lovely slit I shaved for betrays me. My toe catches on the piece of fabric that should have broken away from me when I walked, causing me to stumble headfirst into the never-ending staircase.

My hands shoot up reflexively to save my face from the impact that may never come when I feel a strong hand wrap around my waist and yanks me up against them.

"Whoa there, Five. I've got you."

His voice pours over me, breaking through my panic and the haze of the edible. Roman pulls me upright again, holding my waist to steady me. Every touch of his fingers tingles into my spine, making me want to curl up and live in the feeling. I let all my worry wash away into the strong, calm warmth of his palms on my hips.

"You okay?" He asks.

The words mean more than this moment. This stumble. This night. It digs infinity into my thoughts of all the circumstances I could be in. All the things unsaid between us. I want him to know I'm better now. That his existence changes everything. That I didn't know finding myself would lead me to finding him, too, otherwise I wouldn't have waited so long. I want every feeling I've shoved into corners of my heart to be let out. But I don't have enough time to tell him everything, so I just nod. He offers me his arm, and I happily take it in mine.

Why the hell haven't you kissed this man yet? He's riding in like a goddamn superhero.

I feel Roman laugh more than hear him.

"You'll have to answer that question for both of us tomorrow night."

Fuck. Now I'm saying things out loud that I should only be thinking. I am never taking candy from a stranger again. Not in my life. I ignore the gasps and stares as he walks me to the host. He releases my arm, pulling away smirking, and I fight to stay in place. To not run to the safety of his arms again.

The host greets me away from the mic, leaning in to kiss my cheek.

He softly whispers, "No Andrew?"

I can't speak, so I just tilt my cheek into his in response, his hot stubble like sand on a summer day, making me close my eyes so I can absorb it better. He releases me, allowing access to the mic for the acceptance speech I'm supposed to give on a complete stranger's behalf. I take a deep breath, already mourning the contact of skin on skin.

"Obviously, I'm not Andrew," I say, a trill laugh punctuating my words.

The audience laughs as a consolation. My palms sweat around the glass figure in my hands. I wipe them on my dress, trying not to focus on the thoughts of dropping it that are currently scrolling through my head, the people spinning as I try to fight the high.

"Andrew is currently... unavailable. But if here were here, he would..." I stumble through the lines trying to piece together something worthy of being said through the cotton in my mouth, when I'm interrupted by a voice from the back.

"I'M HERE! That person is an IMPOSTER!" The voice yells.

Andrew steps out of the darkened back tables, pointing up to me. He stumbles through a few tables on his way to the stage, grabbing handfuls off people's plates as he goes, stuffing them into his pockets. He whisper-shouts to the onlookers, "it's for later" before continuing on. I can see a few people trying discreetly to cut him off before the stage, but they are too late. He is up the stairs and in front of me before I can pick my jaw up off the ground.

"Now, Victoria," his breath washes over me, stale and smelling of weed and menthol cigarettes, "you cannot go around stealing other people's awards."

At that he boops me on the nose. Like a dog. And instead of allowing me to leave the stage, his arm wraps around my waist and he leans over my shoulder, shoving his mouth into the mic.

"Hello people!" He sings.

He pulls out a piece of food from his pocket, then quickly shoves it into his mouth, smacking his lips loudly.

"Oh, ugh. Dry. It's dry. Everything is dry," he says, leaning away to whisper directly to me and failing horribly.

He leans back into the mic, "thank you and goodnight!"

With that he bows, before leaving both me and the stage behind. The entire audience is silent. My cheeks flame under the florescent lights and for a moment,

I'm stunned into place. A howl of laughter from the back kicks me out of my stupor. I tap the microphone to make sure it's still on.

"The Last Goodbye has one of the most beautiful scores of music I've ever heard, giving poetry to the background of this love story. I am as grateful for Andrew's brilliance as he is to all of you. He would like to thank everyone who made this movie possible."

I hold up and shake the award to the crowd before backing away from the mic. I rush off stage, following in Andrew's wake, shocked at what the fuck has just happened. Behind the stage is chaos.

"Vip, what happened?" Monica asks me as soon as I get backstage, her platinum bob and cream suit giving her away.

There are crew and people scattered, along with who I assume are Miah and Andrew tucked into a corner, a jacket pulled tightly around their heads as they giggle.

"I don't know, Mon." I shake my head, my nerves bursting out. "He had candies, and I didn't know they were edibles! How would I know that? Then Miah said he'd help, but it doesn't look like that happened. And Kim, Kim said I should accept the award, and, and…"

"Ah! It's okay. It's going to be okay. Did you have any?" she asks.

I nod my head in shame, eyes wide. *What if Monica is mad? What if she's so mad that she kicks me out?* I know I'm spiraling, but I can't stop myself. A full-on panic attack is on its way. I know it.

"Fuck. Ok. You know what? We're going to leave this mess for the professionals. I'm just going to take… that…"

Monica wrangles the award from my hands that are still clutching onto it for dear life. She pats me on the shoulder before turning and shouting to a woman talking frantically into her phone.

"Georgia! We're heading to the afterparty. I need you to take this and get him home. I'll call Beckson and try to explain what's happened on the way."

Her calm, angry words give me a solid grip of reality that steadies me. She grabs my hand, pulling me behind her out into the night. Stan, prepared in his neon purple shirt, opens the town car door for us before we even make it past the venue's door. I smile and try to wave at Stan, but Monica shoves me into the car, climbing in practically on top of me in her hurry to avoid the cameras and reporters.

"Move over, Vip! These scavengers are going to hear what just happened at any moment and we don't need them crowding the car. Or worse, following us!" she gripes, while slamming the door behind her.

Stan jumps in just as quickly and we're gone, not a single person catching on in time to stop us. I'm sliding into my seat properly as Monica pulls out her phone. It barely rings when a sharp voice ticks up on the other end.

"Yeah, Beckson. It was the edibles again."

She rolls her eyes, and the giggles explode out of me.

FIFTEEN

Victoria

I DON'T THINK I could love Stan the Man any more than I do right now. After Monica explained what had happened to Beckson, along with me chiming in to verify that it happened that way, my stomach unravels the knots it is in. The rumble from my hunger is so loud, I'm convinced all of LA has heard me. So, we do what any sane hungry person here would. We go to In and Out Burger.

"This burger is the most delicious thing I've ever tasted," I moan to Monica as she daintily picks at my fries.

"You're a hot mess right now. You're getting grease all over my dress! That's never going to come out, Vip!"

"Sorry! I mean, I've already spilled some soup on it, so what's a little burger juice?" I shimmy in my seat as a few more flecks of oil spill out. "Promise, once I get the check for the script or my payment for tonight, I'll buy you a new one, Mon."

With the plus one income, I wasn't as broke as I expected to be, but I was in no shape to be handing out brand new dresses either. If I was going to actually have a bedroom anytime soon, I would need to save every penny. Not to mention my plus one days were quickly coming to an end. Before long, I would need to sell another script. *And get paid for this one*. My anxiety amps through the fog but nerve endings and the lingering high demand that all of that can wait. Right now, I am calm as a cucumber. And they are cool as hell.

"It's fine," she waves me off, sighing. "Just buy me one when you get more settled. I can't take the lecture I'll get if Cherie knows I took any money from you right now. Not to mention bargaining with you while you're high. She's insufferable enough."

The hamburger almost chokes me as I cough out a laugh.

"That she is. Deal," I say, holding out my hand for a shake.

Monica rolls her eyes and ignores me, leaving my outstretched hand hanging in the wind. I let it idle in between us, feeling frozen in this moment.

"Stan, could you swing by our condo so we can get Alice from Wonderland here a new outfit?" Monica asks. "And for fuck's sake Vip, put your hand down."

She swats my hand onto the seat between us and instantly I feel in motion again. I look between her and my hand.

"Thanks, Mon."

Part of me knows the smile on my face is mad, but most of me doesn't care. I continue to eat my burger one-handed, pieces falling onto the trashed dress with abandon. *Who cares? It's already been downgraded to a napkin. Might as well use it.* I pull up the hem to wipe at my mouth.

"You're disgusting," Monica says, staring daggers at me.

I just shrug, enjoying the hum of the car ride. We make it to the condo in a flash. Or at least I think we do. My burger and most of my fries have disappeared and my drink has been slurped dry. Somehow, I'm still hungry. I'm pretty sure it's because Monica stole way more of my food than I realized. I hate being high. People just can't help themselves from taking advantage.

"C'mon Cinderella. You've got a costume change before you're ready to become a pumpkin." Monica hauls me out of the back and up the elevator to our home.

I get plopped down in the living room before she leaves me to pick out my new clothes on her own. She comes back laying out a pair of my chucks, a fitted long pencil skirt, leather jacket and a retro bustier tank top on the back of the couch, before snapping her fingers at me until I give her my attention.

"Alright, let's do this. Strip."

I get up and pull the silky dress over my head, taking a painful amount of hair with its zipper. She hands me another item, and the world spins as I put that one on, too. Thankfully, I keep myself mostly upright, only needing Monica's help once. I slip on the Converse, then stand as Monica evaluates her work.

"I mean, the shoes are a bit of a stretch, but I can't have you breaking your neck. At least they're black and white and not the bright blue monstrosities you usually wear. I guess it'll do. Normally, I would just scrap the whole night and tuck you in, but I have to go to the party, and I certainly don't trust you to stay here alone like this. We'll do a quick pop in and then we'll leave. Easy."

She pops her hip out like she's about to walk down the runway and I look around confused.

"Are you talking to me?" I ask.

Monica stares at me wide eyed, before mumbling something I can't hear under her breath and heads to the bathroom. From there, I catch a few of her incoherent yells.

"I swear Vip. No candy. What did we. Never take candy. Strangers."

It all sounds like babble, so I ignore it. She must have called someone else over or is talking on her phone or something. As if by magic, my phone blares.

"OH! I love this song." I get up and start moving with the music. "Monica, come dance with me!"

Monica comes out of the bathroom and beelines it for my cellphone.

"Your phone's ringing, dummy," she says to me before answering it. "Hello, Monica speaking."

"Aw! You turned it off, you bitch."

I throw a pillow, which Monica dodges like a ninja.

"You're kidding, right? No, we're going. She's just high as a fucking kite right now…"

Whoever she's talking to is causing the pitch of her voice to change.

"Yeah, ok. But do you think this is a good idea? Fine. We're on our way. Text it to me. Traffic is bad, so we'll be there when we get there. Bye."

Monica hangs up the phone, then looks at me.

"Girl, we've got to fix you up a bit more. Give you some water. Maybe some electrolytes will help. This is going to be such a disaster."

My face falls, pulled down by the weight of the world. But then Monica laughs, and everything feels better again. I laugh with her. She flutters around the apartment, handing me things and touching my face and making me drink lots. But she's smiling the whole time, so I must be doing something right. Before I know it she's leading me back down to Stan and the black sedan he chariots.

We crawl into the back, the sudden pull of the car making my head and my stomach woozy. I grab the leather jacket and pull it around my head, blocking out all the light. I need to stop climbing right now.

"Mooooooonicaaaaa. How long?" I whine.

Her voice comes to me from the heavens.

"Almost three hours, if you took it before the dinner started. You should come down soon. It's okay babe. The wooziness means you're coming down. I think. Here, take some of this."

She hands me a cold bottle and a small pack of mints. I down them both, each mint burning more than the last. I stay under the leather jacket, happy to fade into blackness as I try to ride out this horrible night. The car jolts to a stop and vertigo takes the place of the peaceful emptiness. I can't rip the jacket off my head fast enough. Blinding car lights assault me. I barely catch the two very handsome, excellently dressed men that are sitting themselves in the seats in front of us.

Monica turns to me.

"As you can see, she's a bit of a mess. But I'm not going to fix her until we get to the venue. There's no point."

My hand immediately goes to the rat's nest my hair has become. The lighter haired man laughs with her, but the one directly in front of me looks pissed. I've done something wrong, and in my panic, I desperately want to fix it.

"No, Mon, fix it now," I say desperately.

Instead of her moving to help me, the man in front of me leans in, his hand hanging up in the air between us.

"May I?" He sounds like velvet, making me want to rub my face against the words.

I nod, not trusting my mouth, or my breath, wanting his touch badly enough to still. Gently, he rearranges pieces of my hair, smoothing down sections with the brush of his palm. He pulls back and instinctively I lean with him.

"Much better," Monica says, looking between us.

The car is silent as I'm wrapped in the bubble of this moment. The lighter haired man, being the little prick that he is, pops it.

"I'm Thoren. We haven't officially met yet, but you must be Victoria. I've heard so much about you. Apparently, you are single-handedly responsible for helping to bring this hermit out of his shell." He holds his hand out to me.

His name instantly connects, and I realize the person in front of me must be Roman. The asshole from the tabloids. Boss man in the boardroom. The heartbroken director. And the man who just fixed my hair. A sense of ease immediately wraps around my body. I reach out to shake Roman's brother's hand and catch Roman rolling his eyes.

"Please, Five. You can ignore my baby brother. He likes to embarrass me because, clearly, he wasn't loved enough as a child. Hence the reason we're even here. Thank you, Monica, for giving us a lift. *Someone* offered to drive, only to magically forget his car was getting detailed tonight."

My stomach flips in funny ways at the sound of his nickname for me. I no longer feel consumed with the need for darkened solitude. I have the craziest idea of inviting him under my jacket with me. Thank Andrew's stupid small dose edible that I am not high enough to think that's actually a good idea and manage to keep it to myself.

Thoren offers his hand to Monica as well. I must not be as sober as I think when it seems like he holds on to her a little too long to be friendly. Monica's business frown is in place, but her cheeks are lifted, eyes drawn soft like she's pleased. I've seen her flirt more times than is appropriate and this coy disinterest is one hundred percent an act. I try to file that moment away to bring up later in my garbled brain.

I look back to Roman to see if he caught on to them, too, but he's already staring at me. He's still dressed in his expensive tux from dinner, every piece of him perfectly in place. Hardly even a wrinkle to be found. His fingers flex in and out on his knees. I wonder if he's imaging touching my hair again like I am. I'd curl up on his lap right now and let him pet me if he wanted to. I have enough sense to be embarrassed by my thoughts and look away.

"Thoren, tell me what you do for work?" I ask politely, trying to sound as incoherent as possible.

"Ok, get ready to have the best sleep of your life, Victoria!" He says before diving into a monologue about money, math, and business.

I can't keep up, so I don't even try. *What does it matter anyway?* I smile and nod at what I think are the appropriate places but who really knows? I keep glancing at Roman, catching his eyes every so often and quickly looking away. The high is slowly coming down and my nerves are all that's being left behind. My muscles twitch to get out of this car and away from tonight entirely.

Thankfully, no one expects me to keep the conversation going as the three of them easily chatter back and forth until we arrive at the party. I can finally put enough together to think through the remnants of whatever has been in my system. Just in time for the photographers.

We step out of the car, first Thoren, then Monica, Roman, and I. The lights from the handful of cameras lining the walk to entry are blinding, leaving me with waves of light swirling around my vision bringing on the quiet thrum of a headache. People shout the moment we leave the safety of the car, mostly at Roman. He dips his head, ignoring them. I watch as Thoren offers his arm to Monica.

"After you," he says, smiling.

She begrudgingly takes it as they walk inside, halfhearted snaps being taken as they go. Apparently, the big draw of this vehicle is the two of us that are left. Or, I should say, the one. As foolish as it is, I expect Roman to offer me his arm in the same way Thoren had, helping to guide me through the throng, but he doesn't. Something crushes inside me as he takes a step forward without me, hands shoved deeply into his pant pockets.

He surprises me further as he turns to me and in hushed tones says, "don't stop. Don't talk to them. Just make it inside. I'll go first."

He continues to walk in front of me, making a beeline for the door. I'm a mixture of overwhelmed and disappointed, causing me to fall several steps behind. *It's almost like he doesn't want to be seen with me.* The thought makes me embarrassed and angry. I can hear the crowd around us wondering who I am.

A man much louder than the rest bellows out, "she's no one guys. Just the plus one. Follow the money."

His words shouldn't pierce through me, especially coming down from my high, but dammit, they do. The hurt of being no one, nothing, useless, hanging in the shadow of Roman as all eyes drag away from me. A partner that isn't really a part of the dream at all. Just like before.

Not that I want the fame of being noticed by the photographers and gossipers of LA. It's that I wanted the person I was slowly falling for not to agree. To not leave me behind, without even an arm to hold, at the first opportunity. *I thought we were becoming friends, or maybe even something more.* I'm an idiot. We finally make it in the door, leaving people still shouting at Roman as I step inside.

"What the hell was that?" I ask.

Roman and I are hardly alone, but I can't hold my irritation, my hurt, in.

"I know. They can be aggressive. The best thing you can do is ignore..."

"Not *them.* You. What the hell, Roman?"

His eyes widen at his name before he looks around at the people surrounding us.

"I'm not sure what you mean, but can we talk about this in private?"

He sounds anxious, his body already turning to walk away. *I don't fucking think so.* If anyone is leaving this conversation, it's going to be me.

"No. Let's not. As a matter of fact, let's not talk about this at all. Excuse me."

I storm away from him, determined to find Monica and get out of here as soon as I can.

SIXTEEN

Roman / Victoria

"WHAT'S THE MATTER WITH you?" Thoren asks as I slide into the bar beside him.

"Whiskey. Any kind, anyway," I tell the bartender before turning to my brother. "You know what T, I knew this was a bad idea. I knew it and I let you talk me into it, anyway. When you called Victoria's phone and asked for that ride, I could have refused to go. But this stupid little piece of hope inside me *you* fucking put there, let it happen. And now? The girl I was sure I might, maybe, *possibly*, have a date with—or at the very fucking least a dinner with—just ditched me. So, thank you for that."

The bartender sets the glass in front of me. The look of hurt on Victoria's face slashes through me, setting my teeth on edge. I take a heavy swig from it, relishing the burn as it travels from my mouth down to the pit of my stomach where all my feelings have tumbled to. Thoren waves off the bartender, offering a refill. He turns to me, shoulders lifting to his ears.

"I'm sure it's fine. She's coming down right now. Soon enough, you two can talk it through and everything will be good again. You'll see. If I'm anything, I'm a matchmaker." He looks around the building crowd. "Speaking of, have you seen Monica? She ditched me, too, the second we walked in here..."

I can't help the snort that comes out.

"We're both a bunch of fucking idiots."

Thoren's hands clamp around my shoulders.

"Hey, don't talk about yourself that way, bud."

I smack at him laughing as he dances away from me. "Shut up, you asshole."

He smiles, then comes back toward me. "No, but seriously Roman. Loosen up that tie, take off that jacket, and roll up your sleeves. Girls or no girls, let's at least have some fun tonight."

As much as I want to sulk, he's right. Victoria and I will figure it out. Once she comes down, we'll talk. About the way the media twists good things until they bleed. How I'm trying to protect her *from* me, and all the ways I can mess this up. I'll come clean about everything. Until then, I'm here with Victoria, and I still have a chance.

I pull off my tie and jacket, throwing them behind the bar. Thoren claps his hands against the bar top before howling out.

"Bartender! Another one for my brother and I!" He yells.

The bartender happily supplies us with two more drinks. Thoren clinks his glass to mine, eyeing me until I down the whole thing in one go. I start to feel the warmth of a perfect buzz tying my feelings into a more manageable place. Thoren catches sight of something behind me and cups his hand around his mouth to yell.

"HEY, VICTORIA! OVER HERE."

When I turn to look, she's already weaving her way toward us. I can tell she's unsure who's calling her, her steps unfocused and hesitant. She stops a few feet away, not even glancing at me, focusing all her attention on Thoren.

"Hey! Uhm, sorry, I'm actually looking for someone. Have you seen either Monica or Roman? Monica works for Dreamaway and Roman is..."

Thoren interrupts her. "I haven't seen either of them. But you can wait here with us if you'd like! This is my friend, Captain."

She turns to me and at first, I think she might recognize me, the furrow of her brows not softening. I hold my breath, irritated that Thoren has put me in this situation, and terrified that I'm adding another mistake to the pile. But then the sexy little smile she's been testing on my heart without realizing it was me peeks out and my heart starts beating again.

"Actually, we've met," she says. "Nice to see you, Cap. Save anyone this evening?"

I chuckle, unsure if it's wise to play along with this teased version of Victoria now. It doesn't feel harmless anymore.

"No, not yet. But the night is still young."

For an instant, it feels good to connect with her, to know I'm the one receiving her attention. Then the feeling turns sour in my mouth. "Actually..."

The buzz isn't enough to outweigh my guilt. I know I need to tell her. I reach for her, needing to ground myself for what comes next, but Thoren interrupts me before I can.

"Hey! I think I just saw Monica. Let's go get your friend," he's up and pulling Victoria into the crowd. As if I'm tied to her, I have no option but to follow them.

Thoren stops at the edge of the room, looking left and right like he might have lost Monica's trail. But I know him and the gleam in his eyes tells me he's got something else up his sleeve.

"So, how do the two of you know each other?" he asks Victoria.

"Victoria and I are old friends," I offer, hoping to use the lead in to tell her the truth and cutoff whatever plan Thoren thinks he has to help.

"We absolutely are not. One night, Captain. One does not a friendship make. I don't even know your real name," she says, her words haughty and thin, her focus obviously on finding her friend.

Something in the air has changed, but Thoren isn't deterred. He looks between us, mischief evident, enjoying the secret we share a little too much. Even if she doesn't know who I am, he does. He knows I feel more than I'm letting on. He knows my history with Lauren and my fear of making all the same mistakes. That I'm even wanting to open up again is a miracle.

He should also know that I'll eviscerate his emotional meddling heart if he even tries what I think he's going to.

"It looks like you two have an awful lot to talk about," he nudges Victoria with a shoulder, causing me to instinctively move toward her. "Oh, I think I see Monica! I can go grab her while the two of you enjoy the party."

His shoulders shrug and he backs even farther away from Victoria toward the hall that leads back to the exit. Victoria looks incredulous.

"Oh, no you don't! I'll never find you two again," she says as she follows him.

After the argument we had, I can't let her leave like this. She may not know right now that I'm the asshole she's currently mad at, but I do. And eventually she will, too. I need her to see me, *the real me*, before I tell her. Any chance at a future is slipping further from me every day that I keep harboring this lie. I need to tell her tonight. Every instinct in me screams to follow her, to apologize, to make things right.

Victoria, determined not to lose him, huddles next to Thoren in front of the coat check, her arms tucked tightly across her chest, back angled toward me. She's whispering something furiously to him, but the smile doesn't slip as his gaze flits between us.

"Victoria, I would be happy to help you find Monica since it doesn't look like Thoren's much help. Maybe we can talk in the meantime?" I try wanting to shake my brother and his good intentions without Victoria feeling like I'm trying to corner her.

"No, thank you. I would rather not be indebted to you any more than I am. Besides, he just saw her come this way."

She's still not facing me, and my hands itch to grab her and turn her around. The coat check girl breaks up the conversation, asking Thoren if he has a ticket to retrieve his jacket. I see him lean onto the counter, pulling on his charm, as she blushes and flashes her gaze between Victoria and me. The girl disappears into the aisle of coats.

"She's checking to see if Monica checked anything, you know, just in case she already left," Thoren says to us.

The sounds of the party filter through our awkward silence. I stand there, hands in my pocket, at a loss for what to say to make things normal again. I've never been one to fix the things I've broken, but that doesn't mean I don't want to try. It's the most awkward five minutes I've had in an exceedingly long time, the three of us looking anywhere but at each other while we wait. The girl comes back waving Thoren over while she closes the window with a "back in 10" sign. She exits the half door but leaves it open, without even a glance back.

Thoren grabs Victoria's hand, shoving her in the closet, before doing the same thing to me. Victoria and I are now standing side by side facing Thoren, who looks downright manic. He latches the half door closed. He leans over it, staring at us both.

"I'm going to close this door, and no one is going to come in. I'll be out looking for Monica and I PROMISE to bring her back here. In the meantime, the cameras are down, and the staff is on break. Sort your shit out. You have ten minutes." He gives us both a sly smile.

Victoria makes a sound to protest, but he cuts her off completely.

"Ah. No. One of us tonight should get a romantic moment. This one just happens to be yours. My brother can be an asshole, but you shouldn't let it ruin your entire night. You deserve to feel wanted, Victoria. I expect to read about this exact scene one day. Make him jealous," his eyebrows raise in seriousness toward Victoria before he looks to me. "And you, if you don't kiss her breathless, I swear on all the yachts in the world. Do you hear me?"

He doesn't wait for a response before he slams the top half of the door shut, locking it in place. I expect Victoria to run out of the room, but she doesn't. Instead, she shifts from foot to foot, running her palms down the side of her skirt. I take it as my chance and step toward her.

"I'm sorry about him. He can be... a bit much. Truly. I don't want you to be uncomfortable," I say through clenched teeth.

I'm furious with my brother for putting her in this position. For putting us *both* here. But I have to admit that I want to talk to her privately. And this might be the only chance I get tonight. She sighs and looks up at me, her beautiful hazel eyes framed in black, making them glow in the yellow lighting of the closet. Her hair is wild and loose, swirls of chestnut falling over her shoulders.

"It's fine. Tonight hasn't gone that great, anyway. Honestly, he probably would have taken any excuse to leave, and he's just trying to play matchmaker, even though he is *terrible* at it. I've already been shot down once tonight. I'm a bit of a mess..."

She paces away from me.

"And here I thought this was just your average day," I joke.

She lightly swats at my arm. "Hey! I can be put together! At least, I used to be. California has made me a bit of an outlier, I guess. That and a stupid, infuriating man. But isn't that always the way? Except for, it seems, with you. You seem easy enough."

The air sticks in my throat as I try to swallow around it. I hate that both the men she's talking about are me, and I try not to be insulted at being called easy *and* infuriating. But if I defend myself now everything could be ruined. A line is being drawn that I absolutely cannot cross.

"To me, it sounds like that guy who shot you down is just an asshole. Who wouldn't want you?" I say instead.

She's unsure of herself, fingers rubbing together, pulling at each other as she paces back towards me. I reach out for her hand without thought. If she's falling, I want to be here to catch her. I pull back at the last moment, hand hanging between us. I have to stop this conversation before she unknowingly tells me anymore or I do something incredibly stupid.

"Victoria, I..." I start, needing to tell her everything I've been holding in.

Everything I am.

"Do you?" she says, stopping me.

She reaches toward me, shy in her approach, and the moment hangs in slow motion. I'm so caught up that I lose the ability to fight through my want to do what I know needs to be done. I am weak and foolish. I am my father's son.

"Do I what?" I ask, a hush falling over the words.

I'm leaning before I even have a conscious thought to what I'm doing, trapped by her.

"Do you want *me?*" Her mouth is so close I can feel the tingle of peppermint as I breathe, and I've never wanted anything more.

Her hip slips into my palm, the fabric catching as it does. My fingertips press in as if I can leave their prints all over her by sheer force of will. There's a brief second where alarm bells ring, warning me of a line I'm about to cross, but they fade behind me as I utter a single word.

"Yes."

She pushes into me and I'm out to sea with no land in sight. She catches my bottom lip in hers, the silk dancing over my skin. I can hardly contain my need, but I do, holding onto the sweetness of the kiss. Before I can break it off, Victoria pulls my tongue into hers, sucking at just the tip. I lose all sense of propriety. I let the full force of my want for her out, dragging her mouth into mine.

Her tiptoes teeter in those ridiculous shoes and I growl out of anger that they would dare betray her. I drag my hands down to her thighs, digging into the muscles and lifting her around my waist. Her skirt seams pop in retribution and I release my grip enough that if she wants back down to save it, she can. Instead, I feel her mumble under her breath.

"Fuck it" is against my lips, before fully committing, a slit tearing with the squeeze of her thighs at my waist.

I can't help the chuckle that's quickly swallowed up by her mouth again. Her hands are in my hair, raking against my neck and my back, making time vanish between moans and gasps.

BANG!

We rip our mouths apart at the sound on the door, our chests still pressing into each other. We stare, wild-eyed and mussed, before her laugh rings out, breaking up the tension. It lights a fire in my chest that roars around inside me as I set her on the ground once more.

The skirt falls into a tattered mess along her legs. The slit is clear up to her waist, a pair of black lace underwear peeking out when she moves. She looks down at herself, tears from laughing, falling down her cheeks.

"Oh great. Now I owe her *two,*" she groans. "This is all your fault!" But she's smiling as she says it.

I look around, lost. I have no idea what to do, still reeling from the events of this night. Still unable to believe I kissed her. Again. *And she kissed you back.* I shake my head at her, smiling. She looks around, inspiration striking as she grabs a long trench coat hanging next to her. She quickly checks the pockets as another knock comes at the door.

"One more minute, please!" I yell at the knock. "Should I be concerned your first instinct is to steal," I ask Victoria.

She mocks in offence, "*Borrowing*, Captain. I'll return it tomorrow." She shrugs the coat on before gesturing to the door. "After you!"

At the sound of a nickname I hate so much my stomach bottoms out. *What the fuck have I done?* I grab her hand and head for the door.

"Victoria, I need to talk to you."

The banging on the door intensifies.

"Alright." Worry fills her otherwise radiant face. "Just not here. C'mon."

She opens the door to the wide-eyed girl from before. I pass without a word; Victoria being pulled behind me by my hand that's still wrapped in hers.

Victoria raises her hand in mock salute.

"Thank you for your service!"

She giggles like a teenager all the way down the hall. Emotions war within me. Nothing has ever been as perfect as kissing Victoria. Nothing will ever be. I hope I haven't ruined it before it's had its chance to begin.

We walk back toward the party, the sounds of it floating to us, and I stop, panicked. I can't talk to her out there, with all the people and their judgments. With the phones and cameras and gossip. We can't be front page news before *we* even know what we are. I pull open the first door I see and hurry us both inside.

It's a small staff room, cleaning supplies filling my nose with lemon and chemicals. A light automatically turns on as I reach my hand around Victoria to pull the door closed. She mistakes my advance and runs her hand into my hair again, kissing me softly. I shake out of it.

"Wait, hold, mmf..."

She tries to pull me under again and I want to go. I want so badly to just fucking let go. But I can't. I'm so fucking angry that I've put us in this position. That I have ruined this.

"Goddamn it, Five. Just hold on," I groan, letting my frustration out, the nickname just slipping from my lips like water.

She stops, backing away. Immediately I know I've made a mistake. I've given my hand before I could make a bet and now everything could be lost. I don't want to see the pain in her face, but I have to look up. Her hazel eyes are dazed, swimming in the abruptness of my voice. *I fucked up. I fucked up. I fucked up.* I take one step and see her cringe.

"Roman?"

\#

Roman *fucking* Wheatley. No one, on this entire planet, calls me Five. Has reduced me to a single digit. Has tortured me with such immense want and anger.

No one but Roman.

And now apparently, Captain. Since they're the same fucking person. The name hangs in the air like a shot. Even in the stillness, we both know we're in danger. I want to be a bird in flight but with a hunter near; I don't have that option, so I just wait. Wait for him to say something.

"Five. *Victoria.* I... this is what I needed to talk to you about," he stumbles over his words.

I'm stunned into silence, unable to move. The fogginess from the edible has faded since we arrived, but now I almost wonder if this is a trick. *Am I still high?* I mentally pat myself down, searching the corners of my brain for any lingering excuse why this person in front of me is suddenly two different people. I come up empty-handed.

"I don't understand."

It's so *empty* compared to what I actually feel but the words fall out, anyway. Reflexively, I sort through my memories, trying to piece together the first night at the club, the script edits, this kiss. I want it to make sense; find the connections I've so obviously missed, but so many of the important ones are blank. All I can so vividly remember is the way I felt. The highs and lows. The boldness. The scratch and slide of his mouth and hands.

"I know. It wasn't supposed to happen like this. I was going to talk to you privately about all of this. But then the edibles and the ditching and the kiss. I wasn't supposed to ambush you at a party in the janitor's closet!" He pulls at his hair as he paces. "Fuck! I'm sorry, Five. When I saw you at the club that first night, I didn't know we'd see each other again. I thought it had to be a coincidence that we had even met *again*. I mean, after the whole plane debacle..."

What. The. Fuck.

"The plane... What are you saying to me, Roman?" I yell, stepping forward. "Or Captain. Or whoever the fuck you are or want to be right now."

I'm spiraling. The room slips out around me, and I can't trust myself anymore.

"What the fuck is happening? I cannot believe this, that this is happening..." I spin toward the door, very much needing to breathe. "I... can't do this right now."

The doorknob escapes through my fingers twice before I'm finally able to twist it open. I skip out, thanking Monica with every step that she put me in tennis shoes. I pull out my phone as I'm walking and call her again. She picks up on the fourth ring and before she can speak, my panicked voice cuts in.

"Monica, I need to leave."

I'm rushing into the crowd. Roman calls softly from behind, but he doesn't fight through the throng of people to follow me. Too many eyes watching. At least for that, I'm grateful. A platinum blonde bob pops up next to me, concern flashing across her eyes.

"Vip, it's me," she says.

I'm still fighting through my memories and distrustful of my mind. Even when logic tells me it's her, I have to ask.

"How, how do I know it's you? The code. I need the code, Mon."

Her eyes crease even further in worry. If it's really Monica, she knows what I'm asking. Freshman year of college, at Debby Gordon's party, I had asked her something similar after Debby swore to me we'd never met, then asked about the gossip I'd heard about her. Once I told her everything I knew, she screamed at me in front of everyone, continually yelling, *gotcha*. No one trusted me with their secrets after that. *I* didn't trust myself. Just as I don't trust myself now.

"Nobody puts baby in the corner. Babe, I got you. Is Debby Gordon here? Because I swear, I will kick her ass…"

Before she can tirade, I throw my arms around her.

"Oh, thank God it's you. Monica, this is so much worse than Debby. Can we just get out of here?"

I'm sniveling and on the verge of a complete meltdown. My emotions are so twisted up I don't know what to feel, leaving me with a headache that only numbs the hurt and not the pain. Her beautiful bob bounces in affirmation, the sweet vanilla scent of her shampoo relaxing me. She grabs my hand and leads me out a backdoor. No one follows us. No one stops us. The relief at that swallows any acute disappointment.

Stan's beautiful neon purple shirt glows under the venue lights as he opens the door to salvation. I could just kiss his perfectly shaved head as we slide in. The lights are dimmed inside, and I finally feel like I can fall apart. I barely let Monica settle when I let out a howl of frustration and pain.

"It's Roman, Mon. The guy from the club. The guy from the *plane*. It's been Roman the whole time."

My cheeks flame in embarrassment. I could melt into this seat, a person sized puddle to be cleaned up with the crumbs and whatever other goo is draped along this car. My hands are covering my face, and it takes all my strength to lower them and face Monica. I don't want to hear her *fixes* right now. I just need my friend. To my surprise, she doesn't react.

"Wait. Why do you look so calm? Did you know?" I accuse.

"Honestly, Vip. I thought *you* knew." She shrugs her shoulders as if it's no big deal.

"HOW WOULD I KNOW?" I ask, pushing myself up and into her space.

"I thought he told you. Or someone told you. Or you caught on to the nickname. Any of the literal HUNDRED ways you could have known outside of recognizing his face."

Her nose is inches from mine as she pushes forward too, never one to back down.

"I mean, I obviously didn't know about the plane, which, by the way, is hilarious, but I knew about the first plus one. Beckson told me. That's why he paired you two in the first place. He said he 'felt a spark' and I wasn't to meddle. That if Roman were to calm down enough to do any script, it would be yours. And when you told me about 'Captain' I figured you already knew since his yacht accident was all over the media. The literal headline was, *Hollywood Director Turned Captain in Boat Crash.* We joked about it for days. We even said Cherie should date him."

Snippets of conversations are finally connecting. I'm remembering the exact moments Monica is talking about, almost as if they're now in 3D. But she's apparently not done.

"You even have a picture with him on *social media,* Vip. With comments! How could you not know?"

My forehead crinkles and I pinch at my nose, trying to stave off the headache that's forming deep within my skull. I take a deep breath in, count to four, then let it out again before I speak.

"Excuse me. *What!*"

Disbelief shouldn't be possible now, but it colors my voice anyway.

Monica is quickly scrolling through her phone, furiously looking through to find the photo. Her nails tap lightly at the screen and suddenly she turns it to me, too close to my face. I grab it from her hands and study. The username pops out first, @NICKLEMAY. I notice my straight nose and hazel eyes clinging to them immediately. By my side is a well-toned cheek bone with puckered lips planted on me in surprise. *Nick.*

"That isn't Roman. I remember this. That was my plus one, Nick," I tell her, sure of myself.

That was the night I made out with a stranger. When I finally felt like I was breaking through my shell, ready to live in this new life. Ready to be a new me.

She rolls her eyes. "Yeah, that's Nick kissing you. Look *behind* you."

She snags the phone back from me and zooms in on a face just over my shoulder. Then takes out my phone, using the search bar to bring up a paparazzi photo of Roman. Both men are not smiling, their dark brows furrowed in a perfect arch. Soft lips and five o'clock shadows grace their faces. I would bet anything that dark green eyes hide behind those irises. I drop Monica's phone, unable to look any longer.

"Oh. My. God. I kissed him," I say in a whisper.

Monica looks at me, exasperated. "No, *not* Nick..."

I interrupt her. "Not in the photo. He's the stranger I kissed. MONICA. HE'S THE STRANGER I KISSED."

I fold my head between my legs and breathe. My heart is beating so rapidly that it's going to pound right out of my chest if it doesn't slow down. Monica scoots closer to me, rubbing comforting circles onto my back. The world goes mute, as the only thing I can process is the rasping sound coming from my throat.

Monica lets me spend the car ride back to the apartment hyperventilating and trying to sort out my memories in the soft hum of the road. I try desperately to put together every piece of Roman I missed. Every conversation, every touch, every minute we shared.

By the time we're back home, I'm not even sure it's entirely his fault, even if he knew I was in the dark. When he first walked into that conference room and I was told I would meet *the* Roman Wheatley, I had him pegged. I had read the tabloids and knew that a man like him would never understand me.

Which meant I was wrong, too.

When we finally get inside, I flop myself on the couch. Monica, unable to be silent any longer, brings voice to my growing fears.

"Is it possible he thought you knew?" she asks.

I grab a pillow and throw my face into it, shrugging my shoulders. Monica's weight dips down the cushions and I pull up to look at her.

"I know this sucks. Tonight, we can curse him again if it'll make you feel better. But I, one of your oldest friends, thought you knew. Isn't it just a little bit possible he did too? And even if he didn't, if he hid it, don't you kind of want to know why?"

Before I can answer her, the doorknob shakes from someone trying to get in.

"Shit. I forgot about those two," Monica mumbles. "Do we tell them?" She whispers.

"Yeah," I groan. "You know we have to."

"Have to what?" Cherie says sliding her suitcase through the door, Katie quick at her heels. "Why are the two of you here? Aren't we supposed to be meeting you at the after party?"

"Well, for one, you're late. Second, we had a bit... of a night. Put your stuff in the hall closet and get ready for a story, ladies," Monica pipes in.

"Oh shit. Katie let's take a bathroom break and pull out the PJs. I think the night just went from on the town to on the couch." Cherie says. "Monica, get the snacks."

Monica rolls her eyes at the command but gets up and does it, anyway. I remain still as a statue, the thought of telling them about tonight so fresh that it makes my stomach bubble in nerves. Not that I don't want to tell my friends what's happened, it's that I am still trying to process it myself. My feelings are twisted. Anger, hurt, understanding, excitement. I kissed Roman twice. I laughed with him. We'd fought. Slowly, the Roman I thought I knew was becoming a friend, but now? Now, it felt like so much more.

The sound of the small air compressor whirls in the room as Katie blows up the air mattress. Forest green plastic expands, filling up the entire floor between the coffee table and the TV, its king size providing enough room for all of us to sit. Monica sets various chips and snacks on the table before settling in next to me.

"Ready when you are," Monica says.

"LIKE HELL!" Cherie yells from the bathroom.

"Get your ass in here, then!" Monica shoots back.

Cherie skips her way into the living room, the creak of plastic stretching as she bounces onto the blow-up mattress. Katie falls to her elbow from the force.

"Alright. We ready," Cherie says sweeping her arm in a 'go on' gesture.

"Well... I guess it all started with the edibles," I say before diving into the night, careful to leave out pieces of the mistaken identity known as Captain.

Monica, thankfully, lets me. She sees me crafting a careful story that still relays my mixed feelings for Roman and our kiss, without knowing the whole double identity debacle. As much as I love them, I can't figure this out as a group. I need to sort through my shit on my own first. I finish with kissing Roman using the fact that I kissed the director I'm currently working with as my reason for freaking out.

"Woooooweeeeee!" Cherie squeals out. "You had one hell of a night!"

"Are you okay?" Katie asks, her motherly affection taking over.

"Yeah, I'm... I'll be okay. It's just a lot to process right now. Sorry to ruin your guys' night by being a train wreck," I say.

Both girls move toward me, the air deflating a bit at the edge, so they fall against me a little harder than necessary when we hug.

"It's fine, honestly. We're both exhausted from the flight and getting here," Katie says.

Cherie pipes in, "Yeah! The only thing I really miss about my teenage years is the ability to just keep going no matter where the night took me. But at this point? I'm secretly kind of glad. No good ever came from me pushing forward on an already crazy night."

Monica snorts. "You mean to tell me you don't miss campus police freshman year chasing you down at four-thirty in the morning while you were drunk streaking?" She pretends to be offended. "I mean, who *wouldn't* call that *good?*"

The image of Cherie running down the road through a downpour, butt-ass naked has me laughing until tears come out. Cherie smiles cheekily at Monica.

"You're right, Mon. That was a good night. It would have been an even better night if you cowards wouldn't have backed out of the dare and left me waving in the wind by myself! By the time I lost those two security guards, you all had abandoned me and I had to walk back with Jamie Daminko."

"Oh, like that was such a chore for you! You had a crush on him all of freshman year. You talked about that walk back to the dorm for weeks, Cherie!" Katie says. "Besides, that was the night I met Richard. You wouldn't rob me of my future husband for a redo, right?"

My laugh sobers.

"Cherie, you can rob me of that night for a redo. If you did, I wouldn't have gone on a date with Trent."

The girls all look at me, stricken. I shrug my shoulders, wanting to roll the awkwardness away. I shouldn't have brought Trent up, but memories assaulted me hearing the recount of the night and the uncertainty of tonight with Roman. Trent had been friendly with Richard, Katie's now husband, and once the two of them hit it off, he'd taken his chance asking me to dinner. We'd had a few classes together, so I decided *why not?* How would my life have been different if I had just listened to my gut?

"Oh, Vip..." Katie begins before Cherie jumps in.

"Nope. Uh uh. We're not doing this. *You're* not doing this." She's rocking back into crisscross applesauce. "Just because you've had a weird ass night does not mean you get to dive into your memories of Trent."

"Cherie!" Katie scolds.

"No, Katie, she's right," Monica speaks up. "You're here for *you*, Vip. Don't drag him into this new place. He doesn't belong. And the new Victoria Irene Pencheske? The one who lives in LA and has a script that's being purchased by Dreamaway and makes out with steaming hot directors... she doesn't need him. She *never* needed him. You're exactly where you need to be, bitch. So, breath it out."

We all sit stunned for a second before Cherie starts a slow clap that no one joins.

"Well done, Mon! Couldn't have said it better myself." She turns to me. "Well, Vip? Who are you going to be tonight?"

I roll my eyes at their dramatics but smile, anyway.

"I'm going to be the bad-ass-script-selling-make-out-with-a-hottie-bitch. Obviously."

They all hoot and holler, Monica getting up to grab some more wine and crank up some music that we all shimmy too. Amid the laughter, I promise myself to be those things. And to remember that I'm not that girl who couldn't trust herself anymore.

"So, tell us about this director..."

SEVENTEEN

Victoria

Saturday night cannot come fast enough. Anticipation burns my attention span away, making it impossible to distract myself for more than a few minutes at a time. The girls help by pampering me like a plaything as they prepare me for my 'date'. Monica is the only one who knows it's more of an interrogation than an actual date, so I can't blame them for trying to share in what should be excitement.

Lying to them only compounds my anxiety. It's not very often we keep secrets in this group, and I know the fallout will be explosive. I will probably owe them all weekly deliveries of Frannie's Famous baked goods when I have to earn my apology. Even with unlimited afternoons of groveling in my future, it feels necessary.

Finally, after I convince them all to leave me behind to go to the apartment's gym, I text Roman to make sure he's still planning on attending. My heart beats rapidly, practically on the verge of burning out. The sting of rejection and my own stupidity linger just on the edge, waiting to pounce.

Are we still on for tonight? I feel like we have a lot to talk about...

Thank the universe for technology that I don't need to wait long for his reply.

Yes. Of course. Do you still want me to pick you up?

A sigh of relief karate kicks the worry of him blowing me off. Still, I hesitate. My lip goes raw at my teeth. *Do I?* If he picks me up, I'll be stuck with him until he decides to bring me home. If I get a ride or drive myself, everyone will know something is up since I already told them he'd be driving me before I knew what tonight would be.

Yeah. Just, promise you'll take me home if I ask.

I sigh and throw my phone onto the couch, face down. I hear it's almost silent vibration telling me he's responded, but I ignore it, emotions spent. Roman may have lied, but I don't think he's a creep. I analyzed all the interactions I ever had with him or who I thought Captain was and in all of them he was respectful, if not arrogant and moody.

Sure, he challenges me and makes me furious, but then again, I probably do the same to him. Not to mention I have experience with a certain friend group who do the same. If there's anything I've learned, it's that the best relationships take work. And a whole lot of space, time, screaming into the void, sugar, and Mean Girls. Okay, so the last one might just be for my friend group but I'm sure there's another movie that would work for blowing off steam about Roman, too. Maybe Kill Bill.

I check Monica's clock on the wall, realizing I only have an hour and a half left to get ready. The thought of seeing Roman again, this time with this huge secret laid bare between us, creates chaos in my soul. I cannot help the desire to look my best, no matter which way our conversation plays out. I unfold my hair from the towel it's bundled in and head into the bathroom. By the time I hear the echoing slam of the door behind the gaggle of groans and chatter, it is completely blown out. Shiny curls perfectly styled wrap around my face and shoulders. I start on my makeup just as Katie pops her head in.

"There's our girl. Have room for one more?" she asks.

I nod my head, and she slides in to sit on the closed toilet seat next to me to chat. The door softly clicks behind her. I pat the lotion into my cheeks, the soft slap of skin the only sound between us. She smiles into the mirror.

"You're awfully stoic for your first date since being separated," she says.

I relax my hands on the counter, leaning into the mirror, my breath fogging up the glass.

"It isn't a date. Not really. I told you..."

"Yeah, I know. But you can't really hide from me, Vip. There's more you're not saying. Your nerves feel like a live wire. And the passion! You haven't been like this since 2005 when you watched Pride & Prejudice for the first time."

She doesn't notice her hands resting over her heart, as if she's going to contain it from the sparks. I've tried to hide my feelings, but apparently not well enough. Katie has a way of that. Of feeling things deeper, dipping into the well of feelings from those around her.

She hates the word empath, but it's the closest explanation. She's a bright spot next to my muted colors. The keys to my emotional piano. When things are good, she's the first person I call because there's nothing better than her joy. It's infectious. But when they're not... well, avoid isn't the right word for the intense game of hide and seek, I try to play with her. I shrug my shoulders.

"Of course I'm nervous. This is someone I'm interested in, Katie. I haven't felt that way about a man in too long. But we'll just say we're early in the movie. Time will only tell if he's a Darcy or a Wickham."

She squints at me in disbelief, but lets it go. We both know I'm full of shit, but pushing me a half hour before my date isn't the time. My heart laying vulnerable between us will have to be enough for now.

"Whatever you say, but eventually, you'll have to tell me what's really going on."

She picks up a left behind nail polish from the counter, rolling it between her palms. The soft click of the glass on her wedding ring brings my focus to my decidedly bare hand. I shake off the thoughts as she untwists the cap, applying the subtle pink to her fingers. I continue putting on my make-up, Katie's soft voice telling me how her kids have been since I left. Her stories draping a blanket of calm over my nerves as I finish getting ready.

One thing I miss most about Washington is the predictability of my days. Knowing that Tuesday was Caleb's soccer practice and Katie would pick me up at 4:15 pm sharp so we could dole out snacks and talk about movies together.

Or that on Saturday mornings Cherie, Katie, and I would all pack into the car and drive thirty minutes to the next town over for the "better" farmer's market on Main. Sometimes our husbands, kids, or in Cherie's case dates would come, or when Monica was in town, every other month, she would go. But most of the time, it was just the three of us.

For the first time since coming to LA, I remember all the good that I left behind from my old life. What made it so appealing to keep. Listening to Katie makes me homesick. I turn around, stopping to hug Katie, careful of my makeup and her wet nails. Her arms wrap around me, squeezing tight, not caring in the slightest.

"Ah! Careful of the hair!" I squeal when her sticky painted fingers get too close.

She laughs and releases me. Monica's doorbell rings and know I've run out of time.

"How do I look?" I ask, false confidence puffing out my chest.

"You look beautiful."

Katie smiles her sweet smile that makes me want to unravel my stress and tell her everything. But it's too late now. There's a man with an explanation to give and I think I'm ready to hear him out.

I come out of the bathroom, Katie hot on my heels and stop breathless. Roman is standing between the doorway, the living room and the kitchen. His hands are in the pockets of his dark wash jeans; his navy-blue button down, tucked tightly in against his frame. The damp tips of hair curling around his ears. He must have rushed to get ready, sure that I had canceled. A small twinge of guilt runs up my spine, but I wave it away. A bit of rushing doesn't hurt him and it's the least he deserves.

Monica and Cherie are just staring at him while he tries to look anywhere but. The tension only builds when his eyes find mine. His lips part just enough for his next breath as he takes a step towards me.

"You ready?" I ask, cutting him off from saying anything.

I don't want to have this, or any, conversation in front of the group and if we stay and try to make small talk, I will lose my patience. The culmination of having him and my best friends and all the secrets between us in the same room feels suffocating. The pressure of expectation and understanding amplifying my nerves to a boiling point.

"Whenever you are," he says, his voice low and hypnotic.

I watch as every woman in the room tilts unwillingly toward it. I lean into my movement, grabbing him by the arm, and pulling him through the door.

"Bye ladies!" I yell over my shoulder.

Cherie calls back, "don't bother coming home! We won't be waiting up!" Then in a slightly quieter voice, but still plenty loud, "Hot damn! Did y'all see that man? Trent, who?"

My cheeks burn. I immediately release Roman's arm, feeling the sweat building in my palms. He huffs out a tiny laugh. I shoot a scathing look his way, making him sober. *Good. You're not out of the doghouse, bud.* He overtakes my steps as soon as we're out of the elevator, leading me to where he's parked the flashy green box he calls a car. Like a gentleman, he opens my door, offering his hand to help me in. His eyes search mine as I ignore him, scooting myself into the seat, and he gently closes the door before getting into his own side.

The car is deafening as we pull out of the parking lot and onto the roadway. His fingers twitch on the steering wheel, drumming a beat that isn't there. I'm battling with desperately wanting him to start explaining and terrified of what he'll say. I'm stuck in a moment of suspension, high above what I want and what I need. The fucking tightrope of life.

He breaks the silence for me.

"Should I turn on some music?"

It is a million questions in one. His voice wobbles, unsure. My fear snaps and I need to rip the band aid off.

"Just... Tell me what happened, Roman."

His grip tightens for a moment.

"Now?"

His eyes dart around, looking for an escape, begging for more time. But we don't always get what we want and right now I just need to know.

"Yeah. What you want to be in front of a bunch of people when you tell me and I make a scene?"

I'm trying to lighten the mood, for both of our sakes, but it does the opposite. His face pales, lips drawing thin. He looks absolutely terrified.

"No. You're right. But honestly, Five, I don't want to upset you at all."

"A little too late for that," I mumble, sure he hears me anyway.

His hand comes up and rubs his cheek. "That's fair. I... I don't know where to even start."

His words hang in the air, mostly because I don't know either. He doesn't wait for me to direct him, though.

"I guess the most important thing I should tell you is why. But it's so selfish and... embarrassing. The truth is, I should have told you the moment Beckson introduced us at the club. But when you didn't know me..."

His voice trails off, eyes far away from this car. I let him gather his thoughts, unable to look away from him for even a moment.

"Look, you know me. Or at least, you know *of* me. My life the past few years has been splashed across every cover of every tabloid at one point or another. But even before that my family, well, we're *recognized*. So, when I got into entertainment, all of what I was already used to, heightened." He closes his eyes, looking for the words. "I'm not explaining this very well," he says.

"That's okay. I'm great at reading between the lines. I'm a writer after all." I give him a small smile, needing to know more. "Keep going."

"Ok." He takes a deep breath. "OK. So, when everything went to shit, I thought it might dissipate. Nothing lasts forever, right? Turns out, I couldn't hide from it here. Suddenly, everyone in this industry, in this town, thought they really knew me. They knew my worth. My value. And it didn't matter that I was a Wheatly, that I had a good name. I'd become Captain. A joke."

His eyes glance at me knowingly, punctuating the nickname. It stings and excites my heart all at once.

"So, when Beckson told me you couldn't recognize me? That until I told you my name, you would have no idea of my history? It felt like a gift. Like a chance

I could start over, to see if I really was this unlikeable fuck up everyone told me I was. That I was starting to *believe* I was."

My heart cracks a little for the man sitting next to me. It was part of the reason I came here myself. I needed to start over. Away from what was comfortable. Away from the people who knew me. I couldn't imagine not being able to do that, that no matter where I went, people would tell me who I was. It was awful. But I still felt betrayed despite the understanding.

"I cannot imagine what that's like, but still you used me, Roman."

The hurt pours out of my mouth, like water in a fountain. I can't control the pain from feeling like my entire world is a lie, even though I don't want to lay it all out in front of him. His shoulders tense, a deep frown creasing his face. Regret flashes through his eyes and I want to take it back, too.

"I know. I am so sorry for lying to you. For letting it go on as long as I did. And I know it doesn't mean much now, but I wanted to tell you. Many times. But you were so angry with me when I was Roman to you. I knew if I told you, that was it. I would be that guy to you forever. And that... well, it bothered me."

He takes a deep breath before continuing. "Remember the first morning in the office? I was coming in from a shit night, still hung over. You were the only good thing that had happened at the party when I carried you out and I wasn't sure if, or when, I would see you again."

I can picture the night at the club, feel myself cradled in his arms, a giddy feeling I hadn't felt in forever working its way through my limbs. My memories flash forward to the next morning, waiting for Roman, irritated that he was going to ruin my one shot at Dreamaway and I know what's coming.

I nod my head, whispering, "I remember."

He nods back. "Then I walk into the conference room and there she is. This funny, entertaining, messy girl who infuriated the hell out of me *and* made me laugh. There had been so many times over the last few months I wasn't sure I'd ever feel like laughing again and here you were. Except you weren't laughing. You weren't smiling. You were looking at me exactly the way everyone else, even my father, has since my last movie... disappointed."

Tears prick my eyes. I reach over wanting, no *needing,* to apologize, but Roman cuts me off.

"No. Don't do that. I'm not telling you this to make you feel like the bad guy. I'm the one who lied, Five. You have every right to feel the way you have and do. I know my reputation is a mess. I know my life has been a mess. I'm not innocent here. I'm just telling you because I want you to know the truth. Wherever that lands me. And that I'm trying to be… better."

I sigh, unable to take my eyes off him.

"Aren't we all? I know, I am." I throw him a watery smile. "If it raises your spirits any, my life's a bit of a mess, too."

This makes him laugh, just like I intended. He turns to me briefly, his smile glowing in the sun, before putting his eyes back on the road and maneuvering us into a parking garage.

"You don't say," he murmurs as he puts us into park.

The car hums quietly beneath us, as we both turn in our seats to face the other. I still feel the pain of being tricked, but it's changed. It's morphed into a shade of embarrassment, along with a slice of what could have been if we both weren't so scared. I don't blame Roman anymore. Instead of feeling like we were at war with each other, and he blindsided me, it's more like we were each playing our own game against life and there happened to be a few casualties between us.

I break the silence.

"Let's call it even for now. We still need to work together, and I was starting to enjoy your company."

I leave the obvious unsaid, that I am absolutely drawn to him, whether or not I know his name or his face. Still, I can't let that get in the way of the progress of the script. I let a man come between my career and me once. I won't do it again. He looks at me in thought for a few beats before smirking.

"Sounds good," he murmurs. "Are you still interested in dinner?"

"Are you kidding? I'm starving. Not to mention I have a house full of overbearing women to go back to. I can't exactly do that this soon and this hungry."

He laughs, opening his door. "You're right. Let's get you fed and waste some time."

EIGHTEEN

Hope blooms where a pit had formed in my stomach. *We can do this. It's okay. Everything is going to work.* I push open my door before Roman can beat me to it and hop out, excited now that it's all been laid out. I rush to meet him at the back of the car.

Without preamble or awkwardness, he grabs my hand and holds it. They swing between us as we walk, and my mind spins to find meaning. I silently scold myself to just be in the moment. This can be nice and light. I don't have to rush for this to mean more.

If it's only a moment, I'm going to soak it in.

The elevator dings and we step inside. Roman drops my hand to slide in between the people already there as he selects our floor. We're split up between two children who refuse to move from the middle. My nose scrunches in mock frustration, trying to tell Roman, *isn't this silly* and *are you feeling this, too,* all at the same time. He winks and I know he's heard me.

I take this chance to try and memorize him. My eyes drink in every dimple in his skin, every line of his face. I want to catch his details in my hands even knowing they're slipping through the cracks like sand, but loving the feel of them, anyway. Besides, if I can hold on to just a single grain, it'll be enough.

His eyebrows are dark, strong, providing a shadow that deepens his gaze. He's calm, pupils large but not blown out, letting me see the forest green of his eyes around the edges. A straight nose juts out, falling over gritty stubble that covers just above his lips, cheeks, and chin. They frame a mouth that says painful truths and begs to be kissed. His gaze shoots to mine, catching me mid breath as I take him in. Black expands swallowing his coloring.

I don't feel silly anymore.

The elevator stops, my stomach dropping at more than just the motion, and everyone files out. Roman shakes himself, sweeping his arm to the doors, offering me to step in front of him and I do. His hand hovers just at the small of my back, guiding me kitty corner to a moody lounge. A curvy blonde dangles her leg from a bar chair, leaning into the woman next to her as we walk in. Her eyes drift over to us, coyness tightening her lips as she nods our way to her partner. Roman stiffens beside me, his hand dropping from my back once we're noticed.

Irritation flutters at my heart. I don't know if it's for the blonde or Roman. I just know it's there, burning through my giddiness. When I try to pull it back, I only somewhat succeed. Roman, sensing my curiosity, leans down to whisper into my ear, his cheek caressing my own.

"Are you fine with skipping the bar? I'm not really fond of running into associates."

At the sound of his voice, my skin reaches for him, tiny puckers covering every inch. I dip my eyes in understanding. He's been hiding for months. Of course, he wouldn't want to network. With a glimpse of what he's been feeling, I can hardly protest. I wouldn't want to be friendly either if every fault I had was constantly put on display. If I was talked about as if I wasn't present. I nod, his scruff causing a delicious itch against my skin.

"Lead the way, Captain," I say, poking at him, if only to help soothe the ache of what's mending between us.

I feel his smile.

"You know, I think you are the only person I can even tolerate calling me that."

He puts some distance between us as he leads us deeper into the restaurant. This is the sort of place I would imagine Roman Wheatley to be. The walls are all exposed brick, with windows that climb from floor to ceiling with little concern for the distance. Large pipes laid expertly throughout, an obvious design choice rather than a necessity. Although the décor is industrial, it's anything but common. Everything looks expensively put together.

We stop at a back table; long black drapes pooled at either end, making it easy to wall ourselves off from the rest. I looked around and notice that this corner holds several tables, all with the same feature. I turn my head back to see Roman watching me, cheek twitching. He steps toward me, reaching over to pull the curtain backing us taut. It shields our table from most of the place without being completely isolated.

"That's... odd," I say.

He simply shrugs.

"Not really. It makes it easier not to worry about who or what someone is going to do or say during our meal. The last thing I want, or you need, is some idiot with a camera coming in here making assumptions. The staff are pretty good at stopping it, but they can't be everywhere. This just makes things less awkward."

"But we've been out before, at the cafe, and no one said anything," I retort, not totally convinced this is necessary.

"Yeah, but we were also working. Anyone could see that or hear it, for that matter. And no one said anything, but there were plenty of pictures that ended up as gossip. Mostly just speculation about my next film."

"I am trying to understand Roman, but you've got to help me out. This, *whatever this is*, is confusing enough without you becoming distant and frozen every time people are around. I don't know how to just turn myself off like that. Not to mention that I can't exactly tell when the 'right' people are around versus the wrong ones."

"I know it's confusing, believe me. And I wish it could be different. But especially right now, I'd like to keep us, in whatever context that is, between *just us*. I promise you, going viral is not all it's cracked up to be. Not only will it be a

PR headache, but they'll mess everything up. I've been through this before. As you know, it didn't end well."

We're both still standing. His fingers drum on the back of the chair impatiently. I feel his anxiety at wanting me to drop this, but his face remains calm and stoic. Like there is no argument he cannot win. It makes me want to protest. Even if I know it is childish. I shake myself out of my instinct and register his words. That he's even still waiting for me to end the conversation proves that he isn't dismissing my concerns. I choose to offer him the same kindness.

"I didn't realize... does that happen to you a lot?"

It's a stupid question and I know it. Of course it does. Or has. I've *seen* the stories myself. Laughed about them with Cherie, Monica and Katie. But looking at Roman now, I don't think I'll ever be able to thoroughly, blindly, enjoy a gossip column again.

He looks out the window, taking in the entire city before him.

"Yeah. It does."

He doesn't elaborate like I want him to, but I won't push. I'm not sure it would do any good anyway and our night has already been a rollercoaster. A server comes over as we finally sit, bringing menus, water, and a bottle of wine that she quietly pours for us. I pick up a menu to peruse, but Roman keeps his eyes firmly on the horizon without touching his. I jump between staring at him and drooling over what I'll eat tonight. Each dish sounds more amazing than the last, but as I scour for a price, I come up empty-handed. *Shit.*

"Do you come here often?" I ask, wanting to fish out what I'm getting myself into.

He finally pulls his eyes to me and as if he senses my panic he says, "tonight is on me. There's no use protesting."

He smirks, holding up his hand to stop the words I'm on the edge of saying.

"Besides, I know the owner *and* I picked the venue. It would be bad manners for me to expect you to pay, and I'd hate to tarnish the Wheatley name further. My mother might actually kill me."

I laugh, intrigued by his relationship with his mother, but it isn't enough to distract me. As much as I need to save, I can't let him pay for me. I'm already confused enough about what we are, or what this is. If he covers the bill, it feels like a date and you know what they say, if it quacks like a duck... But then he catches my eyes in his. He pulls my hand away from the menu and cups it gently on the table.

"Five, please. Let me do this."

How can I say no? I sigh, want and confusion swirling in my belly, making it hard to do anything rational. So, I don't. A quiet *ok* escapes on my breath. He squeezes my hand briefly before letting it go. I drag it back to the menu slowly, continuing to search, a blush running from my chest to my cheeks.

The server comes back to take our order and Roman lists his choices from memory. He's so completely put together, knowing exactly what he wants, leaving me completely in awe of him. He is everything I'm not. The order to my chaos. I try to be as concise but can't help the smiles and uhs that filter their way into my conversation. I'm hopeless, but that's okay. Roman is staring at me when I turn back.

"What?" I ask playfully.

"How are you, so... *nice*?" He sounds genuinely confused and I laugh.

"I don't know." I reach for my water to sip. "I guess I just know how it feels to be in customer service."

Lord knows I've had enough jobs in it and one rude customer could ruin an entire day. Roman shakes his head, hands folding on top of the table.

"No, not just to the server. I mean to everyone. The only person I've seen you meet with anything less than a smile was me. That is when you knew you were meeting me."

"Ah," I say. "Well, I can promise you're not the *only* one. If I know who I'm meeting, I tend to let my feelings show. Even if I wish I could hide them. But, if I had to give a reason, I would suppose it's because I never really know who I'm talking to."

"So, it's a status thing?" He nods in understanding, a frown settling in. "I get that. That's something I've seen a lot. Especially here."

"No! I'm not explaining this very well... it's not about knowing what the person does, rather who they are. Like what their intent is. I mean, of course, *sometimes* it matters what they do, like if I'm going to a job interview but mostly it's more like they did nothing to me so I'm not going to do anything to them, situation. I don't know their intentions, so I choose not to judge."

"But what if you *do* know their intentions? What if that server was someone who did something horrible to you before and you just don't recognize her?"

I lean in, gesturing him toward me.

"I'm going to let you in on a little secret I've stumbled upon being faceblind. Unless they know I'm faceblind, which happens but rarely, more often than not, they just think they weren't important enough to remember. That whatever horrible thing they did to me was so insignificant that I cannot even be bothered to treat them accordingly. It drives them mad."

I sit back in my seat, smugness emanating from my cheeks. Roman looks stunned.

"It's the best revenge I can get, really. And I don't even have to try," I laugh.

Roman pulls back into his seat before letting out a full-on bark of laughter, which of course only encourages me more.

"You are absolutely devious, Five, and I can't say that I'm not glad to hear there's a little bit of a mischievous streak in you."

"You have no idea."

Warmth is spreading through me, and I can't help the bit of husk that drifts into my voice like smoke.

Roman's body turns rigid at the sound, eyes narrowing in on my lips, and I know we're both thinking about the closet. So much for this being completely friendly. The memory brings a slight unease back and I shake myself out of it. My heart knows I'm forgiving him, but my mind needs more than an hour to settle.

"Excuse me, I... I need to make a call. I'll be right back," I say, slapping myself mentally at the stupid excuse.

To his credit, he simply nods, but I see a flash of disappointment before I turn away. *Me too, bud.* I make my way to the ladies' room, tucked into a far-off corner of the main dining area. Two giggling twenty-somethings almost hit me with the door on my way in before they're whispering and laughing back toward the bar.

"Excuse you," I whisper to myself.

"Oh, I'm sorry. Did you need this sink?"

I look toward the voice to find two large purses. One sits in the vanity, practically taking up both sinks at the counter. The other hangs from an arm of a woman, fingers paused mid search looking directly at me. She's wearing a beautiful orange dress that perfectly mimics the sunset, and I can't help but comment on it.

"No, sorry, I was talking to the two girls who almost hit me with the door. I love your dress by the way."

She smiles, a full-face smile. "This? Thank you! Orange is really my color, and if you got it, flaunt it. That's what they say, anyway."

I smile back, still standing there awkwardly. Without the vanity to use, I have no reason to be here. Thankfully, she doesn't seem to mind.

"You're totally on a date. I can see it. Things either got awkward, cringe, or too spicy for the table, if you know what I mean." She waggles her eyebrows. "That's fine. You can hang in here. These are okay bathrooms. I mean, they could be better, but they're not the worst in LA, that's for sure. I should find what I need in no time, and then the place is all yours."

"Oh, no, please don't rush. I'm just... taking a breather."

"Ooo. Spicy, spicy," she says, putting a little shimmy in her hips.

I like her. A bit over the top, but she reminds me of Cherie, if Cherie was nice-bubbly instead of opinionated-bubbly.

"Not exact—" I start to say before she breaks in.

"FOUND IT!" she yells, a squeal making my ears ring.

When I look at her outstretched hand, I can't believe what I'm seeing.

"Are those... cupcakes? You do know you can order dessert here, right?"

Dark brown, boarding on black, chocolaty cupcakes gleam from inside a freezer size baggie. The click of the zipper being opened echoes before she offers it to me.

"These are not just any cupcakes. These are *the* cupcakes. Dark chocolate, triple fudge, caramel salted chip, cupcakes. And no one has a dessert like this. Want one?"

They look good, but I've thoroughly learned my lesson about taking sweets in this town.

"No, thank you. But they look delicious. I hope... you enjoy them."

She pulls back the bag to herself, ripping off a sizeable chunk and shoving it in her mouth.

"Mmmm. So. Good," she hums.

Before diving in for another piece, she rounds up the loose bag on the counter and makes her way to the door.

She stops just short of pulling it open.

"You didn't ask for it, but here's my advice: go back out there and give in. Let him have some of that booty, girl. You deserve it."

She flips the door open and dances her way out. I watch in astonishment, trying to catch what just happened, and burst out laughing. I turn to the mirror, catching the pure happiness on my face. There are a million reasons I shouldn't, but the best things are neither easy nor perfect.

"She's not wrong," my reflection says to me.

I turn on my heel, satisfied with where this night should go.

NINETEEN

Roman

TRY AS I MIGHT, I can't stop myself from looking at the dark hallway Victoria wandered down only minutes ago. I know she's probably as confused about us as I am, and that I should give her space, but I can't. Whenever I see her unknowingly bite the edge of her lip, or sneak glances at me when she thinks I'm not looking, it takes all my control not to sweep her up and take her far from prying eyes.

My arm drapes on the seat back next to me as I work not to look like a stalker. I know I messed up. The moment I called her Five, my heart cracked, knowing I deserved the look of confusion and betrayal she gave me. My selfishness had burned both of us, and I'd never wanted to take something back so badly in all my life. I would do just about anything to make sure that look never happen again.

Which is why our privacy, now more than ever, is important. Her soft heart that she tried to hide didn't deserve to have gossip rags dragging up lies about her. I had made the mistake of not shielding Lauren from it, and I wouldn't do the same with Victoria. She was worth more than the mockery that came with this job, and I didn't want her to live with the fear I had of it. She was fierce, there was no doubt about that, but I only ever wanted her to be fierce with *me*. I would happily fight all the rest of her battles.

For now, though, I am relieved she gave me a chance and came on this date. Or not date. Or whatever this is. I will take whatever she is giving. There's no denying any longer that I like her. *I like her.* There has been no one since Lauren. Not for more than a night. And now? Now, I want to be around this girl. I want to laugh and work and play with her. Taking it slow is a gift. One that I won't return. If I have to convince her to work with me again, to talk with me, to kiss me, I'll do it all gladly.

Well, as glad as I can be.

A dazzling orange catches my eye from the hallway, and I see a familiar actress sauntering out. She girlishly wiggles her fingers at me, a not-so-subtle grin on her face. I lift my hand in recognition. She throws her eyes behind her, before giving me a barely concealed thumbs-up. My eyebrow peaks in question. She just laughs and continues on her way, moving out of sight as she wanders up to the VIP bar upstairs. *What in the hell was that all about,* I wonder.

I'm even more focused, but thankfully, I don't have to wait long. Victoria emerges from the dark, her long brown curls separating from the shadow as if it doesn't want to let her go. Her hips dip in and out of her steps like the ocean, making me think of all the waves we can make. She's got her shoulders thrown back, that flirty spark of lust still evident in her stride. I pull myself up and take note, meeting her stare for stare.

Before she can make it to the table, an imposing figure strutting our way grabs my attention. Victoria notices him too. She stops just feet from her chair, turning toward him, looking from me to him, a question in her eyes. He doesn't notice her as he stops between her and her chair. Normally his presence would be welcome, comforting even, but showing up here unexpectedly dread pools in my gut.

"Roman, finally! I have been trying to reach you for days. Why have you not returned my calls?"

He's breathless, although if you didn't know him like I do, I'm not sure you'd noticed. Every hair, every thread, is in place, but the dark rim around his eyes tells me he's been traveling. My brow stiffens as I register his words, trying to place his tone for the type of news he's flown all this way to tell me.

"I haven't received any calls from you." I think, wondering why, since clearly, he wouldn't lie. And then I remember. "My other phone was broken and instead of going through the hassle, I just bought a new one."

"You mean someone pissed you off, and you smashed it? Guess I should have realized. I left messages with Thoren too, but we've been a bit on the outs. I wasn't surprised when he didn't call me back. I *am* surprised he didn't tell you, though. He can be such a child. He probably just wanted to call my bluff and make me fly out here. Thank God he still has a low jack on that monstrosity."

He rolls his eyes. Quinten never stops being the oldest brother. As much as he irritates me, the familiar burn of family also brings comfort in its wake. No matter how he may mock me, he's my brother and will always have my back over all else. Finally, he takes stock of the situation he's intruding on, catching sight of Victoria standing, unsure of what to do.

"You're... on a date?" he asks, the disbelief clear.

"Yes, and you're being rude. Why don't you sit down and I can introduce you." I scoot my seat out and stand, allowing Victoria to sit next to me, curious how the two might get along, but he refuses.

"No, that's alright. I don't want to disturb your lovely date." He grins at Victoria before holding out his hand. "Quinten. Roman's older brother. I am so sorry to burst in like this. Honestly, I thought he'd be eating alone."

"Thanks, Quin. Don't make me sound like a loser or anything," I grumble under my breath.

"If the shoe fits," he shoots back.

Victoria, bless her good humor, laughs, taking Quinten's hand in hers. She trips into him, her arm resting on his chest as she tries to regain her balance. Quinten's grin is bright but guarded, unsure of what to make of the girl in front of him.

"Oh! Sorry about that. I'm a klutz, but *you* can call me Victoria. It's nice to meet you!"

I see Quinten being taken by her. Instinctively, I crowd in.

"Really, you can join us. It seems important," I say as my hand possessively goes to her back, daring Quinten to say something.

He smiles knowingly.

"I promise you; it can wait until you get home. It's just some legal matters. Nothing nearly as exciting as what you have going here." He looks at me, saying *this is Wheatley business*, before he turns to Victoria and says, "You two have a lovely meal."

Before I can say more, he's released Victoria and is on his way out the door, with not even a backward glance. He's never been much for long goodbyes. Or heart to hearts of any kind. If I am my father's son, Quinten is his prodigy. I cannot blame his lack of endearments. Between becoming our father and trying his best to shield the rest of us from his worst, he didn't have a chance to learn.

Victoria watches him go before she turns to me.

"Do you need to follow him?"

I shake my head.

"He said it can wait, so I'll trust his judgment. He is my lawyer, after all." I gesture to her seat. "Shall we?"

She smiles and sits. Curiosity blossoms in her skin and I know she's dying to ask me about Quin.

"Go ahead, Five. I can tell you've got something you're burning to ask, so just do it already."

She blushes deeper.

"That's Quinten, and then there's Thoren? How many brothers do you have?"

"There's four of us; Quinten, Roman, Samuel, and Thoren. You've had the pleasure of meeting the oldest and the youngest and me. I doubt you'll meet Samuel. He's currently somewhere in England, studying for some graduate program. I'd tell you what exactly, but I'm not sure. He tends to jump around from subject to subject. He's a bit of a lifelong student. Married to education, as my mother says. Thoren lives here and Quinten, well, he normally lives in Connecticut near the family home. Currently, he's being groomed to take over our father's law firm. Your guess is as good as mine why he's here."

I ramble on about my family knowing she's asking more in the lines of her question than just what she's said. It feels both odd and wonderful to tell someone about my life, even if it is a small, mundane slice of it. It's been years since anyone has asked such simple things for more than just wanting dirt on me. Victoria's chin tips in toward her chest.

"Wow. Okay. Four boys. Phew! Your mother had her hands full! Any sisters?"

I can't help but smile at her, imagining how she'd react if she knew it was the nannies who had full hands.

"Not a one. Just us four."

"So, there's Quinten, who just left. Then Roman, that's you. Hey, what a minute!"

I laugh because I already know what she's caught on to. It thrills me she's found a pattern so many fail to see.

"QRST. Was that on purpose? It has to be on purpose, right?" she asks.

"You are way too smart for your own good. Yes, it was on purpose. It's... a tradition of sorts, I suppose. Wheatley men in my family get named after our ancestors in alphabetical order. So, Quinten's first child has already been born, and his name is Uriah. The next will be Victor and so on and so forth, round and round."

She sits back in her seat, a look of contemplation taking over. She's quiet for a moment, and I wonder what she could be thinking. I can feel the drip of wealth that's painted my words, and I internally cringe. *Why did I have to tell her all that?*

"What I'm hearing is your family is *old school*. I am getting a very 'steeped in tradition' vibe right now and if so, it explains a lot," she says evenly.

"I mean, steeped in tradition is one way of putting it. Legacy is another. Ridiculous favor of old money and old ways is probably the best way of describing it. I'm not sure if I should be offended that you feel the naming of children in my family explains me. That doesn't seem like a good thing," I say.

"It's really not that bad, Roman. It's not like I didn't know you were rich. If the Mercedes didn't give it away, your Wikipedia page certainly did. You're always depicted as the guy who came from 'a very well-off family'. It's not exactly a secret." She rolls her eyes good humoredly. "I was talking more about the rigidity of it all. The lack of choice that extends to something that is so much yours, such as your children. It just... it makes sense why you kind of come off as a jerk. And why maybe you got a little lost in the partying 'like me' phase when you first started."

Her words don't feel judgmental, but they sting me all the same. I'm ripped open on the table, and I itch to pull and tug all the pieces back under the shell I've created to protect them. I hate that she sees so much with so little and that I have practically nothing of her in return. The weight of knowing is unbalanced, and I desperately need to right it again.

"What about you? You've gotten a serious glimpse into the inner workings of my childhood and, apparently, my recent misjudgments. Now it's your turn to share something personal."

She tosses the possibilities in her mind, weighing what to tell me, and I let the silence hang. I want to push her, hoping to knock her away from giving me too calculated an answer, but I also don't want to break the tentative truce we've made. My embarrassment and uncomfortableness can only be a fraction of what *she* felt at the party when she found out who I was. But in my defense, I haven't been this vulnerable since Lauren and I's split was front page news on the tabloids.

"That's fair." She rolls the words on her tongue, letting them linger. "You know more than you probably realize. You're ridiculously good at finding sore spots without trying and you've read my script. I put a lot of myself in those. But we can start with the newest biggest thing. I came to LA right after filing for divorce. I caught my husband cheating on me with an employee."

My hand shoots out for her as violence overwhelms me. She tuts her tongue, patting my outstretched hand.

"Relax, tough guy. I honestly didn't care," she stops herself and rethinks. "What I mean is, I didn't care about the cheating per se. I cared about losing my husband, but not because I was in love with him. It was more because I didn't want to lose what I had. When we were together, I didn't feel like I was failing at life. At least, I didn't use to think so. I had great friends living nearby. I had a home and a job that I was good at. I had a husband who loved me. Who wouldn't want that?"

Tears are just on the edges of her eyes, but she continues.

"The truth is, I didn't. But I couldn't tell anyone that. It was like spitting in the face of every good thing I was given. Saying it wasn't enough—I couldn't even imagine it. Wanting to be a writer was crazy. My ex didn't understand it since it wasn't a practical dream. Not like his. It didn't fit into our perfect plan. Why, when I'd found somewhere I belonged, did I want to chase something that was full of rejection and heartbreak and struggle? I'd worked so hard just to be comfortable and accepted where I was. So, I tried to sweep it under the contentedness. I let myself have the easy things. But I was never really happy. And apparently, to be in a healthy, lasting marriage, you need that. From both people."

She sniffles, a watery smile lifting her chin, and I think it might be the most beautiful I've ever seen her. It both breaks my heart and mends it. I reach out and begin stroking her palm with my thumb. I don't break eye contact as I do, nor do I give her some platitudes that diminish anything she's said.

"You're absolutely right. I understand that more than you know."

As much as it terrifies me to say what needs to be said, it kills me to leave her out in this memory alone.

"I'm sure you've read all about my breakup. Lauren's family and mine go way back. It was always understood that she'd marry a Wheatley and since I was the same age, everyone just kind of pushed us together. And I loved her. I did. Just not enough. Not like how she wanted or how she deserved to be loved, anyway. I cared more about my dream than our relationship and when my reputation and ratings tanked, I didn't know what to do. Everything I wanted was disappearing. I couldn't take her down with me when I didn't think I could ever love her enough to get us back up. I heard she's met someone, and they're blissfully happy. She never deserved the way it all went down, but I can't bring myself to regret it. And I suppose that makes me the biggest asshole of all."

I can feel her studying me, the deeper parts I keep hidden, and how we're more alike than I let on. I know she wants to refute the last comment I made, but I'm relieved when she doesn't. It's the least of the responsibility I can have. I've taken both the easy and the hard route. I'm still unsure which is better if I'm being honest. But sitting here with this woman's hand in mine makes something click into place. I can't untangle the web of my feelings just yet, so I lock them away.

Before we can go into any deeper thoughts, our food arrives, effectively splitting us apart. Victoria inhales everything, deep breaths bringing her chest up and out. Her eyes drift close while she savors the smell. A calmness washes over me. If this could be my meditation, I would do it every single day without complaint. Her eyes pop back open as the server leaves, all traces of fragility gone.

"I'm starving," she practically purrs.

Me too, Five. Me too.

TWENTY

DINNER IS SPECTACULAR, IF not all that I'm hungry for. For the first time since I met my ex-husband, I am passionately *into* someone, even if I'm not yet ready. Thankfully, he doesn't seem to be in a rush. We've only got a few more edits and a movie to shoot in the next few months. What's a little time crunch when you're having fun?

Even as anxiety nips at my thoughts, I can easily push it away. There's plenty of time for me to drown myself in Roman. I can't be worried when I'm this hopeful. My script is going to be purchased and produced. My friends are waiting to hear all about my night. And Roman. Roman is here looking at me the way he does, with a hint of an edge, as if at any moment the rest of the room could disappear, leaving just us. And that would be completely fine by him.

There's nothing to worry about when a man looks at you like that.

Roman is taking care of the check, his head tilted down to the receipt, quickly scribbling on the paper before gently closing the tab. He looks up, catching my stare and holds me in place.

"You ready to get out of here?" he asks.

Before I can even push back my chair, he's standing off to the side of me, offering his hand. I take it, smiling like a lunatic but unable to stop. All the worries I have are tucked tightly in for the night. Whether this crush lasts the next five minutes or a lifetime, I am enjoying being consumed by it. Giddy bubbles of excitement rise from my stomach to my chest, where they burst into happiness. I feel like they will carry me away if I let them.

We leave the restaurant the same way we came in. A few photographers sit outside on benches, their cameras idly hanging from their hands and necks. They scrutinize us as we pass, a few clicks taking place, but once they see the space between us, they lose interest fast. Apparently, I am not a newsworthy enough scoop for the Roman Wheatley fan. Mostly I'm relieved, but there is a small part that wonders, *what would it be like if they knew this was a date?* It's not the fame I want so much as the honesty of dating Roman Wheatley. Of being able to call it what it is. *Is he embarrassed of me?*

I shake my thoughts from my head. After everything he's shared, everything that I know he's been through, it's not fair for me to ask that of him yet. Possibly never. My mind is slipping from this beautiful moment, and I try to grab it before the spiral.

This is just a date. A single date with someone you're attracted to. It is not marriage. It isn't even long term. We don't even know how this will go with us working together. Enjoy it while it's here, but don't forget what you're doing here in the first place. The script comes first. Your dream matters, not who knows you're on a date with Roman Wheatley.

My mental pep talk has me to rights. I can be caught up in Roman on my downtime as long as I don't lose focus on my career. I need to do this to prove that I can be successful in doing what I love. And to have enough funds to not live on Monica's sofa any longer. I dream of the moment where I can fly back home to visit, eager to talk about my passions without feeling like they're secondary to my job or my husband. Where I feel *good enough*.

Before I realize it, we're already in the parking garage, the elevator door being held open for me to exit. I walk past, but before I can get all the way, Roman snags my hand in his. His palms are warm and large, engulfing mine. All my senses zero in on the feeling and I cannot live outside of this moment, even if I wanted to. He opens my door, waiting until I am all the way in before leaning into me and placing my hand on my lap.

"You okay?" he asks, brow furrowed.

"Yeah, just in my head, I guess."

He doesn't move away. "Anything I can help with?"

I look at his open face, from his brows to his lips, getting stuck on the latter. Another thought takes over and I decide it's the safer option to tell him versus what I was actually thinking about.

"Mmmm. I just can't believe I missed our first kiss. I mean, I remember it, of course. But I don't remember it *with you*."

I want him to understand what I mean as I try sending the feeling from my eyes to his. I'm not sure it works, but if not, he doesn't let on. He just nods, his tongue peeking out to lick his lips.

"Let's remedy that," he says.

I lean in thinking he'll kiss me now. Instead, he backs aways and shuts the door in my face. I'm briefly stunned back into my seat at the contrast of the environment. One moment it's Roman's beautiful face encompassing mine, the next, a car door. I can't help the tiny, irritated huff that escapes me as he climbs into the driver's seat.

"That... is not what I was expecting," I finally choke out as he backs up the car.

His deep laugh sends fireworks through my heart, and I scrunch my nose to keep the giggles from breaking my playful irritation too soon.

"Trust me, Victoria."

His soft smile quirks to one side as he concentrates on the road, but his eyes betray him often with side glances my way.

I huff out my impatience. "Fine. But this better be good, Cap."

We drive into the night, the streets quieter than I've seen them. I watch as streetlights flash past, trying to figure out where we are going. He stops at a hotel, letting the valet take his keys as he walks around to help me out of the vehicle. I stop before my heel can touch the pavement.

"This is forward," I say sarcastically, my nerves getting to me.

It's not that I'm unwilling, it's just unexpected. I didn't prepare for this. As much as I want him, I can't help but squirm with worry. A quickie in a hotel with my director that I am sort-of-kind-of-crushing hard on is not what I expected to make up for our first kiss. But Roman's smile is sweet when I look up to him, melting some of the ice in my veins.

"It's not like that, Five. You should know better than to think our first time would be between dinner and my brother waiting for me at home." He shakes his head as if he's disappointed in me.

My blush rushes to my face and I cannot form words through my embarrassment. I grab his outstretched hand and let him guide me in, careful to keep my eyes down. I'm not ready to own up to my thoughts of where I assumed this night was headed. He escorts me to a bench by the elevators before tilting my chin up.

"Hey, wait here. I'll be right back."

He turns from me but then thinks better of it and instead cups his hand around my waist. My pulse jumps and there's no question he feels it.

"I'm thinking about it, too."

He kisses me on the cheek and rushes to the concierge desk. I touch the cheek he's kissed, lust wrapping around my limbs as I watch him chat back and forth with the staff. He must get what he wants because he's smiling as he marches back toward me, pure determination etched into his face. He doesn't share his plans. Instead, he leads me into the elevator.

We reach the top floor, and a beautiful banquet room opens onto the rooftop. It's empty, all except for the booths nestled into the sides and the shell of a bar with chairs stacked behind it. My steps echo as I move. The dim lights, though turned on, allow the details to hide in shadow. Roman moves around me and starts walking for a far end booth. I follow, gasping the second it hits me.

Roman has taken me back in time to our first kiss. I can almost feel the music pulsing, my feelings of being lonely and wanting to be reckless ebbing in with the beat. He gets to the booth and spins into it, arms stretched out along the back. The shadows hide him and the memory lines up so perfectly, except this time I know who waits for me.

Roman digs into his pocket, pulling out his phone and placing it on the table. A soft thump of dance music fills the air.

"You can't just stand there, or you'll change the course of history," he says.

I walk to the middle of the floor and throw my hands up. My hips sway out and back, rolling through the song like a wave. The pin prick of Roman's eyes on me is like a magnet. I'm drawn to him. My heels click on the floor as I give him my best model walk from the dance floor to the booth. Without hesitating, I crawl in on my knees, careful this time not to bump anything. *If I get a redo, it's going to be perfect, dammit!*

My hands crawl up his chest before resting on his jaw. Instead of swinging my legs down, I tilt my knees up, my chest coming flush with his.

"Married?" I ask.

He smiles awaiting the question. "No."

"Attached of any kind?" I try again, leaning closer as I do, his skin so close to my lips I can practically taste it. The thrill of this night the first time it happened collides with the safety I feel with the man I now know.

"Only to you," he responds.

I guide his jaw with the movement of my fingers, so he's staring up into my mouth before crashing down on him. Our lips meet with ease, forming into the perfect slip of one single entity. He grips his hands around my ass, running them up the length of my hips and back before starting all over again.

The feeling of his hands, his lips, burns into my mind. I will never see this kiss as anything less than this. Roman Wheatley has effectively figured out how to rewind time, how to erase things that don't matter with those that do. I can't stop myself from falling into him. In fairness, I don't think I would even if I could.

For tonight, at least, I'm his entirely.

TWENTY-ONE

Roman

LEAVING VICTORIA IS A new level of torture. The ghost of her lips runs up my neck, her fingertips trailing after. There are so many things I hate about this city but now, I think, it holds one of my favorite hotels in the world. I'm not sure how I got her to kiss me there, let alone twice, but it's got to be a good luck charm. A secret weapon I'll pull out to remind us of how we started.

The night replays as I make my way home, the drive not at all long enough to do the night justice. I'm smiling like a fool when I walk in the door only to see Quinten and Thoren sitting across from one another, staring daggers. The frustration in the room threatens to dim my otherwise cheerful spirits and, try as I might, a scowl takes hold. There's been something bubbling between these two brothers for months, which I've ignored. It isn't my place to step in. Besides, they're both big boys. They can figure it out.

I don't hurry. I take my time hanging my jacket and my keys. Emptying my pants of my wallet and phone. Pouring myself whiskey. Quinten and I get along fine enough. There's a debt I feel for him being the oldest son and sparing me that burden as well, but it doesn't mean our relationship is easy. It also doesn't mean that I am excited he showed up tonight, especially since I'm pretty sure he came as my lawyer and not my brother making this a business meeting. *My favorite*. Only once I've settled myself into the tip of the triangle of the Wheatley men present do I even acknowledge them.

"Quin. Are you going to tell me what you're doing here and why the hell you interrupted my date?" I ask, intensity pumping from every word.

Thoren breaks his death glare at Quinten to smirk over at me.

"Oh yeah! How was the date? I almost forgot, what with His Royal Dipshit over here showing up."

He waves his finger over to Quinten.

I try to keep a straight face, wanting to remain neutral in whatever war is brewing between them, but the thought of Victoria has my cheeks lifting without permission.

"It was good," I say, placating him, before turning back to the topic at hand.

Quinten is furious. The rigidness of his shoulders could cut ice. The way he's staring at Thoren, I'm surprised a murder hasn't been committed in my absence. I'm not sure what's happened, but I wish Samuel were here to smooth it over. He's always been better at mending the wounds we make to each other.

"I wouldn't have even *been here* if you wouldn't have changed your number and T would have just told you to call me. This wasn't family business. It was work, my job as your lawyer, and he should have never ignored that," Quinten growls out.

Thoren's response slices through the air. "And I told *you*, I'm not your messenger. You haven't called or visited in almost a year. You ignore me when I reach out and then expect me to jump when you tell me to? Why the hell should I do you any favors?"

Thoren is seething, but anyone who knows him can see the pain that's laced in his words. Growing up, Quinten was his hero. The brother who could shield him from anything. Fix everything. And yet, for the last few years, he's been busy trying to wear my father's shoes. I knew he had been distant, but in my own retreat from the world I guess I didn't realize how alone Thoren felt without either of us, or even Samuel, to lean on.

The thought cuts deep into my chest, my hand rubbing at the spot as if it is a physical wound. Quinten wants to respond, the excuse and reason for his silence that will surely only start a war on the tip of his tongue. I beat him to it.

"There's no excuse. You're right, T. You're not a messenger and we *both*," I stare at Quinten with hard eyes, "should treat you better. We *will* treat you better. Right, Quin?"

I'm not really asking, the threat and plea clear. It's not much that I'm giving, but I know I need to do something and it's the best I've got. He sighs, sinking deeply into his chair, leg coming up to cross over the other. He fixes his cuffs, just like father always does, before he agrees.

"Yes, of course. I'm sorry I haven't been around much, Thoren. This... I should have come sooner," he says.

Even if Thoren wants to stay mad, he can't. This apology is as good as gold from the oldest Wheatley son. That and the fact that he flew almost three thousand miles to get here. Thoren smiles in acceptance, before waving him on to continue.

"Alright, big bro, I'm forgiving you. Just... pick up your phone." He sighs, resigned to keep the peace for now. "Now go ahead. Get on with why you're here," Thoren says.

I brace my hands on the seat, preparing for the worst, as Quinten turns his gaze on me. I cannot imagine what would be important enough for him to come all this way to tell me.

"Don't look at me like that, Roman. It's good news I bring!" He forces on his business smile. "We made a deal. Found that loophole you were after in your contract."

My breath hitches in my chest. *Does this mean I'm out? No more movies?* Flickers of the relief I've been expecting shoot through my veins, immediately shattered by disappointment and guilt. Victoria consumes my triumph. What will happen to her script if I'm no longer contracted to produce it? What will happen to us?

"You... got me out?" I ask, drawing out the question.

"No. You still need to make the third movie but, you're a sly bastard. When you first put together the contract, you made a direct stipulation regarding creative judgment. Now, because of the deadline for the contract and your tight schedule on work, we barely got the decision changed. It's a onetime, one-shot deal, but we did it."

My brain is having trouble keeping up with the conversation. I cannot figure out what he's done. If I'm not out of the contract, what else is there? I still have to make the movie. I still have to be in California for these events. It appears nothing's changed and yet, the sinking feeling in my gut tells me everything has.

"Speak plainly, Quinten. What did you do?" I say.

He smiles wide, a real one this time. "We got the documentary. I sent the papers last week and you shoot within the month. Your last film will be exactly what you wanted it to be."

My mind races. I finally get a chance at a do over. I can prove to my father, to the critics, to everyone, that I am more than a joke. Then after, I can do whatever kind of movies I want. My pride, my name, my inheritance, all fully intact. It's the next best thing to getting out of the contract entirely. It's everything I want.

Except, it isn't. Not anymore.

"What happens to Victoria's script?" I ask, glare settling into place, eating at the remnants of happiness.

"Victoria? You mean your date?" Quinten asks. "The studio said they hadn't paid her yet and would pull it from the production schedule this week. I assume it'll be buried until they need it or simply released back to the author."

"Oh shit. Roman, you can't." Thoren pipes in, his face mirroring my distress.

I think of the documentary, of what it would mean if it was successful. How my father could finally say I was more than just the second son for the first time in my life. I think about the reviews begrudgingly saying how accomplished the film is. I can see all of it, right in my hands. And then I think of Victoria.

As my dreams lay ready, hers are burning to ash. Best-case scenario, her script would be bought and stored. Waiting for the next director to take it on. But more than likely since Dreamaway hadn't paid her yet, they were going to full on pass. She would have spent weeks preparing it for nothing and, with it being a summer script, she would be almost completely out of time to sell it this year. She would have to abandon the project.

I think about the way her face lights up when she talks about it or walks me through a scene. The way she feels in the crush of romantic moments, her skin flaring pink. I imagine someone else picking up that script and hearing her voice sing through the premise, overpowering them with the want to love. Them looking at her and imagining what could be.

My knuckles pop at the force of my rage, hands tightened deeply into fists. The jealousy is for Victoria, but the possession? That's for the script itself. As much as I fought it, it is just as much mine now as it is hers, and I cannot bear the thought of someone else envisioning those scenes. Of someone else picturing Victoria on that boat. I needed to fix this before she found out.

"Undo it," I growl to my brother.

His eyes widen before narrowing into slits of their own, frustration coating his words.

"I can't, Roman. It took me weeks to get this far and, like I said, it's a one-shot deal. You either do this documentary or you get sued. Those are your options."

I look between my brothers, both fierce in their own ways for their own reasons. Pieces of my father reached all of us and, for the first time in a very long time, I am grateful for it.

"Well, you know what they say," I start, smirking, knowing full well I am about to piss off Quinten to the point I'm unsure if he'll ever speak to me again. "Where there's a Wheatley..."

Thoren smiles wide before replying, "there's a way. What are you thinking, Roman?"

Quinten mumbles, hand rubbing his brow. "Oh, for fuck's sake. I'm not a magician, you impossible bastard! You can't ever just make things easy, can you, Roman?"

No. Apparently, I can't. After all, what fun would that be?

TWENTY-TWO

Victoria

MONDAY ROLLS AROUND WITH a little less chaos. Saying goodbye to my friends never feels quite right, as if a piece of me leaves with them. Although I want to be here, to finally put my biggest dream first, I can't help but be homesick for the people I've left behind. And my favorite Mexican restaurant, *Lucinda's*. I would kill just about anyone for one of her hometown famous enchiladas right now.

I look at the clock above my little desk, seeing it's only 10 am and wonder if Roman is up yet. A bubbling of excitement prickles my skin at the thought of him. We texted briefly yesterday, just to say hello and ask if everything was okay with his brother, but with both of us having people in town, we didn't really get to talk. I didn't want to risk my nosy ass best friends snooping. I would never live it down. But now that they're gone, I can chance it.

Good morning, director.

I hope he reads it as sexy as I do in my mind. Even if he doesn't, it's a safe bet because it can be taken as either formal or flirty. Fear clenches my heart. What if the other night wasn't as romantic as I remember? What if he's already over it, ready to move forward with only a professional relationship? What if this is a onetime thing?

I shouldn't be worried about any of this. We've both been so openly focused on our careers, and we want such different things, I can't expect this to work. Still, my heart doesn't listen to reason. It thumps and stops, as if the minutes between my greeting and his response can kill me. My phone chimes and immediately I glance down.

Morning beautiful.

The traitorous feeling in my chest eases a bit. I set my phone down, determined now that I've made contact to actually start writing for the day while Monica is at work. Knowing he's just on the other end of a phone call or text gives me a rush that can only be memorialized by writing it down on paper. A new story itches at my fingertips. Even though I've sold one, I need to get another polished and ready to sub out. One script isn't going to pay rent for long and staying has never felt more important. My phone chimes again and I reach for it so fast my wrist feels a sting from the movement.

It isn't Roman, instead it's an email reply from Beckson following up on the payment.

Hello Miss Pencheske, completely understandable that you would want to follow up on payment for your script. No need to apologize! Would it be possible for us to meet tomorrow at the office at 11? There are a few things we need to go over. Sincerely, Beckson

Worry nags at my thoughts, but I sweep them away. It's probably nothing, a few t's to cross, and I's to dot. I'm sure everything is fine. Monica or Roman would have told me if it wasn't. I ground myself in the reality of my thoughts, letting my anxiety beat against them before it finally starts settling into background noise. I hold on to the small voice of hope. *Tomorrow, I'll be walking out with my first writer's paycheck in hand.* I squeal a little to myself and wiggle around in my seat with excitement. I'm actually doing this. Despite the obstacles and improbabilities. I'm excited to prove every naysayer wrong, but most of all, myself.

I settle into my seat to write for the next few hours. The words flow out like magic. I hadn't really planned for the story I'm telling before this morning, but at the rate it's being written, I can't argue with it. I bite the smile from my lips as

I slip in a few personal details, things that are an open secret. My heart stutters. *I cannot wait to show Roman.* The thought slips in unbidden, the truth of it sticking to the walls of my ribs. Everything expands and then I exhale.

I don't have long to analyze before my phone rings out, the punchy pop song blaring through the speaker. I don't even bother looking at the caller ID, which is my first mistake. The second is not immediately hanging up when I hear the voice that says my name.

"Hey Vicky. I'm glad you picked up. I... well, I wasn't sure you would,"

Trent's voice is strangled, as if he can't quite swallow what's stuck in his throat.

Is it appropriate to just hang up and pretend I never answered? Probably. I drag air deep through my nose.

"What's up, Trent?"

Impatience drips from every word. My breath huffing out each letter like the caterpillar from *Alice in Wonderland.* I know I sound petulant but compared to what I want to be doing or saying, I'd say I'm exceptional right now.

"How have you been? I heard you've sold a script. Vicky, I'm so, so proud..."

"No. Hell no. Just stop right there." My hand shoots up as if to ward him off with my physical intentions. "Let's not do this. I know we're both at fault for what happened, but that doesn't mean we can be friends. Just... just tell me why you're calling. And don't say it's to catch up."

The line is silent, and I hope he'll just hang up. It would make everything easier if we had distance *and* silence between us. Unfortunately, he doesn't.

"Right. You're right. Sorry, Victoria. I actually have something important, and I guess you're giving me no other option but to just come out and say it. Like always. I don't know why I thought this conversation would be any different," he whines.

I cut him off again. "Trent. Tell me."

"I'm not selling the house," he deadpans.

The words leech in unwanted corners of my thoughts. My mouth gapes, searching for something to grasp. Something to say.

"What?" Is all that I can come up with.

"Listen, this isn't about you. Rebecka and I, we aren't a real thing. Not like us. And well, I need somewhere to live. And, dammit, I don't want to start over."

He sounds lost, untethered, but all I can hold on to is the fact that he's fucking me. Again.

"You can't. You *legally* can't. Sell the fucking house, Trent. It's *over*." I say.

"That's not what my lawyer thinks. He said that I can take ownership of the house. That it was purchased in my name, and used as collateral for my business, so there is a certain claim..."

"You fucking dick. It was *our* home. Our business. I gave up everything to make sure you had your dream. Just because it was your name on the paper doesn't mean it wasn't *my sacrifice* that gave it to you."

Angry, confused tears are creating rivers on my cheeks, and I don't even try to staunch them.

"I'm doing this, Victoria. You'll get the paperwork in the mail in a few days, but I thought I'd give you a heads up. Sorry that you'll have to come back home for court until it's all settled. Everything will be all laid out in the paperwork. I know you were waiting for that money. I thought it only fair to let you know it isn't coming. But you seem to be doing fine without any of it. Have fun while you can down there, Vicky. I'll see you soon."

The line cuts out, and he's gone. I scream into the screen, anyway, noticing a text notification as I pull back.

Have any plans today?

I had lovely, beautiful plans of writing another love story, but those are in tatters now from the wake of Hurricane Trent. I won't let him ruin this, too.

What do you have in mind?

Anything is better than wallowing in my afternoon. I'll just have to deal with Trent when the paperwork shows up.

Well, I ran into Monica and invited you both to a private beach party thrown by some of Thoren's buddies.

My mood immediately perks up at the thought of relaxing on a beach, Roman spread out in the sand next to me as we soak up the California sun. The image shines so brightly that it burns out the lingering frustration of Trent.

I'm in.

He shoots back a final text in the blink of an eye.

Good. Monica is on her way to pick you up now. See you soon.

I quickly shoot an email to my lawyer back home relaying the nasty bits of my morning, knowing that getting ahead of this is my best plan. Armed with renewed determination to stay and the reminder that I have more than one reason to, I look for my bathing suit and an outfit to match my newfound confidence.

If anything can wash the taste of talking to my ex and all the shit he's trying to pull out, it's a private party with Roman. Not to mention Monica is probably driving a hundred miles an hour to get here. She loves exclusive invites and will never turn down an opportunity for both a party and the chance to network. Roman has now earned infinite brownie points for inviting her.

I am just washing up my face from the earlier meltdown when she races in the door. She shoots directly into her room and begins tossing things around. I lean against the open door and watch her, aghast at both her ferocity and the amount of things that can fit in such a small closet.

"Hey, going somewhere?" I tease.

She takes enough time to shoot me a glare, then wrestles herself into a smoking hot, red bikini.

"You may have found someone to bide your time with, but some of us are still looking. And the Wheatley brothers, they know people. So, yeah, I'm going."

I laugh at her rarely shown frazzled side.

"Mon, it's just a party. No big deal," I say.

She stares at me like I've grown another head, "Nooo, Vip. This is **the** party. The Mid Som Beach Party is one of the most exclusive invites you can get. This isn't a celebrity party. This is an *old money* party. People who make or break entire careers, entire lives, will be there. And they'll have the best of the best of everything—food, drinks, music..."

She looks awestruck, a fog taking over her eyes. Then I say the dumbest thing, that immediately snaps her out of it.

"They have that kind of party on a Monday?" She completely freezes at my question and looks me dead in the eye.

"You're an idiot, Vip. A lovable, frustrating, confusing idiot. These people don't have jobs. They have enterprises. Monday is just another Friday for them," she says before continuing to get dressed.

We both work to make ourselves up, constantly changing and switching clothes between each other. The energy's chaotic nature is undeniable. There's excitement and nerves. My expectations are empty for a party like this, so I take my queues from Monica. If I trust her for nothing else, her ability to read a room and fit a setting is unequaled. She's a chameleon, especially when it comes to elegance and wealth. While I cannot hide from myself and will undoubtedly stand out in a crowd. Her phone's alarm beeps.

"Shit! Ok, look at me one last time." She runs her thumbs under my eyes, then pinches at her cheeks in the mirror. "We're good. Let's go!"

She grabs my hand and pulls me out the door. We're zipping down the highway as if we're sixteen again, her windows and top firmly in place so as not to mess up all our hard work before we can even get there. She's also brought along a slim black duffel bag filled with just in case and emergency items. I learned years ago never to ask what the extras are, just to know there are no bounds to Monica's preparedness.

We pull up to a long-gated community, the GPS telling us to continue straight. Monica hands over her phone to the security guard, along with her ID. She must have done everything right because they let us in without another glance. Large, customized mansions sit above ornate driveways and fences as we pass down the road. I don't know where we are, but as we slide downward, I can smell the salt of the ocean through the car vents. I roll down my window just enough to let it in its crisp, stinging salt, making me feel alive.

Insanity. That's the only way to describe what's happening at the last house on this road. If you can even call it a house. I see nothing else for miles and if I have to guess, I will say it's a hotel more than a home. The gates are thrown open, several security guards sitting in front of them running through the same checks as the previous one had. The anticipation of just being inside makes my fingers twitch and the men chuckle as they see the nerves. When we're through, lights and cars are everywhere. Not another home is in sight, but the one we're going to is enough to house plenty.

Monica pulls the car up to the valet and lets them take it. She also gives them the duffel and receives a ticket, along with instructions on how to retrieve it when needed. The whole affair is so organized, leaving me feeling wildly out of place. Before I can back out, she's guiding me away from the car. I squirm in my sun dress and wedges; not sure I've achieved the proper dress code when met with the valets in their starched shirts and dress shorts.

Thankfully, once we get inside, everyone's wardrobe is casual. Relaxed dresses and shorts. Tees and tanks. It truly is a beach party and not a black-tie affair, as I feared. The wide hall in the entry shoots directly through to an open glass wall that reveals a large backyard party. Tables stretch from end to end filled with food. Attendants float around, providing drinks and attention. Everything is so beautiful. So intentional. Awe and surprise consume me, that people actually live like this and it's normal for them. I don't think I'd ever get used to this. Even breathing feels difficult, with so much opulence in front of me.

Men and women are huddle in groups outside, laughing amongst each other. Some are playing yard games that are scattered about, while others lounge next to an Olympic sized pool. Children and teenagers form their own cliques and meander through the food tables, heaping piles onto their own plates. They rush off to claim their seats around the fire tables. My stomach protests loudly in jealousy. I pat it subtly to let it know we'll eat soon.

Entire areas are closed off, attendants standing every few feet in front of them to guide wayward souls back toward the party. Right inside of the doorway, an enormous ballroom sits empty but ready for the outdoor-adverse party goer to find refuge inside. It's the kind of place I would normally find myself propped up in at a party, leaving the outdoor beer kegs and barbequing to the true extroverts.

Monica pulls me into the backyard where everyone is as if she can sense my thoughts. As we step outside, I lose track of the details, only catching small pieces of a rather large flutter of activity. There's too much to capture it all.

The only thing that keeps my attention is the ocean lapping at the sand in the distance.

"You should probably text your man to let him know we're here," Monica says, nudging me.

"Don't call him that," I hiss, worried someone has heard. "It's not like that and I don't want anyone getting the impression it is."

More like I don't want anyone to think *I'm* under that impression. Not before he tells me he is, anyway. My head swivels, trying to catch anyone who may have heard. Embarrassment colors my cheeks, but the only person I catch is Monica rolling her eyes. She waits a beat for me to get myself together, then pointedly stares at my purse. I sigh and retrieve my phone, but it isn't needed. A warm breath at the base of my neck pulls my eyes up.

"Hey, Five. You look nice," Roman says.

I turn around to catch him, my lips lifting as I do. I'm not sure if I'm supposed to hug him, so I don't. We both stand there, arms dangling oddly at our sides, until a guy in bright salmon shorts pops up next to Roman.

"Hey Vip! Nice to see you again."

He leans into me to give me a squeeze. I laugh and hug him back; certain I know who this is.

"Hey Thoren. You should probably do a better job of announcing yourself. I could've maced you just now." He laughs at the joke, then I catch on to what he called me. "And when did you start calling me Vip? How? Why?"

Only Cherie, Monica, and Katie had ever called me Vip. I like hearing him use the name, as if we are more than just passing acquaintances. He smiles sheepishly, first to me, then to Monica.

"Well, Monica called you that, so I figured it's a friend's thing. And since you're the first girl in a *very* long time to make my brother smile, it seemed appropriate."

Roman swipes the back of Thoren's head with his palm.

"You should ask if it's OK before you call people things, T." Roman says, exasperated, as he flicks his fingers at Theoren's head.

"What like you did when you called me Five?" I ask, innocently.

Roman eyes heat as he flicks them to me.

"That was different, and you know it," he says.

Thoren coughs out an *ACK*, which Roman meets with a deathly glare that seems to shake even his brother's resolve as Thoren's hands pop up in supplication.

"OK, OK, big bro." Thoren grabs my hand in both of his. "Victoria, would it be alright with you if I call you Vip?"

"I would love it if you called me Vip!" I say, flicking my eyes to see Roman's reaction.

"You hear that, Roman? She would *love* it!"

He's smiling so hard his face might break from the strain as he bows his forehead down, kissing my hand in the process. I cannot suppress the giggles that shake me.

"Enough, Thoren. You shouldn't encourage him, Five!" Roman says as he pulls Thoren back from me.

"Ack. Get your own girl, hot shot, that one's taken," Monica shoots as my cheeks burn red.

Thoren's head flips up, a mischievous look in his eyes.

"Oh, I plan too. Hey, Monica. Interested in some dessert?"

Monica's arms fold, and I watch as her eyes dance over Thoren's features before she tightens them to her chest.

"You wish trust fund."

Before I can jump in, she swivels away and heads toward the food, Thoren quick on her heels.

He turns to walk backwards, shrugging as he says, "I'm only doing what the lady says I should."

I look between where Thoren and Monica are and Roman.

"What in the hell did I miss there?" I ask.

Roman shakes his head, clearly entertained.

"I have no idea. But it looks like Monica may be in trouble now. Thoren is insufferable when he has a crush."

We both smile like fools, and I can only feel vindicated at the justice that Monica is about to be served, if that's true. I file the incident away to tease Monica with later and instead focus all of my attention on Roman. Butterflies flap furiously around my chest at his proximity. I want so badly to wrap my arms around him, feel his skin on mine. The inaction of my thoughts is both intoxicating and incredibly agitating.

"So, friend's party, huh?" I ask, nudging him with my shoulder.

He shifts his weight right back into me. "Yeah. They're family friends. Thoren stayed close with their son and comes to this every year. I haven't been in a few though."

His brow crinkles, smile slipping. Whatever memory those years bring robbing him of the here and now. My hand instinctively brushes against his waist as I try to break him out of it.

"Want to grab some food? I'm starving."

I pull my hand back, pretending to hold in my hungry stomach with it and he laughs.

"Let's get you something to eat!"

We walk over to the tables of food. Thoren and Monica are a table away from us, but I can hear Thoren's obnoxious attempts to get Monica's attention. Her cheeks match the little red dress she's wearing and if I didn't know any better, I would think she might be upset. But I do know better. Monica is enjoying it. I smile back at Roman, who's also staring.

"Should I intervene?" He asks.

"Nah. Monica seems tough, but she's a sucker for a good time. Besides, if you only knew, this is the least of what she deserves for the shit she pulls on other people."

He huffs a laugh. "One of these days, you'll have to tell me the stories. Thoren means well, but if he gets to be too much, just let me know." My heart melts at his willingness to step in. Hardly the asshole I thought he was. "Would you like to share plates? I can hold them while you fill them up so you can try everything. The food at these things is always spectacular. If it was socially acceptable, I would take home leftovers."

I cough out a laugh that's a little too loud. Quickly, I bit my lip to keep it from escaping again. Roman's eyes glitter with mirth. With every interaction, he's surprising me, becoming more real and less a caricature of his status. Even though I respect he doesn't always sugarcoat his words or treat me with kid gloves, I love seeing this softer side of him, too. He picks up a plate in each hand, nudging them to me as if asking permission.

"Yeah, that sounds good," I say.

We stroll along the line; me piling the plates full as they sit in Roman's hands. When it doesn't appear that a single thing more can fit on them, we break from the tables, leaving behind at least half a dozen untried items. I look back longingly.

"We can always go back, you know."

Roman's deep honey voice soothes the fear of missing out, and I leave the tables behind me completely.

He leads me to an open picnic table. The wood is polished, shining a deep mahogany brown. I'd bet this table costs more than my car back home did. The thought twists at my heart as I sit on its sun-warmed surface. Roman takes the seat across from me laying the plates directly between us and scooping a piece from one of them into his mouth. His deep moan of pleasure negates everything around us, pulling through my body like a living thing, until black orbs blink open, staring directly into me.

I clear my throat and look away, digging into the food myself even if the hunger now zipping through me is not for the plate in front of me. That is, until I take a bite, leaving Roman momentarily forgotten. It's better than any I've had before, and now I understand why he kept insisting I add more. Everything is amazing. Perfect. Crisp and gooey and bursting with flavors so unexpected, I wish I could meet the chef to demand he tell me what they are.

We're quiet as we sort through the first few bites, happy to enjoy them. The sounds of the party around us filter in, but it does not break the peaceful bubble encasing us. It's refreshing to feel at home with someone new. Someone safe. Someone who will grow with me, instead of trapping me in who I've always been. I almost forgot what it was like to drop the pretenses of who you should be. It's nice.

The vibrations of the bench dipping down as someone sits beside me and Roman draws my attention. Monica's red mini dress is a beacon in the fog of her face, and I give her a smile she doesn't return. Instead, she digs into her own plate. Her eyes close in bliss and I'm not the only one who notices. My attention turns to Thoren, whose mouth falls open, watching her. He sees me and knows he's caught but just winks at me, unfazed.

He turns to Roman. "So, Roman, what do you think the odds are that we can talk these two lovely ladies into playing a game of corn hole with us?"

Roman rubs his chin as if he's seriously contemplating the possibility.

"I'm not sure T. Their attitudes make them seem tough, but I doubt their egos can handle a loss like that. Especially not publicly."

Monica tightens next to me at Roman's obvious baiting. He doesn't realize how good of a job he's doing, but if I know Monica, she'll be throwing down the gauntlet in three... two...

"You two couldn't get your bags in a hole if the fate of humanity was riding on it," she seethes.

"How would you know?" Thoren tempts.

"Oh, I can just ask any of your ex-girlfriends. I'm sure there's at least a dozen here."

Monica stands, as if to go look for them. I grab her hand, yanking her back down, enjoying seeing someone get the better of her. She scowls at me as if I am a traitor, but I've got something better up my sleeve.

"Well, if you two are so confident, how about we make a little wager on it," I say, my voice husky with the sway of a risk.

"What do you have in mind?" Roman asks.

Their eyes are trained on me, waiting.

"If we win, you two have to run naked into the ocean. Tonight."

Monica laughs outright, the lilting bells of it filling our table. Thoren smirks while Roman remains completely neutral.

"And if we win?" he asks.

"What do you want?"

He thinks, looking from Thoren to me and back. My hands pull at each other under the table. The longer he takes to think of something, the more nervous I become. Finally, he settles.

"If we win," he pulls his gaze back to me. "You both have to stay over here tonight. There are a few families who claim the guest wings, and Thoren and I just happen to have two suites."

His eyes sparkle, daring me to object or back out of the bet. But I don't. I slap my arm on the tabletop, hand outstretched. Monica snickers beside me, her game face slipping at the thought of what's coming. Roman doesn't notice or doesn't care and shakes my hand with enthusiasm.

"It looks like we have a game, my friends!" Thoren chants.

TWENTY-THREE

Victoria

THOREN POPS UP FROM the table, jogging over to an open set, sorting the bags for play. Roman insists there is a cleanup service here, so we leave behind what's left of our meal and make our way over. He walks beside me, our hands brushing easily against each other, but never meeting fully. A rush of excitement bubbles up my skin, but my eyes never leave the blonde bob bouncing in front of me.

Monogrammed initials *H. C.* shine gold on the custom boards and bean bags. The bags are not the traditional red and blue of retail store brands and instead are a deep teal and royal purple. The boys take the purple bags, handing off the teal to Monica and me.

"Purple, huh? Big Tinkie-Winkie fan?" Monica taunts.

Thoren just smirks, tilting his head down to be directly in her face.

"Purple, beautiful, is the color of kings."

Monica's eyes narrow as she lightly shoves at his chest.

"I think, *trust fund*, you mean it's the color of Jesters."

She stands to the side of the angled board and, with no fanfare, throws, perfectly sending the bag into the center hole. Thoren's mouth is agape, hand stuck in midair.

"Hey! That doesn't count! We haven't started yet," Roman says, the tinge of challenge coloring his voice.

Clearly, the Wheatley brothers are competitive. Monica just shrugs her shoulders as I pick up the bag and toss it back to her.

"That's fair. You can have that one for free. But keep your wits about you boys and let's get started!"

She winks at me, and I laugh as both the guys' faces fall, clearly suspicious of us now.

For all my clumsiness, I am fantastic at corn hole. The four of us throughout college played constantly and would often hustle poor unsuspecting frat boys for our drink money on the weekends. Throwing the silken bags here with Monica makes me feel twenty all over again. Even though Roman and Thoren can hold their own, there is no question of who is going to win.

"Roman, we've been hustled man," Thoren complains, not for the first time.

Roman chuffs back at him, concentrating on his throw. His bag makes it a quarter of the way through the hole before stopping. I sidle up next to him, my hand clamping around his shoulder.

"That was such a good throw! Honestly, I thought it was going in," I say, seriously.

He tilts his head toward me, a strained smile in place. I can tell everything in his competitive spirit wants to rally around this loss and yet he fights with the fact that it's me and Monica he'd be rallying against. Even though it's not funny, I can't help but want to laugh.

"Honestly, how did you get so good at this?" he asks astounded.

I shrug. "Years of tricking boys just like you, just like this."

"Not *just* like this, I hope," he says, closing his arms around me.

My mouth tilts up in a taunting smirk as I shrug my shoulders, unwilling to give him the reassurance he's asking for. His eyes narrow and he pinches my sides causing the hum of laughter to swell out of me as I twirl to get away from his attack. I dance away and wink, before letting him scoop my hands back up into his.

"The two of you are trouble," he says.

"I second that thought," Thoren yells, eavesdropping.

Monica throws her head back with an ease that's so unlike her it leaves me entranced by her joy.

"You have no idea," she adds.

The loud ringing trill of a phone goes off, Roman fumbling in his pocket to make it stop.

"Hey man, are you *trying* to sabotage us? Wait to have your phone ring until it's one of the girls throwing," Thoren says.

"Sorry, sorry. I've been waiting for a call." He looks at the screen then back to me. "I have to take this."

I nod. He immediately answers with *this is Roman* before wandering off toward the house. I look after him until he disappears inside, then focus to my friends behind me.

"Looks like we're stuck," I announce.

Monica snorts. "Honestly, we didn't need to finish, anyway. We all know who was going to win."

Thoren protests that they could have made a comeback, arguing that there's no way Monica and I have won fairly when we didn't even finish the game. They're both so engrossed in their play fighting over the validity of the bet that I feel invisible. I don't want to insert myself into their conversation and mess up the vibe Monica has unsuccessfully been trying all day to deny.

"I'm just going to get some food while we wait," I throw over my shoulder as I walk back toward the now picked over meal, neither of them seeming to hear me.

From the tables, I pop random bits of food into my mouth, sure by the sideways glances I'm getting, it might be inappropriate. But right now between trying to kill time until Roman gets back without having to talk to anyone and keeping the nervous energy about *who* he could be talking to, this looks to be my best option. Besides, mostly the area has cleared out, party goers instead opting for the beach, the pool, or the lawn.

There are maybe a hundred people present, which I'm sure will grow as the night goes on. Everyone is familiar with each other, leaving me the odd one out of the conversation, if not stares. I grab for some sort of jalapeno kebab, curious about what was taking Roman so long, when a lanky redhead swishes up next to me. She reaches over me to grab the kebab spear first. Her long delicate arms easily beat me out.

"You must be the writer," she says in greeting.

My skin prickles at her tone, her words heavy with judgment.

"I am a writer. But *the* writer? I'm not sure I can own to that," I say, my friendly tone not quite convincing.

She huffs out a laugh like one would cigarette smoke.

"Honey, anyone that shows up with a Wheatley is *the* one." She eyes where Thoren and Monica are. "Unless, of course, it's that brother. You're just one of many if you show up with him." Her nose swivels high in the air.

I've dealt with people like this before. Rarely has it worked in my favor and with the setting I'm currently in, I think my track record won't be broken tonight. I let the drive to defend my friends shimmer. Being here makes me weary of my words, so I swallow any comeback I might have, choosing instead to excuse myself before I say something I can't take back.

"Good to know. It was nice…"

She doesn't let me finish. "So, are you saying you and Roman are an item? I find that hard to believe."

My head jerks back in disbelief and irritation. I am not having this conversation. Not here, not now.

"Obviously, you don't, otherwise you wouldn't be here worrying and prying at the new girl, having a completely inappropriate conversation with someone you just met," I say, backing away. "Now, as lovely as this has been, I have someone waiting on me."

I don't give her the chance to respond. My steps are quick but confident, unwilling to give her the satisfaction of knowing she rattled me. Or that I have nowhere else to be. The shadow of the open house falls over me and I decide it's time to find Roman. Even if he's still on the phone, it'll be better to wait there than take the chance of being peppered with questions outside again.

Inside, there are a few people milling about, drinks in hand. Conversations are low-toned and serious, more business than casual. All except one. A commanding voice comes from the room down the hall. There's no attendant outside of it like the others and the door is ajar, light shining from inside it. I step up to it as Roman speaks curtly into his phone.

"I don't care. No excuses. This shouldn't have happened. Someone should have talked to me before the paperwork was filed. You can't just change my entire life whenever and however you feel like it!"

A heady silence fills the room as he listens to the other side of the line. I push forward to hear better, my face directly against the crack in the door. If Roman turns at all, he'll see me.

"It isn't some fucking girl," he yells as he spins on his heel.

I jolt backward at the aggression on his face and we both startle at being caught by the other. I am stepping away from the door, turning to go back to the party, when I hear him say *this isn't over*. His footsteps are behind me before his hand is on my hip, spinning me back to him. He doesn't know what to say, his eyes searching me as if the words could be written somewhere on my skin.

"What was that about?" I ask worrying it might have something to do with me.

He sighs. "Quin. He has some business contracts we're dealing with. They... well, they want to take me out of LA. Which is a good thing, but... you and me. We're just beginning to figure this out."

He's leaving. That's why he doesn't want to tell me. They're filming somewhere else. Somewhere I'm not. It's not as if the screenwriters are always this involved. I should feel lucky I'd gotten this much time with him.

My heart feels like it's shattering into pieces, which cannot possibly be right, since this is nothing compared to my dreams. Sell a script. That's what mattered. Not an elongated, not-even, one-night stand. A few stolen kisses. Everything will be alright even if he leaves. It doesn't mean everything is over again. I'm not sure what he sees, but his arms wrap tight around me, and he leans down to whisper in my ear.

"I'm figuring it out, Five. This is a beginning, not an ending. I want to see where this goes, too. Trust me."

His heart thumps against my cheek and I inhale his vetiver scent. His confession was enough to allow him to hold my hope in his hands a little longer. *This isn't an ending,* I repeat to myself as my head bobs against his lips. *OK,* my body says. *I'll trust you.* He plants a kiss into my hair at my answer. It's intimate and sweet, two things that are slowly weaving their way into Roman Wheatley. As if this version of him is just for me. For *us.*

I step back a fraction to look up into his face. He gently guides a loose strand of hair behind my ear, watching himself stroke the strands. I desperately want to lean up and kiss him, but the redhead's words drift in, squashing the thought. I'd rather save those moments from her, or anyone else here's, scrutiny.

"What now?" I ask.

He smiles softly at me, catching my eyes. "Now, I think we have a game to finish."

I laugh. "You mean you have one to lose?"

He laughs too; the competitiveness drifting away by our closeness.

"Yeah, something like that."

He snags my hand, leading me back out to the party. I drop it as we get to the open doors, aware of all the eyes on us now more than ever. He lets me with only an eyebrow raise. By the time we make it back to the game, another group has taken up residence and is playing. Roman spots Monica and Thoren snacking at a nearby picnic table and leads the way over to them.

"Hey guys! Way to guard the game," Roman says.

"Someone," Thoren points directly at Roman, "took too long."

"It doesn't really matter. We all know who lost here," Monica chimes in.

Both boys look displeased, almost offended at the statement. I jump in.

"Don't be sore losers. You Wheatleys don't want to be known for welching on bets, do you?"

The boys look at each other, shrug.

"Best two out of three?" Thoren asks.

Monica shakes her head, laughing. "No way. Pay up!"

Roman moves towards the pathway that leads to the beach, a slog he's playing up as if he's on his way to the gallows. The sun is setting, orange and pinks lighting his frame as he goes. Slumped, he turns to Thoren and says, "A deal's a deal, T."

Thoren gets up from the table, mirroring Roman like a shadow. Monica and I take up the rear, giggling to each other.

"Dead men walking!" Monica whisper-shouts behind them.

I swear I hear their own snorts of laughter, but neither turns around. Chaotic beach grass waves and slaps at our calves, sand kicking up around every step. The lawn disappears behind beach dunes; the path winding through brush and driftwood, leading us to the water. We step off the path into the hot, sifting sand, the entire landscape flattening out in front of us. It spreads to the sides of my feet, threatening to sink me. I pull off my sandals and see Monica doing the same. The dry grains are ragged against my soles, and I wiggle my toes in deeper to the damp chill beneath.

The beach is empty. Only a few families and a group of teens are brave enough to take advantage of the space. They sit off to our right with umbrellas and lounge chairs, watching children run and scream into the crashing waves. Roman veers left. Only two people sit on this side using a large log as a bench. We pass by them and continue to the farthest point we can while still having the pathway in view.

"Alright. You two have passed by all the people and now are far enough away that no one but us will see your Little Willies," Monica says, eyes gleaming mischievously.

"You are about to be surprised, beautiful. There's nothing little about this willy," Thoren jokes.

Roman rolls his eyes. "I cannot be here for this, standing between the two of you. It is wrong on so many levels."

Monica shrugs. "Feels right in a lot of ways, Roman. Maybe it's just the winner in me, but it *feels right*."

I laugh at both of them. The sun and sand feel so good that I don't want to be left out of dipping my toes into the ocean—even if I'm clothed. I pull off my sundress to reveal the metallic blue bathing suit beneath.

"What are you doing, Vip? We won!" Monica moans.

I throw my dress into her face. "Yeah, we did! But it's hot and I'm sweaty and just look at that view! Doesn't it make you want to take a dip?"

Both boys smile at each other before they strip down to their swim trunks that very much resemble boxer-briefs to me. The fabric stretches against Roman's thighs, putting his legs and backside on full display, and suddenly, everyone else disappears. They're navy blue with small waves stitched into the seams that I adore; my eyes moving with the ebbs and flows of the thread. He pulls my attention away with the yank of his shirt revealing tight, toned skin, just barely touched by the sun. His chest is awash with dark, finely curled hair, making my hands twitch with the need to run them through it.

His muscles ripple, skin puckering under my gaze. I realize he's stopped moving and I look up to see that I've been caught. We stare at each other, neither one of us moving, as the air around us cackles with the sudden need to have hands all over each other.

"Get a fucking room!" Monica shouts before taking off toward the water.

"Hey! Don't leave me with them," Thoren shouts after her and they're gone.

We don't chuckle or acknowledge them. I should be embarrassed but right now all I have room to feel is pure, unfiltered want. He holds his hand for mine and it is not nearly enough.

"Shall we?"

I take it, twining my fingers into his. He pulls me to him, covering his mouth over mine like lightning. I don't have enough time to comprehend the kiss, let alone truly enjoy it, when he pulls me into a sprint toward the ocean. My breath is pulled from my lungs, cheeks burning with the force of my happiness. The water hits my legs, and I gasp out in delight. Thoren picks Monica up, legs in his arms, as she kicks out to get him to release her.

"Don't you dare!" she screams before he drops her into the ocean.

"They are so cute," I whisper to Roman.

His eyebrows shoot up, and immediately I try to run. He's too fast, grabbing me and dunking me under. The chill of the water stealing whatever thoughts I had held. I pop up for air.

"Oh, you're dead. Do you hear me, Roman? DEAD."

His laughter makes me feel anything but.

Our walk back to the party is slow and sloppy. We are all wrung out by the salt and the sand, the ocean's scent thick on our skin. Beach grass cuts at our exposed skin, but none of us can bother to care. Clothes are haphazardly hung, sticking to bathing suits that are still wet. Thankfully, it's dark enough that no one can see the mess that I'm sure my makeup is or the frizz my hair is turning into. At least until we get to the lawn where lights are strung, and a fire is lit, providing a bright glow to the night.

Roman keeps checking his phone, the frown on his face deepening with every glance. I already miss the smooth spot between his eyebrows that appears when he stands, eyes-closed, letting the water lap at his chest. He sees me staring and pockets the phone, but the damage is already done. Thoughts of him leaving take root in the places only passion had been moments before. Like the shifting of sand, we're different now.

"I can't believe how late it's gotten," Roman says as we get closer to the house.

He's rubbing at the back of his neck, and I know he's reaching for a way to say goodbye. I think Monica senses it too and is more than happy to help him along.

"Yeah, I have an early morning tomorrow with work and all. You about ready to head out, Vip?" she asks.

I'm not. I don't want this night to ever end. But how do I say that when it's clear both Roman and Monica do?

"Sure. I have a meeting in the morning, anyway. Might as well get some shuteye," I say.

The tone is somber, all the electricity faded out by reality, as Monica collects her bag, and we make our way to the valet. My heart aches, unsure how much time we have left and not wanting to waste it. As Monica searches out the valet to get our car, I lean into Roman.

"You know, it doesn't have to end. I know we didn't lose, but if you're still up for company tonight..." I let the offer hang in the air.

Roman's eyes blow out to full on black. He bites at the inside of his cheek as he studies me. Then he turns away.

"I wish I could Five. You have no idea how badly I wish you could stay, but…"

"But you can't." I finish.

I am humiliated by my eagerness. I thought we were finally on the same page, but I was wrong. His hands shrug off as I step back.

"It's fine, really. I'll just… talk to you later."

Monica's car pulls up, saving me from this dumpster fire of a conversation. I move completely away from Roman, feeling numb. He beats me to the car door and opens it, leaning in before I can sidestep my way into the front seat. He wraps me in his arms, and it makes me want to burst into tears, or hide for the next century, or anything that would suffocate this open vulnerability.

"I will text you tonight and I'd like to see you tomorrow," he says.

"Ok," I say, slipping out of his arms.

He lets me go and closes the door softly behind me.

"Bye, Roman!" Monica waves before taking off, leaving him standing in the driveway behind us.

She looks at me, no doubt seeing the stricken look of someone who's been overexposed. She grips her steering wheel, continuing to glance my way.

"What did the bastard do to you?" she asks.

Nothing. And that's the problem.

TWENTY-FOUR

Victoria

ROMAN TEXTS BEFORE I'VE even made it home and continues texting me until I fall asleep around one o'clock in the morning. At first, I was determined not to answer, but after the fifth message, I caved. He not only apologized, but he told me all the ways he would make it up to me, causing the knots in my heart to unravel and bloom. *Trust me*, he'd said. And I wanted to. So instead of crafting stories and reasons why this wouldn't work, I let myself have a beginning.

When? I asked.

Soon, he texted back.

And soon couldn't come fast enough. My mind ached for it. I play over the conversation in my head all the way to my meeting at the studio. The Uber takes longer than usual, but thankfully I arrive with plenty of time to spare. I give my name to the receptionist as I walk in.

"Oh, Miss Pencheske, you can go right into the conference room. Mr. Beckson will be in there shortly. I'll page him now," she tells me.

I give my thanks and make my way upstairs, familiar with this routine by now. The conference room motion lights come to life as I get closer. I'm just about to go in when the voice I've secretly been listening for, the one I dreamed about all last night, floats down the hall. I may not recognize his face, but with his presence fresh in my mind, I could pick up on his voice anywhere.

He's angry, the thick honey sound turning to tar in warning. He's not yelling, but his strong booming voice makes me sorry for whoever it's currently aimed at. I sneak a peek inside the office, feeling guilty that I'm openly eavesdropping on him twice in as many days, but not enough to stop.

Inside, the men have their backs turned to me, a conference phone between them and a projection screen in front. One has features that are dark, a tone of authority coming out with his words. *Roman*. The other, I look down to catch a gregarious gold pinky ring dangling from his finger. *Beckson*. There's a third man that I can't recognize sitting on the other side of the room, who I decide to ignore.

Roman stops speaking long enough for the conference call to crackle to life.

"What Roman is trying to say is that you will make more in the long term with this deal we're offering. You'll get another contract, and you can stay in line with the plans you've already agreed to before the new documents were filed," it says.

Beckson shakes his head.

"No dice. We already bought the rights. The minute you sent that paperwork over your firm should have known we'd be under direct recommendation to comply. We're not in the business of losing money, boys. We can't just change things and open ourselves up to lawsuits. No matter how *honorable* you think you're being."

"What if I sign a liability form? What if I take the ability to sue out?" Roman asks.

"Roman," the speaker cuts in warning.

"No! If that's what they want, Quin, that's what I'll do."

Beckson turns in his chair to look at Roman directly.

"Look, I told you. This was your last shot. Dreamaway is done with your drama. You want to come in here with your high-powered lawyers and do whatever you want, but that's not how this works. I think you could sign a hundred forms and contracts, and they'd still say no. And this little stunt you pulled to get the script you were working on scrapped, and the documentary slipped in... well, no one upstairs is happy with you. No one wants to work with you anymore."

The script you scrapped. The words repeat, getting louder and louder in my head each time I hear them, gut dropping with every word. It would be my script. I'm the script that was scrapped. This wasn't a meeting to get paid. This was one to *fire* me.

"It's my script," I say, forgetting where I am.

Everyone in the room turns to me. I stare blindly at each of their faces, then double down.

"It's my fucking script that's scrapped!" I yell.

Roman snaps out of the shock of seeing me jumping up from his seat. I stop him in his tracks.

"Don't you fucking dare."

My tears swell, heart shattering into a million pieces at his feet. It's the last thing I want to do; to cry in front of them, but I have no control. I've lost response from my body.

"Who's that?" Quin asks from the speaker.

No one answers him, the silence hanging us all. I turn to Beckson, wanting nothing more than to ignore Roman entirely.

"Is it true? Are you firing me?" I ask him.

Beckson nods, eyes sad. "Sorry sweetheart. I was going to tell you at our meeting today. I just found out myself. It's not a firing; we're just passing on this script. But you bring me your next one and I promise I'll read..."

I turn and bolt from the door before he can finish. There's nothing anyone in that room could say to me to make this better. To fix what has been destroyed. Any thought of professionalism is out the door along with me.

I can feel Roman's steps more than hear them, the sound of the world taking on a dull shape in my ears. He pulls at my arm, turning me and I immediately rip from his hands.

"Victoria, wait. I can explain what's happening. Just... wait," he pleads.

"Is this why you wouldn't sleep with me last night? Too consumed by your guilt." I yell. "Maybe I should thank you for being so fucking *noble*."

It shouldn't be what I'm focused on, but with the embarrassment from his refusal fresh and the gut-wrenching news, it's the first thing I can think to say. It's the least of the evils that I have the capacity to accept.

"I... I..." He stumbles.

"You couldn't fuck me two ways, Roman. Is that what this is? Roman Wheatley living up to his reputation, everyone. "

People come out of their offices, leaning into the hall to see what is going on. Two men from the office I just left are standing behind Roman, arms crossed, and pity etched into every crevice of their backstabbing faces. I turn my focus from them, disgusted by myself as much as I am with anyone in this building. Anyone but the person right in front of me. I direct all my anger to him.

He stumbles back when my eyes meet his before he hardens his stance.

"I can explain all of this. It isn't what it sounds like. I am finding a way..."

I slice my hand through the air between us.

"Just stop. You and me? We're done. In every *possible* way. There's nothing to find a way for. I don't need you. Not as my friend. Not as whatever the fuck this was. And I certainly don't need you to sell my script." I breathe in deep, finding every scrap of confidence and dignity I have left. "Don't call me. Don't look for me. I want nothing more to do with you."

If this were a scene in one of my scripts, the main character might turn back. She might look at the mess of a man she's leaving and see that he's falling to pieces, too. She might suck in her tears to appear strong, giving him the goodbye glance she'll need to make it through. Only, in my script, it wouldn't be goodbye.

She would pull that memory out and see it anew. She'd find all the heartbreak and love that she let slip through her fingers when she was too busy turning into her fears. Forgiveness would find her, in a day, a month, or a year. The audience would know her story doesn't end in pieces.

But this isn't a fucking script, and I can't take any more. My dreams have been trampled in this hall. My tears don't reign in; I couldn't make them if I tried. They carry with them the poison my heart is so desperately trying to purge, stinging my cheeks as they fall. I turn, the sound of the fragile fragments of my soul-shattering as I do. For my dream. For the hope of what this was. But I don't turn back. I can't.

The heartbreak Roman questioned me feeling so freely blooms to life, and the irony is not lost on me. So, I run. I run from the script I've passionately written. I run from the studio that's been stuck to my dream board for years. I run from the man I have unwillingly but fiercely wanted. Who I thought I could finally fall in love with. And through all the chaos in my mind, through the pain laced with fear and devastation, all I can think of is Roman asking me to trust him that this wasn't the end.

TWENTY-FIVE

Roman

THREE WEEKS.

It's been three weeks since Victoria broke to pieces. Since she ripped out my heart and scattered it in the hallways of Dreamaway. Three weeks where I've been trying to make things right. While I'm very close to finding a way to clean up the mess of our careers, I'm not sure I'm any closer to getting her back.

"Are you sure you want to do this, Roman? It could ruin you," Quin says on the other end of the phone.

I'm already ruined.

"What if I just give you a day or two to think it over? Make sure it's what you want before we do something we can't reverse. Two days, max," he pleads.

"Okay," I relent. "Two days."

I hang up the phone and immediately hit speed dial. *You've reached Victoria. Leave your name and number and I'll get back to you.* I disconnect before the beep blares in my ear. I throw my phone to the other end of the couch, flopping my head back onto the cushions. The light from the windows blazes into my eyelids and I live in the spots that dance across my vision.

I'm sure by now she's blocked my number, but I can't stop myself from trying. Maybe Quinten's right. Even if I could somehow get Victoria to listen, I'm not sure it will make a difference. At least right now, with my career, I'll be able to put all of this behind me after the documentary. But if I do this fix and she still says no? I'll be stuck in this hellhole without her.

"You look... rough."

Thoren's voice breaks through my thoughts and I open my eyes into the sun.

"*Fuck,*" I whisper at the pain before covering my face with my hand and sitting up.

Thoren stands in front of me in one of his best suits, done up to the nines for his day. His hair is freshly cut, almond shoes shined, and tie perfectly knotted.

"Where are you off to?" I ask.

"Out," he says as he fixes invisible imperfections in the window. "You should do something about that."

"About what?"

He gestures to the whole of me, eyes not missing the beard that's a little too grown in and the three-day-old sweats.

"I know you're dealing with work remotely, but you can't let yourself go like this. It isn't you, Roman. I've never in our lives seen... this," he says.

I sigh, knowing he's right. I get up from the couch, deciding the least I can do now is shower, but he stops me before I get past the couch.

"It isn't like you to just sit around and wait either, brother. Anytime you've ever wanted anything, regardless of what our family or our father thought, you went out and *got it*. You're the most fearless, determined person I know. Even when you buried your head in the sand after Lauren, I knew you'd come out of it. Just like I know, you'll come out of this."

He's looking at me like the six-year-old kid who begged me to teach him to hit a baseball, all bright hazel eyes and admiration. It tugs at my unhealed chest painfully.

"And look at where that's gotten me, Thoren. Dad thinks I'm a disappointment. Lauren and I broke off our engagement. The world thinks I'm a joke." My throat closes at what I have to say next, but I can't stop now. "And she's *gone*. I don't think I'll get out this time. I'm not sure I deserve to."

I once told Victoria what I thought heartbreak felt like. And I was so fucking naïve. So, completely and utterly, wrong. I could never put this into words.

There is no feeling better. There are no moments of possibility. I'm trapped in a windowless room of all my failures and every regret. Stuck in knowing that the only person to blame is me. I could have had everything and instead, I chose this. Purgatory be thy name.

Thoren grabs me by the shoulder, forcing me to face him.

"Don't go there. I see you torturing yourself and I cannot take it any longer. Did you fuck up? Yes. Yeah, of course you fucking did. You could have made different decisions. Maybe things would have turned out differently. Maybe not. But you didn't and you can't change that. What you can change is this piss poor attitude you're carrying around."

He shoves his forehead to mine, and I close my eyes instinctively. His breath burns across my cheeks and lids as he continues.

"We're all fucked up, Roman. You. Me. Dad. Even Victoria, God love her. Everyone makes mistakes. But you deserve to be happy. You deserve to feel and be and receive love. And we both know that girl loves you. The real, angry, closed off, sweet as a fucking kitten, spiky as a damn urchin, **you**. She deserves to see this filthy thing you have growing on your face and your stinky ass clothes because you're heartbroken, too. As much as you deserve to be loved, she deserves it, too."

He throws my head away from his by the back of my neck, and we stand square, staring at each other.

"I, on the other hand, do not deserve it. So, take a fucking shower, get dressed, and go fucking get her."

He doesn't give me a chance to respond. He's striding to the door, slipping his keys off the hook, and he's out without the slightest hesitation. I look after him, wondering when in the hell my baby brother got so smart. I stand there for a few more moments digesting everything he said.

He's right about all of it. If there's even a chance that Victoria's heart is breaking like mine, she deserves to know she isn't alone. I force my body into my standard routine before everything fell apart, getting my razor and towels ready. In the mirror, I see someone I hardly recognize and pray that she isn't doing the same. I'm not worthy enough to be the reason she's in pain. I promise to myself to do everything I can to change that. No one will love her like I will. I can only hope that everything I'm doing will prove that.

I pick up my discarded phone from the couch. It only takes one ring before the other end picks up.

"I don't need two days. Do it now, Quin. It's what I want. It's *all* I want. Make it happen. The contract should be in my inbox no later than tonight."

I hang up the phone without waiting for a response, knowing how pissed Quin will be, but not caring. It's time to make things right. My pride be damned.

I'm coming for you, Five.

TWENTY-SIX

Victoria

The fresh air outside of the courthouse licks at the sweat that's been building on my neck. *I shouldn't have worn white.* I think for the millionth time. All my clothes are in storage or at Monica's, except for the few I packed when I fled. I didn't expect to be here this long, but Trent wasn't lying to me when he said his lawyer thought they had a good case. Thankfully, not good enough.

"The paperwork will go through in the next week and then he'll be required to come up with your half of the house value or sell. It should be smooth sailing from here, Victoria," my lawyer says next to me.

I force a small smile for her, which my lips barely agree to.

"Thanks for everything, Dana. I really appreciate you dealing with this last minute."

She's nodding her head as she walks away from me toward her car.

"Please, it was a pleasure. I can't believe he even tried this. Call me if anything else comes up."

She waves goodbye, which I reciprocate as I start down the steps after her to my car.

"I don't know how you've always been so lucky, Vicky," a voice comes from behind me. "Ever since I've known you you've just had this way of making things happen. Of getting everything you want."

I turn toward him. "This isn't luck, Trent. We had already agreed to this. When we got married, we agreed to share our lives and when we got divorced, we agreed to split them."

Trent's chin falls to his chest in defeat.

"I thought it was til' death do us part? I never agreed to lose you, Vicky."

He slides down the stairs without a backward glance my way. Still, I whisper, if only to myself, "I didn't agree to lose me either."

The courthouse is about thirty minutes away from Katie's, where I'm staying while I'm here, but I don't feel like going back just yet. Seeing Katie's kids has been a balm to my soul, but even their cheerful faces can't patch up what's broken in me. My friends have helped keep the darkest moments at bay, making me wonder what happens when I go back.

Maybe I just stay.

It isn't the first time the thought has crossed my mind. With the money from the house, I can afford a nice enough apartment for a while before I need to land my next gig. In the meantime, I can always submit my work online. I don't need to be in LA to follow my dream.

I can almost make myself believe the lie, but the truth is funny that way. It can twist to try and fit into what makes you comfortable until it's no longer what you wanted at all. By the time you realize that, though, it's usually too late. I did that. I let it bend around a life that wasn't really mine for ten years before I figured it out. Am I really willing to lose another ten and hope I'm wrong this time?

I'm no closer to an answer than I was yesterday, or the day before.

I see the sign for Grocer Save and veer off, deciding to pick up a few snacks and staples for the Monson family for letting me stay with them for so long. The parking lot is full. I have to drive around twice to find a spot, but I'm determined not to be any more of a burden. Buying a few groceries is the least I can do.

I snag a small cart out front and beeline it to the snack aisle. I try to avoid looking too long or giving anyone the impression I'm noticing them, for fear we know each other. Being faceblind has few perks, but one of them is unknowingly snubbing someone when you actually don't want to be bothered. You can always tell them you didn't notice them and mean it. The problem with being back home is that a lot of friends know this about me and, therefore, will approach me without hesitation or doubt. So, giving off aloof, in a hurry, vibes are my only shot at missing an interaction.

My luck runs out as I'm sorting through the macaroni and cheese aisle.

"Vicky Penchescke. I should have figured you'd be back."

The woman who addresses me is a short blonde with a voice that tickles the back of my mind. Déjà vu hits with a vengeance, but I can't picture the memory clearly enough to know why it's familiar.

"Hi. It's me! And I'm not *really* back, back," I say. "I'm sorry, but I've got somewhere I need to be."

I try to be polite but firm. She doesn't care about that either.

"You're not back, back, *yet*. You will be. I mean, I'm the idiot who thought I could get between you two. Who thought she had something real. But I should have listened. Everyone told me you two had too much history. That you were his first love. But it felt like bullshit. If you two were so perfect, why would he give in to me?"

For a split second, I think she's talking about Roman. After all, who else is there? Then an inky, sick feeling crawls up my stomach and into my throat. I know the person in front of me now and it's the last girl I wanted to run into. Rebecka's eyes fill with angry tears that she swats at. Her pink sweatshirt turning dark with the mascara she wipes away.

"Rebecka, it isn't like that at all. Trent and I are not together. I don't know what you heard," I try.

"Yet. You're not together yet. But you will be. Like he said when he dumped me, you are *perfect* for each other."

I feel so much sympathy for the woman standing in front of me. If she only knew that perfect doesn't exist. That it's an image made up by people too scared to find the things that matter. That being palatable is never better than being real. I want her to know that there's someone out there who will see her, push her, in a way that doesn't feel like she's checking off a box, but that the box itself doesn't exist.

Instead, I rest my hand lightly on her shoulder, steadying her as our eyes connect.

"You deserve so much better than him," I say.

Her tears glisten and I think she might break down right here in aisle seven. Somehow, she snaps herself out of it and shakes me off.

"Fuck you, Vicky," she squeals before walking off, head held high.

Stunned, I watch as she goes, unsure what I'm supposed to do now. Finally, I decide the best thing I can do is leave my cart and head straight to my car, my arms empty. I sit there, unable to start it and drive off. Unable to do anything but cry. The tears stream freely, and I can feel the goopy mess they're creating with my makeup.

Every part of me wants to find Rebecka and force her to listen to me, to understand that Trent and I will never be together again. That she wouldn't want to be with him, either and that perfect is overrated. That when he cheated on me with her, I didn't even feel it. I couldn't break down because nothing had been built up to begin with. We didn't work because we were meant to be; we worked because I was scared to go after anything else. We worked because I could suppress and settle. And I couldn't do that anymore. I couldn't do that ever again.

I pull myself together enough to drive to Katie's. I make it in the door, the rambunctious screams from the kids filling my ears. They each race by me, slowing only enough to hug around my legs and waist before dashing back off. Blissful and absorbed in their lives as they are, they don't notice the tear tracks as I kiss them on their heads. I dart into the room, hoping I've missed the roving eye of Katie. I should know better. A knock rings on my door.

"Can I come in?" she asks.

Directly on the other side, my hand still holds it closed between us.

"I just need a bit. I'm okay, I promise," I whisper, hoping she'll hear my need.

"Okay, Vip. But if you need me, you can come out here or text me or anything. I'll come. Whenever."

I release the breath that I'm holding as she pads away. I run to the bed, curling myself up in its covers, letting loose every pain and fear in my heart, knowing what I want but having it be completely out of reach.

My bed sinks down, a hand coming up to cup my face. Leaning into it, I stretch awake, feeling puffy and with the sharp sting of a headache that's coming my way. I hate crying and the fact that I've done so much of it in the last few weeks irritates me. My eyes lock on the person holding me's face, a blond bob throwing me off from who I expected it to be.

"It's Mon, babe. How are you doing?" she asks.

"Monica? What are you doing here?"

The grog and disoriented sleep from crying exhaustion is making it hard for me to grip reality. Monica doesn't come home randomly. We practically have to drag her here.

"I'm here for you. It's time to come home, bitch," she coos, so unlike her normally rigid self.

"I'm dreaming. You can't take me home. I'm already home. And you wouldn't come here just to drag me to LA."

I close my eyes again and snuggle up into my pillow, sure that I'll wake up and she'll be gone. Instead, the bed sinks deeper and more voices appear.

"I told you it was dire. She needs an intervention, girls. I can start. I've written this letter..."

"WAKE UP, BITCH!" Monica yells, shaking me wildly, all sweetness gone.

I immediately shoot my head up only to smack it against something hard, a thick WAP ringing out.

"OUCH! What the fuck!" I scream, grabbing at my forehead.

"THAT'S WHAT I'M SAYING VIP! That hurt!" Monica yells, holding her collarbone.

"Okay, you two, settle down. Everyone alright?" Katie's sweet voice breaks in.

"I'm doing great, never better! Is that a new candle, Katie?" Cherie says.

Monica and I glare daggers at Cherie, who just smiles innocently. She is fooling no one. Monica turns her glare to me, rubbing at her neck and chest.

"Get your shit. We're leaving," she says with no wiggle room.

"What? Now?" I ask, confused.

"Yes. It's obvious you're wallowing and we," she points to the surrounding circle, "will no longer enable this behavior. This isn't home, Vip. Not right now. Home is LA where your dreams are fucking waiting. So, get packing and let's catch a flight."

She's already getting off the bed. I grab her and pull her back down.

"Wait, wait, wait. What time is it even? It has to be late."

My mind is still trying to catch up.

"It's eleven thirty and if we get moving, we can catch a red eye and not sit in the airport for hours. Let's. Go."

I know it's the wrong thing to do, but I can't help it. I laugh. Full on, snort-through-my-nose, laugh. My heart and lungs and ribs rack together in a pain that feels so, so good. I laugh until the tears come, the only ones that belong on my cheeks, and my breath runs short.

"We've lost her. You cracked the fragile little egg, Mon. Congratulations! You want to pull a *Taken* now or some shit and stuff her in a suitcase or something?" Cherie asks.

"I didn't do this! You two let her be comfortable for too long. This is on *you*." Monica is sticking her finger in Cherie's face in accusation.

"Oh, hell no. Get your dragon claw out of my face!" Cherie yells.

Katie puts a hand on both of their faces and shoves them away from each other. My laugh dries up, the smile fading but not completely disappearing.

"Guys, stop. I'm not cracked." I take in a deep breath. "I know I can't stay, and I know I have to go back. Even though it hurts."

My eyes water and Katie can't help but pull me in.

"It's going to be okay, Vip."

"I know." I wipe at my eyes. "I really don't even know why I'm crying so much. So, they passed on my script. It happens all the time to every writer ever. I should be excited to be part of the professional's club."

I sniffle, hoping to stop the leak from my nose. The three of them look back and forth from each other, before Monica settles on me like I just said drinking coffee is a personality type.

"You are seriously going to lie to yourself that hard right now?" she says.

"Mon," Katie warns.

To my surprise, Cherie comes to Monica's defense.

"Nah, Katie. It needs to be said."

She looks to Monica, waving her hands out.

"Proceed."

"You are in love with Roman Wheatley, and he broke your heart," Monica says, no inflection in her tone.

"No, no Mon. That's crazy. I liked him, sure, but my script is all that matters," I plead.

Cherie looks at me. "It does matter and maybe it started out that way, but all of us know that's not true anymore. You light up for that man, Vip."

"And we're sorry he royally messed up. Believe me, it is on the top of all our lists to kill him, but in the meantime, you've got to recognize what you're grieving for so you can move on." Katie says.

They all look at me expectantly. I try to wrestle my feelings back into the lockbox I've been pushing them in, but they refuse. My heart thumps with terror, a shiver of panic threatening to pull me under. The thought of sixth grade Jimmy Parker flashes through me. Of how we sat in a circle just like this when he asked Jennifer P. to the Friday night dance and how I promised these girls that I'd love him forever, no matter what. I haven't thought about him since he moved the next year and something about that realization breaks me all over.

"What if I don't want to?" I whisper.

The thought of forgetting Roman tears at something deep. I don't know if I can ever forgive him, but I cannot imagine never remembering. Everything I write about, everything I've imagined feeling, intensified in reality. He's the only one who got that. The girls all look at me with the same look of pity they used when I confessed my undying love for Jimmy.

"Maybe not now, but when you're ready to, you can. We'll be here." Katie says.

I nod, head hanging down. I concentrate on breathing. *In. Out.* Holding in everything I don't understand and don't want to feel.

"We'll go back, Monica. But can you give me until Friday? Let's just spend two days together, like the old times. I'm sure Katie won't mind a slumber party," I plead.

Katie shakes her head. "Not at all. You're all welcome to stay as long as you'd like."

Monica rolls her eyes. "Fine. If that'll make you happy and willing to get on a plane with me, I'll do it. I can't afford another flag from TSA, anyway."

I snort. "Fine, it's settled."

"Hey! I didn't agree," Cherie interjects.

"No one asked you," Monica responds.

Katie doesn't have time to play referee as Cherie slams a pillow straight at Monica's face and then all hell breaks loose as swears, laughs, and fluff explode into the room.

TWENTY-SEVEN

Roman / Victoria

"Thoren, just call her please. I know you have her number, and I don't know where I'm going. If you do not call her and text me in the next five minutes, I'm going to paint your favorite car yellow."

He gasps in my ear, clearly enjoying this.

"You wouldn't. You know how much I hate that color! Fine," he relents. "I'll call her. And Roman? She's going to forgive you."

He hangs up the phone, and I breathe out. *I sure fucking hope so.* The airport bustles with people, unusually busy for a Thursday morning. I make my way through baggage claim to the rentals desk to pick up my car for the next few days. The keys jingle in my hand nervously, as I try to pay attention as we check the car for any scratches, but honestly, I couldn't care less. As soon as the guy gives me the go ahead, I jump behind the wheel, hooking up my Bluetooth to the radio.

A notification on my phone goes off almost immediately. Thoren with an address and a peach emoji. It dings again, *Go get 'em tiger*. Gee, thanks, bro. I don't respond to his antics, instead I set up the GPS and floor it. The car roars to life and I hate to admit that Thoren was right choosing a sports car. I don't want to waste a second more than I have to getting where I need to be. I've waited long enough.

The car eats up the road and I'm outside the house in what both feels too soon and too long. I haven't felt this nervous since the first time I told my father I wanted to be a director. How long ago that feels. How juvenile. All the things I've had to do since, without my father's permission or approval, would make younger me die from shock. Just the things this week would be enough to cause it. But older me couldn't care less.

Monica stands in the yard waiting for me. She has tucked her blonde bob behind her ears and is wearing relaxed-fit jeans. If I didn't know better, I would think she belonged here. My fingers itch to take a picture to send to Thoren, but I don't want to test my luck or her patience. It's a pleasant distraction from the nerves doing a river dance on my insides. *Today is not the day.* I store the memory away for later to tease my baby brother with endlessly.

"You've got real balls showing up here, Wheatley." She says, walking right up to me before I can take too many steps from the car.

"I know, but Monica, I swear I'm trying to make it up to her. That's why I'm here," I plead.

Her arms are crossed as she studies me.

"Yeah. Thoren told me. Did you really do all that he said you did?"

"Yeah. I did."

Her hands go to her hips. "You were a giant dick. You lied. Twice. And we're not talking about tiny, white lies. These were bombs, Roman. Why should I help you? What makes you think you deserve her?"

Her words wash over me, causing my arm hair to stand on end. I had asked myself the same question, wondered if I really should get another chance. If she had asked me this a couple of days ago, I would have told her I didn't. Maybe some part of me still didn't believe I did. But Victoria deserved me to try. Even if I failed. And there was no backing down now if I wanted to stand a chance.

"Because I love her."

The words aren't enough, and I know that, but I hope Monica can see and feel the truth of them. That she knows what I've done to get here, to say that out loud. My confession hangs between us for several moments. I'm scared to move and break whatever hope still lingers. She doesn't look away or fidget. I feel like she's trying to find a secret I'm keeping. But I have laid everything bare; there's nothing for her to find.

Finally, she sighs. "Alright, you big ass. I'll help you, but I swear to God, if we have to go through this again…"

"Never," I promise. "The three of you can castrate me if it comes to that."

I try for a smile and am rewarded when I get the sliver of one. I'll take it. She needs to be on my side if I have any chance of getting Victoria back. Monica gives me the address for a local park, which I immediately type into my phone. I add a quick stop to the grocery store and settle on thirty minutes from now as the meet time.

"Are you sure she'll be there?" I ask.

Monica just rolls her eyes. "You just focus on getting yourself there, on-time."

With that, she walks away to the house, and I slip into my rental, eager to get everything in motion. I swing into the parking for the Grocer Save and take it as a good luck sign that I've been blessed with upfront parking. My grocery list is few, but necessary—boxed wine, bags of snacks, a few candies. Before checking out, a golden bouquet that reminds me of Victoria's eyes grabs my attention, so I get those, too.

"Woah. That's either one big occasion or one hell of an apology," a guy about my age says from the checkout line.

"It's both," I say, carefully laying my items on the checkout belt.

The guy finally looks at me instead of my wares, recognition lighting his face.

"Hey, aren't you that director guy? You did *The Running of Christopher Saints*, right? I loved that one!" He exclaims.

I nod noncommittally, preoccupied with the fact that I'll soon be in front of Victoria, begging for our future. He takes my silence as the brush of it is.

"Well, whoever she is, she's a lucky girl! Maybe you can post some tips online for us poor saps if it works. I have an ex-wife that I think needs an apology to win back."

He winks at me as if we share a bond now. I want to ignore him, but a nagging in my gut, and the sweet face of the girl I love, demands that I answer.

"Actually, I'll let you in on a secret someone very close to me shared. She said that for an apology to matter, I'm sorry is the last thing you should say. To really mean those words, you need to have accountability *and* action to prevent it in the future. Give her that and you've at least done the best you can."

The cashier rings up my items while casually eavesdropping. Both look stunned by my words, the man's face souring as if I've said something he thoroughly doesn't like. The tension between us rises, but I cut it like a knife when I grab the outstretched bag in front of me.

"Thanks," I say to the cashier. "Good luck. I hope it all works out," I tell the man who still stands frozen. Maneuvering my way around him, I exit the store, knowing now more than ever that I'm exactly where I need to be.

After carefully placing the bag in the car's trunk, I take the short drive to the park. It's only a few minutes, making me arrive early. I run through some breathing exercises, gripping my hands to the wheel, but it's no use. Everything inside me shakes, my nerves having a field day on my body. When the confines of the car start to make me claustrophobic, I get out and decide to wait in the open for her.

And then I see her, our picnic completely forgotten. Her friends fan around her, but they lose my attention immediately. She's wearing a pair of black leggings that suck to her curves like a racecar to the track. Her thighs and hips sway and dip, forcing my breathing to follow suit. Her hair is down, the loose spiral curls cupping her ears, her shoulders, her breasts. They fall into her body with ease, a silken thread through a needle.

She talks to them, oblivious of me, her gaze not even straying my way. *Is this what it'll be like if she doesn't say yes? I live in a world where all I see is her and she just forgets me.* The thought beats through the broken bit of my heart and I take a few steps toward her automatically. I can't accept that without trying. I can't always wonder.

My movement must catch her eye because suddenly, I'm trapped in them. She's staring at me and although I know she doesn't recognize me yet, I feel the connection snap into place. Her friends fall behind, letting her continue to walk this way with only Monica by her side. Monica leans into her ear, whispering something, before falling away too. She's alone when we meet.

"Five," I breathe like it's my last chance at air.

\#

It isn't fair how good Roman looks. How warm and spicy he smells. How his voice pulls at the knots in my stomach, begging to release them. I knew the moment Monica whispered for me to give him a chance, who was walking to me, but when he calls me by that name, I almost fall completely apart. I know he sees the shiver that shakes me by the crinkle in his brow. He's everything I left behind. Everything I want. It hurts to know it's too late.

"I... I called, but I couldn't get through," he says lamely.

His hands twitch and dance at his sides as if he's forcing them to stay. *I wonder what he'd do if he let them loose. No,* I tell myself. I cannot be drug into this again.

"I blocked you. Why are you here, Roman? Wasn't LA enough? Don't you have somewhere else you need to be?" I ask.

I'm trying to hold in the tears, but they're barely listening and if this goes on much longer, I won't be able to stop.

"No. It'll never be enough," he whispers, then shakes himself out of it. "I'm here to make things right. I fucked up. I know I did. I should have told you the minute Quin told me what he'd done. But I just... I wanted to fix it first. I didn't want you to think that's what I wanted anymore. And I have, Five. I got a new deal."

He's running out of breath trying to get every word out, one on top of the other, worried I won't let him finish. And he's right to be worried. I wanted to stop him right after *No* but didn't get a chance and now I'm hooked. None of what he's said makes sense and I'm lost in the explanation. My heart thumps wildly, the traitor seeing hope in the spaces where there is none. But it's not my common sense in charge. Not anymore.

"Slow down. What deal? And what are you talking about what Quin did? *You* did it Roman. I should have known it was coming. You were honest in our first meeting about not wanting to produce my script, but I was too dumb to listen. That's on me. You can't *fix* anything. Dreamaway *passed*."

He takes deep breaths, eyes closing just long enough to get himself together. The crease between his brow's releases.

"I'm getting ahead of myself. Remember when Quin, my brother, interrupted our date?" he asks.

I nod, telling him to go on.

"Well, he wanted to tell me he found a onetime loophole to get me the documentary I had been wanting to director as my last movie with Dreamaway. Since he couldn't get ahold of me before the deadline, he filed the paperwork without my permission. Because he thought it was what I wanted. Because at one point that *was* what I wanted."

He looks at me, eyes begging for me to follow along with the train of thought he's not saying.

"But that's not what you want now?" I ask.

He shakes his head, a small smile playing on his cheeks.

"No. That's not what I want. Not at all."

I feel my body knit itself back together at his words. *If he didn't want to scrap my script, that means...* I quickly shake myself out of the thought.

"No. That changes nothing. I lost a very big opportunity *because of you*. I've been through this once, Roman. Always putting my goals, my dreams, on the back burner. I won't do it again."

As much as it hurts to say, it's true. I can't start my next relationship by giving up on myself. He reaches for my hands, which surprises us both when I let him take them.

"I know. Victoria, I know. I don't want that either. Believe me. That's why I quit my Dreamaway contract. They're suing me."

I look into his eyes, searching for the lie and seeing none. His face is open and even with the horrible news, he's *happy?*

"What? Why! Why would you do that? Roman, just because you tanked both our careers doesn't mean I'm going to..."

I squeeze tightly to his hand, ready to unleash fury on behalf of both of us. *He's an absolute dumbass. You fell in love with a dumbass, Victoria.* He just smiles wider.

"I got a new contract. I signed with Idyll Fun Studios for the next four films. The first one, if you say yes, will be yours. They've also agreed to sign a first options contract with you for the next two scripts you write."

My hands go numb and I'm not sure how I remain standing. I'm trying to comprehend what he's saying, but can't quite wrap my mind around it.

"You sold my script?" I ask.

"Technically, you sold your script. I had it sent to them through a third party, and they loved it. Our contract hadn't even been offered yet when they asked for your contact information."

"*I sold a script?*" I ask.

He pulls out a piece of paper from his wallet and hands it to me. The *pay to* line boasts my name with an amount that will definitely pay some bills. In the memo it says *Sailing Single*. I look from the check to Roman and back, unsure of what to believe. He nudges my hips with his hands, holding me up when I'm sure alone I would be flat on the ground.

"So, what do you say, Five?" he asks.

"You want to make my script as your first movie? I thought you hated romances?" I know I'm pushing my luck, but I can't help it. A coy smile lifts his lips, drawing me to them.

"I do. All of them except yours. I can't seem to hate anything you do," he says.

My heart swells, everything falling back into place.

"What are you saying, Captain?" I ask.

"I'm saying that I love you, Victoria Irene Pencheske. I am madly, and irrevocably in love with you." He pulls me closer, and I stare up into his face. "So, please, put me out of my misery. Will you make a movie with me?"

I shove up onto my tippy toes, allowing myself to fall entirely into the man I've been writing all my life to love, with the sounds of my cheering, backstabbing, crazy-ass friends behind me.

EPILOGUE

Victoria

I CAN HEAR THE crowd through the curtains and the pounding of my heart. Everything around me has movement, but my mind is still. Even though press tours are terrifying and I hate public speaking, I'm stuck in a glimpse of a dream, and I never, ever want to get out.

A PA glides around me, carefully setting my microphone and wires into place. Sasha, with her makeup brush, lightly fluffs powder around my chin and my cheeks, sopping up what I'm sure is the dew of my nerves. If I release my twisted-up hands from each other, I know they'll be shaking, so I don't. They stick to the front of my dress like they were designed to be there.

I peep down at my shoes, turning them sideways so I can catch the red bottoms beneath. The power of that color and the knowledge we've come this far together, allows me to breathe deeply for the first time in hours. An arm wraps around my middle, pulling me in close from behind, palm laid flat on my stomach where a custom beaded ring he's taken to wearing rolls across. The feeling of its small indentations makes everything else disappear, recognition instant. I turn into him.

"I thought you couldn't be here this time, Cap?" I ask.

The pleasure that he is outweighing any concern. He sighs into my hair, his breath causing wispy flutters to dance across my skin.

"You know, I tried, I really did. I had a meeting that I was driving to and somehow, I found myself here instead." He dips his head down to me, lips close enough to feel. "Are you really going to make me wait, Five?"

No. To hell with the makeup.

I push up on my toes and press my mouth to his. His smile curves into mine before the wail of my makeup artist has us jumping apart.

"NO! WHAT HAVE YOU DONE?" she squeals.

I know I should be ashamed, but I can't when I'm wrapped up in so much love. She grabs my hand, spinning me to her, working quickly to disperse the red that has undoubtedly blurred outside of my lips.

"Four minutes, Victoria. We have four. Minutes. You couldn't have waited," she mumbles.

The nerves dive back in.

"Sorry Sasha. I know I should have. But it's Roman's fault. *Really,* this time. He wasn't even supposed to be here."

As cold-blooded as Sasha can be, even she has to smile when Roman does something ridiculously romantic like this. She loves a good love story as much as the next one. It's why I hired her. That and she kind of reminds me of Monica. While I'm on my press tour, I can't think of anyone better to wrangle me in.

"Two minutes, Victoria," someone says to me.

By the tablet they're holding, I just assume they're in charge. Sasha finishes up, mumbling the entire time about how delusional she is thinking she could use lip color this time. I try not to smile, which would only make her angrier with me. Roman squeezes my hand as someone whisper yells, thirty-seconds.

"You've got this, my love. Remember, the host is a friend. Feel free to be a little more open with this interview," he whispers to me.

He's coached me for this meeting since he wouldn't be attending it with me. It differed from all the others, making me glad to hear his reassuring voice before it begins. Smacking a small air kiss to his cheek, I leave him behind and go to my marked spot by the curtain's opening. I try not to fidget as I wait for my introduction.

I have many mantras I use now when I'm doing press, but the one I choose tonight is *don't trip*. It's simple and easy to remember. I cannot have a replay of the Chicago stop from three nights ago where I ate it walking across the open floor. It wasn't my fault someone had folded the rug. But that didn't matter to everyone who posted the pictures online the next day.

I wasn't happy with the studio's decision to put me on tour with Roman, but they insisted. *You're selling a romance with romance, Victoria. That's too good an opportunity to pass up.* They weren't wrong, I just hated public speaking. It caused the air in my lungs to become stubborn and my nerves to stand up on a cliff's edge. Roman has been the only thing that's kept me going. That and the fans who are so kind and swept up in our love. The kind of fans that I used to be.

My name is announced and I follow the steps from rehearsal, walking out into a blinding light. It takes my eyes a few moments to adjust, but I keep moving, a smile plastered on my face. A tall man, with bouncy brown hair and a huge goofy smile, walks up to greet me on stage, his hand already stretched out for mine. I oblige, but instead of the handshake I'm expecting, he pulls me in for a hug.

"You are doing so good," he whispers before pulling back and guiding me up to the couch.

I stand for a few moments as the crowd goes wild, welcoming me. I'm a bit surprised since Roman isn't on stage with me this time. Usually, the crowds come for him, but I'll take all the love I can get. I don't need fame or recognition, and I certainly don't envy him. After seeing what it did to Roman, I can do without all of it and just be behind the scenes, but it's still nice when I'm this nervous to feel like the audience is on my side. As our host speaks up, they finally quiet and I carefully take my seat, twisting in it to face him.

"Welcome, Victoria! Or, as I hear, Vip to all the important people in your life."

I laugh in a way I've perfected for these interviews.

"Thank you so much for having me! I'm excited to be here."

As many times as I say it, it never stops being true.

"I know you're here to talk about your new movie that just came out in theaters this week, but I have something a little more personal I'd like to talk about. Is that alright with you?"

The goofy smile is back, making him look on the cusp of laughing, but in a way that makes me feel inside the joke. My stomach sinks at the thought of this conversation turning into a deep dive into my love life. My eyes try to flick backstage to where I think Roman may be standing but see nothing. I know he and Roman are friendly with each other, so how bad could it be? He has to know what's going to be asked after prepping me for it to become more personal. Since I see no way out, I go through.

"Sure," I say, my smile less bright than before, nervous energy eating me up. "What you got for me?"

"Well, Vip." He leans into the table toward me. "Is it okay if I call you Vip?"

He waits for me to nod my consent, and then he continues.

"I have it on good authority that you have a special reason for using nicknames. A superpower, if you will."

His face is expanding, getting more and more excited at the joke he'll reveal. I'm surprised. This wasn't at all what I expected to be talking about tonight. It's kind of an open secret that I'm faceblind, and it hasn't really been a topic of interest yet. Mostly, everyone knows Roman and I's relationship is off limits. We agree on what goes to the public and in our movies. That doesn't stop interviewers from trying. But this is the first time someone has brought up something so personal about *me*. Normally, they're only interested in diving into Roman's life, him being the phoenix of bad Hollywood reputations.

"Oh, um, yeah. I guess I do have a bit of a superpower. Different people use different nicknames for me to make it easier for me to tell them apart since I'm faceblind," I say.

It seems like a harmless enough answer, but he looks like the cat who just ate the canary.

"That is so interesting! I did a little research so I could be prepared for this interview and also found out that before you signed your writing deal with Idyll

Fun Studios, you were a celebrity plus one to make ends meet. Is that right?" he asks.

I relax in my seat. I see where he's going, and it's fine. He wants dirt on who I dated, and I am in no jeopardy of giving that away. The anxiety of how this conversation would turn dissipates and I am more than willing to give the scoop that I know absolutely nothing.

"Oh yeah, that's right. I went on a few dates. It was a wonderful way to network when I was new in town."

I am careful not to include the studio that shall not be named in my response, stubborn not to give them any undue credit or publicity. I'm relaxing in my seat, letting the suspense of the crowd build. They think something big and juicy is coming, and while I hate to disappoint, I can't help but feel safe knowing there's no danger here.

"Can you tell us anything about who you went on dates with? Any interesting stories you'd like to share?"

He's leaned so far over I can smell the coffee and mint battling on his breath.

"Actually, I'm sorry, I can't! Even if I wanted to. I don't know who any of them are."

I shrug my shoulders and smile harmlessly, happy to indulge in this nonsense before the actual interview begins. He leans back with a look of defeat. Just when I think we're going to move on, he shoots up from his chair, startling me, giddiness taking back over. Anticipation cracks through my limbs.

"That's ok! Because tonight, we have an audience full of people who can help."

"I-I'm sorry, what?" I ask confused, chills making my fingers twitch.

"We invited all your plus one dates, family, and friends to join us in studio tonight Vip, to help celebrate," he's smiling from ear to ear.

I look around to see everyone begin to stand, clapping at me. Even though I can't recognize any of them, I feel it. I feel the connection, the love, the shared history. Tears threaten, brimming just at my lash line. I laugh at the thought of Nick or Andrew, or even Logan being out there. I'm excited to see my godparents and Cherie, Katie, and Monica, hoping they all made it, too. My heart swells. By far, this is the most perfect audience I could ever ask for. Hope lights up inside me, but he's not quite done with me yet.

"And we have an extra special guest for you all! Drum roll, please!" He pats on his tummy, then announces, "You know him as the director of *The Running of Christopher Saints* and his newest movie, *Sailing Single*. The one. The only. ROMAN WHEATLEY!"

Roman struts out from behind the curtain with a wink and a smirk just for me. He looks like he should be a movie star under all these lights, and my heart can't stop fluttering at the sight of him walking this way. I stand to greet him at the stairs to the platform. He grabs my hand, holding me there, unable to break eye contact.

"Victoria Irene Pencheske. I know things have been a whirlwind. A dream in the dark. We're both passionate about what we want to do with our lives—it's one of the reasons I fell in love with you—and I couldn't imagine doing any of it without you."

Roman gets down on his knee, sliding open a blue velvet box.

The diamond ring inside shines blindingly in the studio lights. My breath catches like the first time I saw it, on the empty hotel rooftop weeks ago. While that will always be my *real* moment, I can't help but love this one, too. Surrounded by my future and my past. I wasn't expecting it, and the surprise is like a gift. And even though this isn't the first time he's asked me; I can't help but respond like it is.

"YES!" I yell, pulling him up by his collar to kiss me.

The audience goes wild as he wraps his arms around me, dipping me back into a swoon worthy picture we both know will be plastered all over every tabloid tomorrow. Neither of us care. We cut it off after what feels like too soon and make our way to the couch.

"Wow! That was some entrance! You should be up for an award for best kiss," our host says, winking at us.

We laugh. "Let's hope so, my friend," Roman says.

"Now, before we move on to our standard fair about the newly released movie, I have one more question for you, Victoria."

"Shoot!" I say, now ready for anything.

"Will your love story ever make it to the big screen?"

The whole studio feels like it's holding its breath, weighing the silence of my answer. I look to Roman, whose strong presence makes me feel like the entire world is at my fingertips. I don't know what answer I would've given if the room wasn't filled with my friends or if Roman wasn't by my side. But they are, and he is. The smile starts slowly as my eyes stretch from person to person, all waiting. Finally, I land on our host, the whites of his eyes gleaming under the studio lights, and I lean into the desk between us with barely a whisper. It doesn't matter because right now, on this set, you could hear a pin drop and I know it'll be splashed across every headline in the morning, but I don't care.

"Never say never."

* * *

ACKNOWLEDGEMENTS

I NEVER THOUGHT I'D write a book about being faceblind. When I first had the idea of Victoria and Roman, there weren't many faceblind main characters in fiction. To be honest, there still aren't. And while you'll mostly find them in mysteries, I always thought faceblindness was more than a vehicle to forget the face of a killer. I thought it was funny, thought provoking, and romantic in the way it demanded trust from everyone around. And to write this book, as someone who knows its quirks intimately, I needed to have that same trust. From my friends. From my readers. From *myself*.

Needless to say, this funny little sad girl romcom, wasn't created in solitary. I began writing this book three year ago, and while a lot has changed in my life in that time, my acknowledgment of all those who helped me on this journey, has not.

Thank you to the round one WWTS retreat group. You read and critiqued the early pages of this draft and listened while I worried my way through how I could write a character that couldn't remember the faces of the people she loved. Thank you to Isabel Ibanez, who was my mentor during this retreat, and helped me settle on the format of my POV and dual chapters with Victoria and Roman.

Thank you to the early beta readers who cooed and swooned over the pages. Who continued to message me asking when they would see this book on their shelves. You're the reason this is here, now.

Thank you to Sapir Frozenfar and Ashley Rankin. I am so lucky to call you both friends. Your constant support and continuous enthusiasm for my writing (starting with this book) is humbling. I can only wish other writers have friends like you.

Thank you Michelle Donovan who has been in my DMs from the beginning. You are the biggest, brightest cheerleader and I am so very grateful to know you.

I am *always* going to thank Jess Robling, my guiding light in life. My sister from another mister. I would be lost without you. Thank you for the many times you've read this book. When you've dropped everything because I had procrastinated again and needed help. You are better than I deserve.

Thank you to Parker Peevyhouse who asked the most important question of all, *why are you obsessed with this crying baby?*

Thank you to my readers. You have been phenomenal. I could never have guessed so many people would highlight, share, comment, and talk about something that I created. I am blown away by your support and love and I am so, so beyond grateful that I can bring you more books.

And, of course, to my husband. Who doesn't know when to quit and therefore would never allow me to either. You are everything.

ABOUT THE AUTHOR

Samantha Jon is an upmarket fiction author whose work blends gothic romance, mystery, and evocative emotional depth. Her most notable novel, **The Truths We Make**, debuted in November 2024 as the first installment in the House of Poe Duology. The book has been praised as "heartbreaking," "visceral," and "as if Poe had written it himself." Samantha's highly anticipated sequel, **The Lies We Keep**, will release soon, taking the series' gothic longing and lyrical prose to the rugged landscapes of the West.

A poet since the age of seven, Samantha's early works have been featured in contests and anthologies. She wrote her first novel at 25 and has been writing passionately ever since. As a Writing with the Soul alumna, Emerald City Romance Writers member, and founder of an indie author networking group, Samantha is committed to fostering community among writers. Her first love is poetry and the classics, and she strives to make these timeless art forms accessible and engaging to modern readers.

Samantha's writing reflects her distinct voice, marked by lyrical prose, dark humor, and deep emotional connections. Her stories explore self-exploration, bone-deep love, and finding peace in life's imperfections. She aims to leave readers with a bittersweet ache and characters that linger in their minds long after the final page.

Outside of writing, Samantha loves hockey, trying new things, music, and baking bread. She enjoys hosting events and making thoughtful gifts, even if she insists she's terrible at it. Samantha is active on social media, where she connects with readers and fellow writers, building a vibrant, engaging community.

You can follow her on Instagram @samanthajonwrites or email her at samanthajon@gmail.com.